Praise for *Once This River Ran Clear*

If, at the end of Twain's novel, Huckleberry Finn does in fact "light out for the Territory," the sixteen year old narrator of *Once This River Ran Clear* might be his grandson. On the lowest rung of society, he tries to make sense of the larger world and attempts to solve a mysterious crime. Novelist Peter Martin leads his self-taught narrator through picaresque adventures as he discovers injustice and develops his personal ethos.
David R. Solheim, author of *Riverbend: Poems*

A good heart in muddy waters, the oft-renamed narrator guides us along his seventeenth year on earth as his life meanders towards an unclear future. His wry, earthy humor punctuates this not-so-matter-of-fact tale of Haves and Have-nots, secrets and suspicions, heartache and heartbreak, while the turbid river divides, provides, and eventually reveals. I laughed a lot, I cried a little.
Roland Trenary, author of *The Songs of Roland* and *Mahlon Blaine's Blooming Bally Bloody Book*

Once This River Ran Clear

Peter Martin

Buffalo Commons Press
Dickinson, North Dakota

Once This River Ran Clear.
Copyright © 2020 by Peter Martin. All Rights Reserved.

This is a work of fiction. Names, characters, places, and incidents are the products of the author's imagination or are used fictitiously. Any resemblance to actual events, locales, or persons, living or dead, is entirely coincidental.

Cover design by ZAQ Designs
Interior design by Modern History Press

Library of Congress Control Number (LCCN): 2020941071

ISBN: 978-0-9972293-1-8   paperback
ISBN: 978-0-9972293-3-2   hardcover

www.BuffaloCommonsPress.com/

For Adrienne, Bryan and Astrid

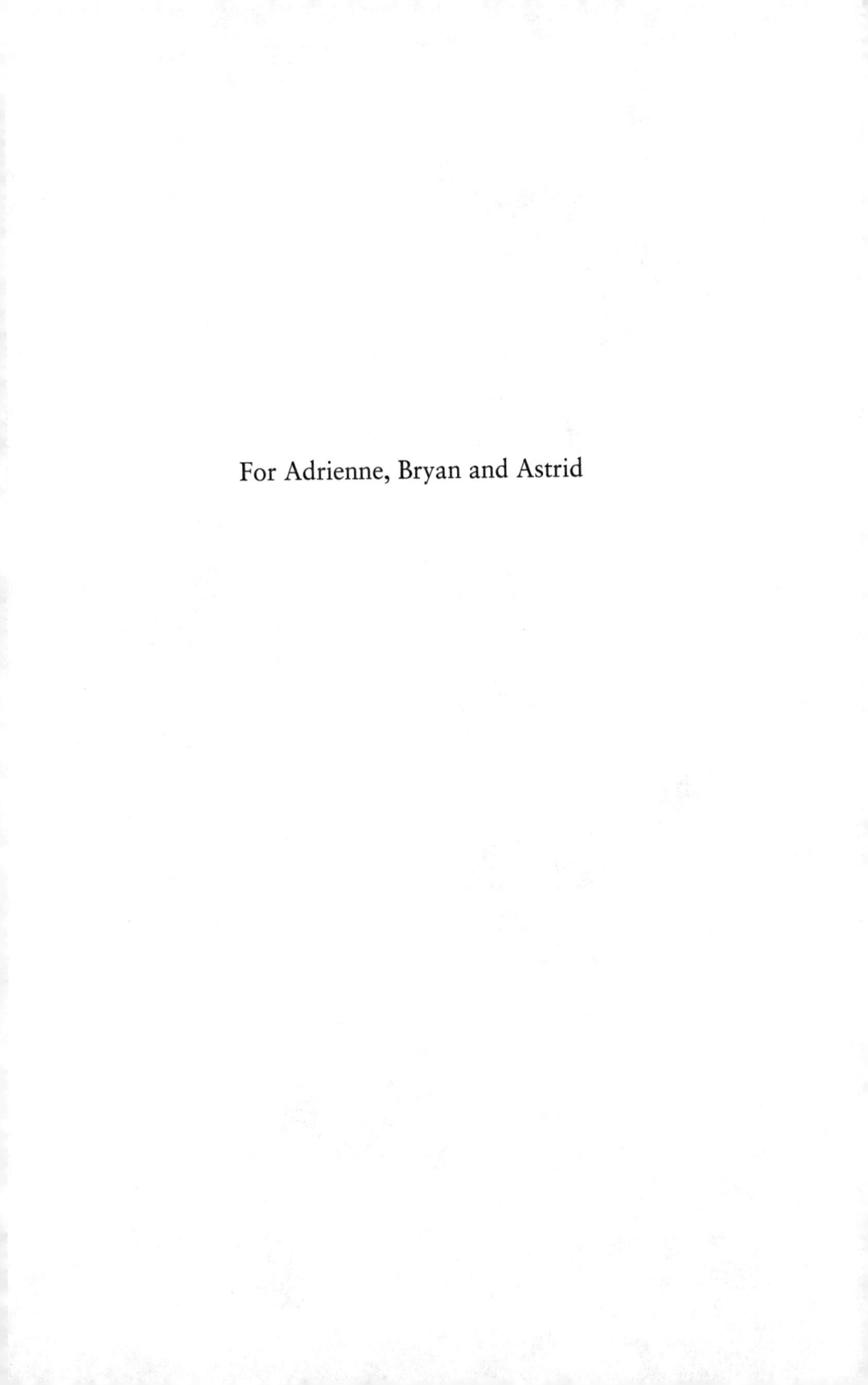

≈ 1 ≈

If I knew the misery Laurence Larkin the Third was gonna cause I'da shot him dead the first time he showed up at our cabin.

It was the end of June. Urs and me were down by the beach, watching for the one ten freight train, hoping Viv'd be on it, along with one or two of the other hobos. I was reading in the Bluffton Graphic about Truman sending the army to Korea when a car stopped by the breach where our trail opened onto County Road 33. "Shit," Urs said. He was naked from his dip in the lake.

The man who got outta the passenger side was dressed like he came from church: light colored suit, vest, bow tie, and a stingy brim hat that wasn't good for blocking the sun. Tough to imagine he was comfortable in that getup in the hot weather but some folks choose looks over comfort, making 'em stupid in my book. He helped out a lady in a pink dress and a scarf around her head. Around front came a tall man in a dark suit. The guy in the hat pointed toward the lake like he was explaining something important. Turned out that was Larkin.

They started down the muddy trail to the cabin. You couldn't make out their words but you could tell it wasn't happy talk as they slipped in the mud and tiptoed around donkey shit. When they got across the train tracks at the bottom of the hill, Otis and Tyrone caught sight and ran straight for 'em, causing the lady to scream and hide behind the men. From the beach I saw the tall man kick Otis in the head. The men rounded the corner of the cabin and found Urs in the porch chair he liberated from the Mercantile trash. It was a big chair but Urs's hairy body was bigger and you didn't know how the chair could hold him.

"Are you Mr. Urs?" Larkin asked.

"Mmm," Urs mumbled.

"I'm Laurence Larkin the Third," said the man; "call me Larry, though. I developed Cherry Grove Estates over in Pressworth; you probably heard of it." He stretched out his hand. Urs pretended not to see it.

"It's okay, Eunice, he's got pants on," said Larry. Eunice peeked around the corner. The tall man helped her onto the porch. "That's my secretary Eunice and that's Borg."

"He kicked Otis in the head." I was up to the cabin by this time. Urs got up and stared at Borg, who stared back, working his mouth so his hollow cheeks sank in further, making his nose look even longer.

"Mr. Urs, we're here on a business matter," said Larry, "I know it's the Lord's day so I imagine you're resting, but I couldn't wait to tell you about something that's sure to interest you. You see that island right there?"

"I been seein' it every day for twenty six years."

"Of course. Well as of last Tuesday it belongs to me—bought it at an auction." Urs just stared, so Larkin kept going. "And I'm going to do something that'll put us on the map—you, me, your boy here, the town of Hertzville, all of us. It's going to make us proud and you're going to be in on the ground floor."

Words spewed outta Larkin so fast it's hard to remember it all: "We're going to make that island into a paradise. People from all over will come here to luxuriate in the embrace of nature." Whatever else he did, Laurence Larkin the Third was adding to my vocabulary. "There'll be a big lodge right there where the ground swells up and it'll have an observation deck on top. Clear away some of those trees and you'll have the best view in the state. And there'll be a path around the whole island, just right for an afternoon stroll after we lay down some boardwalk."

Larkin paused for Urs to say something, but Urs just started a slow circle around the three of 'em so Larry started up again: "I know you're wondering what this has to do with you. Well, let me tell you. The access to the island will come right across this piece of ground we're standing on. We'll grade out a road down the bank over there—it'll be steep but people will enjoy the adventure—and we'll dig a tunnel so cars can cross under the tracks and we'll throw up a bridge to the island. People can drive right up to the lodge and porters will take their bags. They'll be Indians to add to the mystique; we'll make sure they're some of the good ones."

Urs continued his slow circle during Larkin's jabber and I saw his intention. A family of spiders lived in the porch rafters and a big one was making its way down a thread. Larkin started up again: "Now I'm a generous man so I'm going to make you a generous offer, Mr. Urs. I've drawn a check for five hundred dollars to pay you for this property—Eunice, get that check, would you—and all you have to do is sign a paper deeding the property over to me. Eunice, get that too, please."

Eunice fumbled for the paperwork while the spider inched down and Urs closed the circle. Larkin spewed on: "We're on the cusp of something big, Mr. Urs. It's going to be God's blessing on the town of Hertzville—and by the way we're going to change that name, sounds like a town in pain." Larkin laughed at his joke, which I'm sure he'd told a thousand times. I told myself to look up the word "cusp." And "mystique."

"Here it is," said Eunice. She turned to show Urs the check, found the spider an inch from her nose, and let out a scream that rattled the window glass. She let the papers fly and ducked behind Larkin. Borg made a swipe at the spider but Urs caught his wrist and the two of 'em faced off, wrist and hand clamped together. Borg's lip curled up.

It must've been one ten cuz the freighter shook the silence like it did every day. "Those spiders belong to us!" I yelled over the racket. Finally Urs let go and Borg backed off, his yellow eyes locked on Urs.

"Are you okay, Eunice?" She didn't answer Larkin, just bent down, sobbing, for the papers. "We need to go but you think about my offer, Mr. Urs, it's a good one."

"Mmm," said Urs.

Larkin the Third, Borg and Little Miss Muffet made their way over to the tracks, hounded by Otis and Tyrone, then up the muddy trail and squealed off in the cream colored four door Mercedes One Seventy V with a 1.8 liter engine. I didn't know much about cars at the time; it was Larkin's son Winthrop who educated me later on.

Otis and Tyrone were goats. They burned up in the fire.

2

The cabin sat maybe two hundred paces from Lake Delacroix, which bulged in the Nawaakamig River like a rabbit in the belly of a snake. That's two hundred of my sixteen year old paces; for Urs it was probably a hundred fifty paces since he was a bear of a man with a stride like Jesse Owens and the strength to carry twelve foot logs over his shoulder. I counted eighty of those logs in our cabin and they were thick as Urs's leg from his crotch to his knee. In the summer of 1924 he cut and notched and stacked those things into the walls that stood sturdy against the wind. He said once the work sweated off his war memories.

Urs wasn't near as fast as Jesse, though, which made me wonder where I got my foot speed. I could outrun the freighter for a quarter mile. I'd run alongside until the dirt path disappeared into a tangle of backwater branches. Viv taught me how to run. Actually running might be in my blood, but Viv taught me how to breathe.

There was a rock ledge on the cliff above our cabin where I went to dream of riding the river, hide from the pain of huge losses, and plan a murder. I'd scramble up the bank and swing over on a scrub tree growing crooked and stubborn outta the rock. I could see over the island to the west shore two miles away and I could see the whole eight miles of the lake, which was cradled by bluffs on either side.

The tracks divided my ledge from the river. You didn't wanna tumble down the bank in front of the train cuz the engineer couldn't stop. The only thing he cared about was taking the bend a quarter mile north slow enough so he didn't launch into the backwater and fast enough so he could make the rise after the bend. That worked out for Viv and the rest of the hobos cuz they could jump off their boxcar on the slow stretch and hike back to the cabin.

What little money Urs had resulted from fish. Every day after the ice was out him and me staggered out at sunrise, pissed on the compost pile, pushed off in the rowboat, and hauled up three nets strung between our land and the island. Each one was fifty feet long, give or take, and we'd pull up ten feet at a time and lay it in the boat, along with fish flopping and sucking air. We threw 'em in one tub for carp and another for walleyes. We'd get maybe ten carp and a stray sheepshead for each decent walleye. The bony northerns had to be long as my leg from the knee to the foot before we'd keep 'em. Penny didn't use northerns at her restaurant so we threw 'em in our soup and picked the bones from our teeth. The walleyes, on the other hand, were good eating. If the catch was heavy—say seven or eight nice ones—Penny's be damned, we'd keep a three or four pounder for dinner. We ate good in the spring and early summer when the high water drove fish into the nets.

We could usually clear the nets before the boat had more'n six inches of water in the bottom from its approximately million leaks and the runoff from the nets. We hauled the tub of carp—probably thirty or forty of those suckers—to the donkey cart. Same with the tub of walleyes, which had to have water in it cuz Penelope wanted her fish live when they got to the restaurant.

Dash usually kicked the air when he saw me drag the harness from the barn. "Stand still you son of a bitch," I said every day. Once his hoof connected with the cart and splintered one of the planks.

"I'll have your hide for that!" Urs yelled. I know he was thinking how would donkey jerky taste, but who'd pull the cart? Looking at Dash's sad eyes, I wondered sometimes if he'd prefer to be jerky. Three seasons a year, six days a week, he pulled that loaded cart to town, then back again, heaped with whatever Urs could beg (and sometimes steal) from town. Sundays was Dash's day off, not cuz he believed in God but cuz everybody in town did. In winter he shivered in the barn and coughed like an old Ford.

We'd lift the cart over the tracks, then Urs'd curse Dash up the steep bank to the road: "Pull, you son of a bitch." Dash didn't do much of anything till he heard the words "son of a bitch." On County Road 33 Urs walked behind, steering with the handle bars in back and cursing the donkey every time he stopped in front of a pothole. For all his rough ways, Urs had humor, naming him "Dash"; that lazy donkey did anything but.

They did the mile and a half to Hertzville in forty five minutes, give or take, depending on the weather and depending on what you took as the actual border of Hertzville, cuz Ho Chunk Flats, as the people in town called the tangled mess of a hundred or so trailer houses, either was or wasn't in the city limits and definitely was mislabeled cuz it was built on a hill. According to Urs, the sign saying "Hertzville, population 1743," was deliberately put between the Flats and the town proper so the Indians couldn't vote in city elections and so the city didn't have to keep up the dirt streets that worked their way up the hill. You could imagine a big rain washing the streets away and the trailers with 'em, which woulda been just fine with the decent folks in town. The people who lived in the flats were called "Chunkers" but they didn't like that name. Ho-Chunk Flats and Onawah, which was a few miles upriver, were the reason people called us the "Indian side of the river."

I said the folks in town were decent but that was sarcasm in case you didn't catch it. Most of the decency was a thin coating over a core of ugliness and supersition. You could count on one hand the number that were actually decent. Most of them hung out at Turlough's Tavern. Okay, two hands cuz you'd have to include the McDonalds. And Louise.

Urs's first stop was Werner's mill, where he'd dump the carp on a scale and collect a penny a pound, maybe forty cents a day. Werner's chopper spewed 'em into fertilizer. Later that summer Werner said he couldn't use any more carp.

Most Mondays I would go along to help with the heavier load resulting from the two days catch cuz nobody but God did business on Sunday. I was needed to pull on Dash and yell "son of a bitch" if Urs tired of it. Dash coulda pulled the cart a lot easier if it had better wheels and some axle grease. Or if he had a better attitude. Or if he was a mule.

Next stop was Penny's Kitchen on Main Street. It was urgent to get there at least an hour before lunch so Penelope could write "Special today: fresh battered walleye" on the chalkboard by the front door. She had maybe ten customers every lunch and they all wanted the walleye so she didn't have to cook much else besides mashed potatoes and gravy. If she ran outta walleye, she'd throw in a perch and nobody knew the difference cuz of the thick beer batter and the spicy dipping sauce. I'm not saying it wasn't good cuz it was; Penelope was famous for her fish. Also for her loose hanging blouses that flopped down when she bent over with the plates. Urs's fish and Penelope's tits kept Penny's Kitchen in business. Most of her customers were men and she knew how to keep 'em coming back. If you're ever up north you should take a look for yourself.

Urs and Dash would wheel the cart through the alley to the back door. He'd slide the fish onto an oak board, slit it under the gill and down its length to the tail, press the knife flat against the skin and the skin flat against the board, and separate the meat so there was nary a bit of meat left on the skin and nary a bit of skin on the filet. He was the best at cleaning fish and everybody knew it, though they had trouble giving him the credit. Penelope wanted the heads and backbone for the fishhead soup she froze to serve in the winter when fresh walleyes were scarce. That soup was famous too, but for a different reason.

Urs's reward for the filets was twenty cents a pound and a peek down Penelope's blouse. He'd stick around to trade funny insults with her but Penelope's cook Jenkins'd run out in his dirty apron, squealing "there's people comin' in and who on God's green earth is gonna take the orders while I keep the gravy from boilin' over goddamnit." Jenkins was wiry with a squeaky voice and there was good reason Penelope kept him in the kitchen away from the customers. He hated everybody and Penelope had to beat him with a potato masher once for spitting in the batter. Maybe I shouldn'ta told.

Across the alley from Penny's was Virgil Dickerson's bait and fuel shack. Urs'd pump twenty cents worth of kerosene for our lantern, but only if I was with him to bring the twenty cents inside. Virgil had no trouble displaying his dislike for Urs, owing to the fact that Urs caught his fish in nets insteada buying bait from Virgil. There was also a gas pump but we didn't have a boat motor. And I know Virgil had his eye on Penny across the alley, wishing it was him, not Urs, who went upstairs with her after she closed on Saturdays.

Dash didn't need urging to continue through town. He looped around to Main Street, clopped past Christianson's Hardware, where Jerry was probably tipped back in a chair out front and his teenage daughter Louise was probably looking out the window; past the Mercantile, which usually had valuable stuff in their dumpster; past the front door of Penny's Kitchen; past Vera's Bakery with a balloon of a woman—Vera—eating a fresh bun while kids pointed at cookies and donuts behind glass; past the beauty salon with Lavinia the owner and a woman in curlers staring out in disgust at the large, hairy man and his donkey; past Syd's barber shop, where men chuckled at seeing someone more miserable than they were; past the two room hotel where Hotel Harriet had no renters but sold ice cream; and stopped at Old Man MacDonald's Grocery, where he knew Lettie MacDonald had a wormy apple nobody was gonna buy. Urs would tie him to the porch post and spend the day's earnings on whatever we needed, usually flour, beans, salt, coffee, and the like. Really, the name of the store was "Old Man MacDonald's." It was painted on a board above the door. His first name wasn't "Old Man"; he just got a kick from outliving everybody. And it was good advertising too, cuz kids would sing "Old MacDonald had a store."

Lettie would feed Dash the apple, and scratch his ears as Urs meandered to Syd's barber shop. "In the barrel," Syd would say, and Urs'd paw through hair clippings to retrieve the day before yesterday's newspaper and whatever year old magazine Syd had decided to toss, usually something like *Field and Stream*, but if we were lucky there'd be a *National Geographic*. There was normally a man or two waiting in chairs and, the times I heard it, the conversation went something like:

"How's fishin', Urs?"

"Okay."

"Big ones?"

"Bout average."

"Carp's filthy, huh."

"Assholes!" If you thought Urs was calling the carp "assholes," you'd be right cuz he hated 'em in spite of the forty cents a day they fetched. And if you thought he was referring to the guys in the barber shop you'd also be right cuz their comments were said with snickered looks. Urs coulda shut that down with one of his lethal stares backed up by the fact he could mash your skull with one hand, but he always let it pass.

If Levi Nelson happened to be in the barber shop he'd likely say something like "How's Penny's tits?" but he'd say it in such a way to suggest Urs didn't deserve to be one of the people squeezing 'em. Levi was big with muscles, but if he thought he could take Urs in a fight, he'd be wrong. Urs just ignored him. Levi hung around the church in the late afternoon and watched the kids get off the school bus. It gave me the creeps thinking about him watching Louise walk down the street to the hardware store.

Later that summer Syd quit throwing his used magazines in the hair barrel and burned 'em instead.

Past Old Man's and just before the church was the smallest library west or east of the river. We'd go inside for my book of the week but not if the library lady saw us first. Ever so politely she'd block the door so our rough looks wouldn't disturb the one or two people searching the one or two reference books on the shelves.

"Hello, Mr. Urs. Can I help you find something?" she'd say, blocking the door.

"We need a book for the boy."

"What do you like to read?" The first time she saw me I know she was thinking I needed one of those Dick, Jane and Spot books for beginners. It was known about town I didn't go to school so she assumed I couldn't read. What she didn't know is I was getting a first class education from a couple hobos named Viv and Felix, as well as Urs.

"Adventure," I said.

She came back with three books. To her amazement, I chose the hardest one. After that she had a book ready for me every week. We didn't have to check it out cuz we'd have to come inside to register. "Just bring it back in two weeks," she'd say. There were actually two library ladies; library lady Gertrude was nicer than library lady Frances, who was older and meaner looking cuz she squinted over her little round glasses. Urs said she just needed a good poke.

There was only one side to Main Street. The same big hill separating our cabin from the road ran the length of the lake. Whoever laid out the street in the last century forgot to allow space for stores on the west side. So if you're down at the beach looking east, there's a ten foot bank which was riprapped for erosion and which supported the railroad tracks, followed by the steep hill up to Main Street, then a gentle slope fulla houses leading to the rocky bluff standing vertical and proud, with Big Baasha—a huge rock—threatening to break loose and crush the town.

The one sided street was okay for the business owners, who appreciated the clear view west to Bluffton, wishing they lived there insteada Hertzville, but it was not okay with the shoppers who had to walk the whole length of town to get from the post office on the south end to the Catholic church on the north, assuming they had business in both places. One day Mrs. Goodwin, an elderly widow, had to mail a letter and also needed to visit the church. It wasn't Sunday so she musta had a troubled conscience. As she left the church she grabbed her chest and dropped dead. If only the church was across the street from the post office, she might be alive today. Her house sits empty cuz it was rumored the widow Goodwin was not as nice as her name implied, and had, in fact, poisoned her husband, who was found slumped over a bowl of chicken soup and whose ghost cries for revenge. Her house has a picture of a ghost painted on it that nobody's painted over, probably from fear.

There were other pictures on buildings around town. There was a wolf on the back of Harriet's Hotel but the best one was a horse with fire in his eyes painted on the south side of Christianson's Hardware. I thought it was awful good but Jerry painted over it and the word around town was he'd fill the bastards with buckshot if they did it again. He could save a shell, though, and just gore 'em with his flat top hair, which stood up so stiff and sharp it could hold a dictionary. I hope he never does, though, cuz I like the kids who did it. They got to be famous and me along with 'em.

Just after the church was Prospect Drive, which wound up to the top of the bluff. You couldn't see over the edge of the bluff but you had to know only rich folks lived there. Once in a while you'd see a little red car hauling ass down the road and you'd wonder how it didn't fly off the curves.

Across Prospect Drive from the church was Turlough's Tavern and pool hall, the only place in Hertzville, other than Penny's and Old Man's, that welcomed Urs. He'd go in for a beer on the house, that generosity resulting from the fact he could tell funny stories once he was lubricated. Urs didn't talk much but when he did he was worth hearing.

By the time Urs left town Dash's cart usually held odds and ends dug from trash barrels or found by the road, such as pieces of rope, coat hangers, scrap metal, and tires, along with the goods from MacDonald's store. He'd bring home twisted boards from where a house or shed was tore down. We'd pound out the nails, straighten 'em with a pliers and hammer, and nail the boards over the holes in the barn. Urs'd go by job sites when the workers were at lunch so he could pick up a new two by four or some rebar and add it to the pile by our barn. Some people would call it junk; to us it was the stuff Urs used to ease our hardship like when he rigged sheet metal to reflect the winter sun through the cabin window.

    The Saturday after Larkin offered us the five hundred bucks, our fish nets got tore up. I think it was on purpose.

3

The island was shaped like a crab with its claws pointed west. On summer Saturdays the Delacroix Queen sidewheeler cruised around the far side at dinner time, carrying fancy dressed people digging at plates of food. Captain Jack would pull into the cove between the crab's claws and turn off the engine. Over the loudspeaker he'd tell folks to appreciate the sounds of God's creation, which they did for twenty seconds, then resumed yacking about anything but the grand and mysterious creation surrounding 'em. On a still evening the water carried their noise and I heard the demands and complaints of fat cats and their kin from way up on my ledge.

The Saturday after Larkin's visit Urs was late from town as he was on most Saturdays. After we pulled Dash and the cart over the tracks Urs handed me forty two cents that I ran to the Prince Albert can behind a chink in the cabin wall. Urs headed for the outhouse. I had to go too; it was a two holer and we had some of our best discussions in there. "Assholes," he muttered as he handed me a Bluffton Graphic with a story about the draft and how young men had to go fight in Korea whether they wanted to or not. "You gotta be eighteen." His words hung in the air like they needed explaining, but he said nothing, just tore pages outta *Field and Stream* to use for their real purpose.

"How's Woof?"

"Good, I wrapped her foot." Woof was a stray dog that adopted us when I was a nipper. We figured her and me was the same age.

"You shovel out Dash's stall?"

"Yup."

"Shell some peas?"

"Yup." Peas, along with cabbage, were some of the earliest truck from the garden. Stuff don't grow too early in the north. We were just a hundred or so miles south of Canada.

"Tomatoes?"

"Small ones. First of the summer."

"Plant the potatoes?"

"Yup." We planted the second crop in late June for spuds to last the winter.

"You read that book?"

"Almost done."

"Any words you don't understand?"

"We got a dictionary, Urs. And it's a simple book. Stupid too. Did you ever see a bear out to kill a human? It's a grizzly, though, so maybe that's the difference." It was that book about Danny and the dog and the bear. The book was silly in some places and downright sad in others. I don't hold with killing animals for their skins, which is only one step better'n killing 'em for the fun of it. I've killed plenty of squirrels and raccoons and a deer, except I ate every one of 'em.

"There's a walleye on the stringer."

"I know."

"You clean him."

"That's for you."

"You gotta learn."

"I'll butcher him."

"Then I'll whup the tar outta you." I laughed cuz Urs never laid a hand on me; he just liked to joke.

Once This River Ran Clear

"You can whup me but I ain't gonna feel it; your swing's as weak as ..." There was a noise from the lake.

Urs looked out the door. "No! No!" he bellowed. "Stop!"

The Delacroix Queen had glided in, then started its engine, obviously intending to run the channel. As the paddlewheel started churning, Urs stumbled from the outhouse, holding up his britches with one hand and pounding the air with the other.

As the fancy people on the boat stared at the maniac running toward 'em, the wheel ripped up our nets and spun 'em around itself. Since their attention was focused on a huge, hairy man trying to hold up his pants, nobody noticed the disaster unfolding around the sidewheel till fish started slapping 'em in their bugeyed faces.

In situations like this Urs would hurl the most vicious yet comical cuss words. A writer might want to use some of his curses to tickle the reader's funny bone even in the midst of a tragedy. The run to the shore happened fast so I may not be remembering the exact words, but it was something like "Stronzo! Drittseck! Turn the engine off, you hairy arschloch! Those are my nets you're ripping up, you fuckstick weasel!" I don't think folks on the boat heard this over the thumping of the wheel but they could tell something fearsome was happening due to Urs's clenched fist and his drooping pants, which exposed him briefly but often.

I was halfway to the shore when the engine shut off and I could see it wasn't Captain Jack at the wheel but a kid about my age. "Back up this barrel of shit and get this bucket of pickled dicks out of here!" Urs shouted.

"Sir, there are children on this boat!" came from the crowd.

"Well, get those little snot nuts outta here too!"

The young man started the engine again and reversed the wheel, which chewed up the nets and wrapped 'em tighter around the axle. "Turn off the engine!" hollered Urs.

"How am I gonna back up if the engine ain't on?" the young man yelled back. That left Urs speechless cuz the young man was right. "Dad says you don't own this channel!" yelled the young man as he backed out, turned the boat around, and churned back toward Bluffton. Urs sank to his knees and buried his face in his hands. There was a lightning flash to the west.

In the next week's Bluffton Graphic, Urs was described as part man and part bear, estimated at forty to fifty years old and about three hundred pounds, with a vicious dog and a young accomplice. He was a heathen shouting words'd make a sailor blush and should be arrested for indecency. The people on the boat supplied the information. They were half right about one thing: Urs's name has something to do with bears. Felix supplied that moniker.

The vicious dog was Woof, who ran arthritically behind Urs. Her only claim to viciousness was she could lick you to death. And of course I was the young accomplice. If they could see into the future they woulda wrote something more sinister, cuz the next summer the devil took control of my soul.

The most impressive part of the whole incident was Urs could say "asshole" in Italian, German and Norwegian. Beneath it all he was a cultured man, unusual for the son of an illiterate father, but his momma was a school teacher before they left Norway to work in the iron mines. Some of it rubbed off on me, which is why I have such a magnificent vocabulary. I learned "moniker" from Felix, who was smart as could be in spite of being a hobo.

Urs sat on the shore till it poured. He slogged up to the porch, the thick hair on his head and chest matted and dripping, kicked off his boots, and stripped off the wet britches, leaving him buck naked. "Where are those tomatoes?"

We ate by lantern light while wheels spun in Urs's head. Sometimes that was a good thing and sometimes bad. More'n once his brain hatched a plan that saved us hellacious grief, like the winter he patched a hole in the roof by shoving an old stove pipe in it. He flared out the top so when it snowed the water would collect and trickle down to a bucket so we didn't have to run to the well for water. Of course he made the hole himself when he climbed up to shovel off the snow and stuck his leg right through.

I don't mean there were actually wheels in his head; that's just a manner of speaking. I guess you knew that.

Urs wrapped up in a blanket and sank into the stuffed porch chair. I slept on my mattress inside. In the morning I got the walleye off the stringer and cleaned him while Urs slept. I split logs to get at their dry insides, built a fire in the pit by the beach, spooned lard onto the cast iron griddle, and sliced potatoes onto it, then onions and cabbage and the walleye filets.

The smell musta woke Urs. He came to the beach carrying soap, threw off the blanket, and lathered up in the lake. Bathing was like starting over. In winter we couldn't wash up except by the stove, so when the first warm day came round we'd jump in the lake no matter how cold the water, and dry off in the sun, our lives beginning fresh.

Urs walked outta the lake dragging three pieces of net that hadn't got wound up in the paddlewheel. He tied loose ends together and launched into his carp tirade: "Asshole fish. They don't belong here, shit brown, mud sucking fuckers. When I was a kid I never saw a carp. It was walleyes and northerns and perch—none of these garbage eatin' fish. River's gettin' to be a cesspool."

He shut up when I shoved a fork into his hand. For ten minutes nothing made any difference except for the taste of the fish and the potatoes and the onions and the cabbage all mixing together in our mouths and warming our stomachs. Urs grinned when he had to spit out a bone I missed.

Did he already know what to do about the nets? "We're goin' to Bluffton," he said. I wondered if someone was gonna die.

↯ 4 ↯

We decided to wait till Monday to go to Bluffton cuz we probably wouldn't find Captain Jack on a Sunday. Instead we climbed up the bluff to find mushrooms. At the far end of a corn field was a thicket of ash trees that sheltered a patch of morels. We always made it unseen, but this time the farmer caught us cutting across his corn, which wasn't tall enough yet for cover. He intercepted us on an Allis-Chalmers as crusty with rust as he was with wrinkled skin.

The man spat tobacco from a mouth containing exactly one tooth: "This here field belongs to a fellow named Claude Pease. That'd be me and I don't allow nobody in my field." He shifted his look down to the shotgun holstered on the side of the tractor. "Now git."

So we got. But we waited over the lip of the cliff till the son of a bitch looped his smoke spitting tractor around a bend and the engine noise faded, then we worked our way along the tree line to the ash grove.

When people talk about the finer things in life a lot of 'em mean cars, big boats, and vacations in the sun. For Urs it was fish on the griddle, stories around the fire, big tits on foul mouthed women, and morel mushrooms. For an hour we pushed aside leaves, snipped off the pecker shaped fellows, and put 'em in a mesh bag, all the while listening for the tractor and watching for Mr. One Tooth in case he decided to walk back with his shotgun. We got maybe two pounds of morels and on the way back Urs cut a huge pancake fungus from a rotten stump and threw it in the bag. I eat stuff like that and I'm still alive.

I guess that's obvious since I'm standing right here telling the story.

We slid down the bluff and found Woof waiting by the tracks. She led the way to the cabin but stopped suddenly and darted into the woods to an uprooted tree with a branch tangle around it, sniffing, digging, and suddenly jerking back with a squeal.

Outta the twisted branches charged a buncha skunks, blinding Woof with their spray.

"Save the dog!" yelled Urs. She was yelping.

"Who, me?!" I yelled.

Urs threw down the mushroom bag: "Follow me!" I ran in after him.

At least a hundred skunks attacked us. I exaggerate, of course, but it was too many to count. I got hit from two directions: "They got us surrounded!"

"Grab Woof!" Urs clubbed skunks with a stick, which really made 'em mad.

I bent down to hoist Woof onto my shoulders and got a direct hit in the face. "He got me, Urs!" When Urs told this story, he said I yelled "I'm a goner, Urs, save yourself!" but I didn't.

Urs shoved me toward the trail, still waving his stick. In my version Urs brandished his sword yelling "take that, you motherfuckers!"

We got to the trail and ran. "Wait, the mushrooms!" Urs ran back for the bag. The mushrooms were stinky but they were morels so we saved 'em and hoped the smell would die off.

We stumbled through the brush to a backwater pond. I lowered Woof into the drink, then submerged myself. We soaked for a few minutes and climbed out, still skunky.

"Take off your clothes. Leave 'em here."

"These are my best pants," I said.

"We'll get 'em when the smell fades, take 'em off."

We headed home naked except for our boots and Urs's mushroom bag. The strap was looped around his neck so the bag swung back and forth covering his hairy privates for an instant on each arc.

"Did you really say 'they got us surrounded?' Wait till I tell that story." Urs broke into a huge laugh that froze in the air when he rounded the corner of the cabin and stopped short. I peeked around the corner and saw Little Miss Muffet paralyzed into a horror-stricken statue, one hand holding a folder of papers, her wide eyes watching the mushroom bag reveal Urs's hairy privates for a second on each swing. Behind her was Borg and Laurence Larkin the Third, faces locked into an unbelieving gawp.

Eunice screamed and threw the folder—apparently a reflex of hers—and ran. Due to the non-stop screaming, we could only guess Otis and Tyrone were at her heels.

"You are ... this is ..." Larkin stuttered and shuddered. "You owe Eunice an apology, you ... you ... savage!"

"She was trespassing, same as you."

Woof eased herself onto the porch, and rubbed her skunky body against Borg, looking for some love. She was not a great judge of character, however, cuz Borg had no love to give. He kicked her hard in the ribs, bouncing her down the steps. Urs launched himself into Borg's stomach, sending 'em both to the floor. Borg jumped up and kicked Urs in the nuts. He pulled a club from inside his coat and was ready to use it, but I busted around the corner with a two by four and stood between the two. Borg snarled and bared his teeth. I'm sure he coulda grabbed the two by four and knocked me upside the head with it but he didn't, cuz he'd never live down the story of how he beat up a naked sixteen year old (I'm guessing).

Larkin stood to the side, moon-eyed, and finally stammered: "B ... B ... Borg, go help Eunice!" He picked up the papers, ripped and crumpled 'em as he yelled: "That's it, you son of a bitch! You see this?! That was a check for a thousand dollars! Now it's confetti and you're getting nothing! You think ripped up nets is bad, you just wait for what comes next! You'll see! I'm building a resort on that island whether you like it or not! You'll see! You'll see!" Laurence Larkin the Third kept yelling "You'll see!" until he caught up to Eunice and Borg halfway up the hill.

I saw to Woof and Urs rubbed his nuts.

5

Bluffton's on the other side of the river three miles south of our cabin. To get there you follow County 33 north past Farmer Fred's Petting Farm and the power plant, cross the Bluffton Bridge, and head south eight miles on River Road. We called it the Bluffton bridge even though the people in Bluffton wanted nothing to do with it. Unlike Bluffton, the bridge was beat up and ugly and Bluffton folks almost never crossed it cuz they had no use for the Indian side of the river.

Or you could cut across the lake, angling to the southwest, which is four miles as the crow flies. We ain't crows, of course, so we had to use the rowboat, the same one we used to haul up the nets. The same one with a million leaks, give or take. The same one that woulda been chopped up in the waves raging on Monday morning. It was a north wind, unusual for that time of year, which woulda pushed us right to Bluffton, but we had to get back. Our boat woulda been chewed to pieces and we'd be Alliconda's dinner. That's nonsense, of course, but some folks in Hertzville really believe an alligator mated with a giant snake to form a monster that haunts the lake under the full moon.

Urs put tar he'd chipped off the highway into a cast iron pot over the fire. When it softened we turned the boat over and spread it on the worst cracks. "It's still gonna leak," I said, "and now the pot's ruined."

While the tar hardened and Urs took a dip, I got snow peas, new potatoes, and onions from the garden, cut 'em onto the griddle, then ran to the barn for eggs. We were down to three hens due to the dining habits of foxes, so we got maybe two eggs a day. There shoulda been more but those sneaky hens would sometimes lay 'em out in the open as a sacrifice to the foxes and weasels, I suppose, so they'd be too full to bother with chicken meat.

While we waited for the wind to die down we trimmed Otis and Tyrone. Urs turned 'em over and sat on 'em while I shaved the hooves with my jackknife. Urs paid actual money for that knife so I kept it sharp to skin squirrels and chop veg. I'd use it that winter to break into a gun cabinet but I didn't know that at the time.

About noon we decided the wind wasn't gonna let up so we put off the Bluffton trip and cut an acre of hay instead. It's agony, even though we took turns swinging the scythe. By then the day was shot. We threw a stick for Woof but she just looked at us like we were crazy. The three of us collapsed into sleep.

The next day broke clear and calm. We dragged my mattress to the porch so Woof'd have a soft bed outta the sun, and shoved off. The boat creaked and the oars squeaked in their sockets as Urs pulled 'em. His back was to the front so I directed from the stern, heading us straight west, counting on the current to take us south, all the while bailing with a rag and coffee can.

Urs took a breather every hundred strokes and for a minute we lay crosswise on the seats, feet in the water, enjoying the whoosh of heron wings against the silence. Except there wasn't as much silence as you'd like cuz of the unusual number of boats.

Bluffton's set on a broad plain extending east from the western bluffs. Unlike Hertzville, there was no threat of a huge rock splitting off a cliff to crush the town. The flour mill stood tall and white at the back end of town. Two church steeples poked the sky, one for Catholics, one for Lutherans. There were other churches but you couldn't see 'em from the lake cuz they didn't have enough money (I assume) to reach up toward God through the blanket of trees.

"This is Tuesday, ain't it?" I asked.

"Yep."

"Then why's there so many boats on the lake?"

"Damn if I know." It wasn't like the lake to be busy on a Tuesday. The rich doctors and lawyers from Pressworth who owned the big cruisers and sailboats didn't normally travel the two hours to Bluffton except on the occasional weekend. Boats big as small houses passed us with oily women in swim suits pointing fingers and cameras at us.

We oared around a point and into the harbor, bouncing in the wake of Mama's Mink, Sea Senora and Beeracuda. Almost every yacht slip in the harbor was empty causing me to wonder again: "You sure it's Tuesday?"

We beached the boat, walked past dry docked sailboats with masts sticking through canvas covers, and headed for the harbor office cuz Jack was the harbor master in addition to owning the Delacroix Queen.

"Where's Jack?" Urs didn't exactly shout it but the sharpness of his voice caused the man behind the counter to grab the phone.

"Mister, when you come in here like that I'm thinking I better call the police." The man was old and sticky, no match for Urs in a fight.

I mean he was built like a stick, not that things stuck to him.

"I ain't gonna hurt anybody," said Urs, "just tell me how to find Jack. It's about my nets."

"Oh, you're the bear," the man chuckled. Urs didn't think it was funny. "Jack's not here."

"Where is he?"

"Don't know."

"Where does he live?"

"I don't ..."

"Your name's Bob Duffy, right?" His name was sewed to his shirt.

"Yes."

"And his name's Jack Duffy, right?"

"Yes."

"Is that a coincidence or are the two of you related?"

"I'm his father." Bob's face got red.

"And you don't know where he lives?"

"Is this man bothering you, Bob?" There was a greasy man in the doorway, holding a beer.

"We just need to talk to Jack," said Urs.

"What's it about?" Another greasy beer drinker walked in. He blew cigarette smoke toward Urs.

"That's between me and Jack," said Urs.

"It's about the nets," said Bob. He went in the office and picked up the phone.

"So you're the asshole who messed up the wheel," said cigarette guy. "We been here three days pulling out pieces of your net. Had to miss church on Sunday, huh, Mitch."

Mitch took a step toward Urs, who stood his ground with his hands by his side. In cases like this Urs used his eyes to tell folks they better rethink their next move. I was considering my move, too, which was gonna be to kick Mitch in the nuts and hit him with an uppercut when he bent over in pain. I learned that move from Viv two years before when Three Finger Eddie and Viv were on our dock. Eddie ran his hand up inside Viv's blouse so I pushed him in the lake. He crawled back on the dock and grabbed me by the throat only Viv kicked him in the crotch, kneed him in the chin, and pushed him back in the lake. I didn't realize till a year later that Viv left her blouse hang loose so Eddie and the other hobos could do that.

Bob came out and gave us directions to Jack's house: "Main Street to Lyon, up a block, right on Oak, third house on the left, white with gray trim."

As we left I shouted back at the two assholes: "If you're here when I come back, you'll be sorry." Actually I only thought it.

At Main Street, Urs stopped short. The street was lined with people in lawn chairs in front of the curb, others standing behind 'em, some with kids on their shoulders. They were looking to the south, where a big crowd of teenagers, dressed in red, white and blue uniforms, marched toward 'em. They wore stupid furry hats with tiny visors that didn't block the sun, and swung musical instruments back and forth.

"It's the Fourth of July," said Urs. I knew about Independence Day, of course. Urs and Viv and Felix all educated me about history. The Fourth was a day for parades and beer drinking. The mystery of the big boats was solved: The fancy people from Pressworth had descended on Bluffton for the long holiday weekend.

When the band reached the bulge in the crowd, a young lady in a glittery costume blew her whistle four times and music blasted out. Sweaty teenagers passed in neat rows. After the band there was a gap cuz the Boy Scouts were horsing around so we hurried across the street in front of 'em. I saw heads turn toward us and wondered if anybody recognized Urs from the Delacroix Queen incident three nights before; maybe if his pants were down to his knees.

We pushed down the sidewalk, which was choked shut by the crowd and the merchandise sitting out. Bluffton had more stores than Hertzville: a clothes store just for men; two stores for women; a store selling only shoes; Serge's Hair Styles for both men and women (and there was a man working on the hair). You could buy a Ford or Chevy in Bluffton and you didn't have to go far to compare the prices since they were across the street from each other. The Pit Stop sold donuts, the soup of the day, and gasoline. They had a sign saying "eat our food and get gas." The joke was ... oh hell, you know the joke. Between buildings was a wrinkled man with a wooden leg sitting in front of a red, white and blue wagon with a sign that said "War is hell—eat popcorn. Ten cents."

Best of all, Bluffton had a movie theater. It was playing Cinderella, which is a dumb story. Viv read it to me when I was a nipper and I thought the girl was stupid for putting up with that shit. Up to that point I hadn't seen any movies, but I have now, including one Felix told me about, where they burned Atlanta. I bet most of you have seen it.

We took the left on Lyon, away from the crowd, and looked down a long wide street with large white houses and trimmed bushes. There was a park with a statue of a man on a horse with a copper plaque saying "Colonel Burton "Buster" Pritchitt, 1881–1918, 18th Cavalry. Buster led the charge up Insanity Hill, giving his life for your freedom."

We turned onto Oak Street, which was misnamed, since it was arched by elms. The third house on the left was all the way at the end of the block cuz the houses on this street took so much space. Captain Jack was sitting in his porch swing, working a piece of wood with a jackknife. He looked up when we were at the steps: "Afternoon, Urs."

"Afternoon, Jack."

"Grab a seat."

We sat in wicker chairs. Through the big front window I saw the kid who drove the Queen through our nets. He ducked away.

"You ain't at the parade," said Urs.

"I saw it last year and the year before that. Been here waiting for you, got a phone call," said Jack. "Arlene!" he shouted. A woman with poofed up hair appeared behind the screen door. "Get these gentleman some ice tea, would you, honey."

"Not for me," said Urs, "we ain't stayin'." She disappeared. "You need to buy me some nets," said Urs.

"What makes you say that?"

"You drove your damn boat through my channel."

"I have to quibble with you on several grounds, Urs. First of all, it's not just a boat, it's the Delacroix Queen. It gives this lake some style. It brings a lot of commerce to this fine town of ours. Second, I was not the one driving the Queen …"

"No, it was that bonehead I just saw behind the window."

"That's my son, Urs, careful what you say. Third and most important, it's not your channel. Your property ends where the lake begins; after that, the lake belongs to everybody."

"I've been fishin' that channel for twenty five years; that's how I make my livin'. People know to steer around the other side of the island."

"You call that a living? Look at yourself, Urs, the way you're dressed, the way you live, the way you're raising this boy. What's your name, son?"

"Danny," I said. I got that name from the book I just read but Jack bought the lie. Truth is Urs just called me "son" or "hey" and said I could make up my own name if I ever needed one.

"There's a basketball hoop out back and it's got a cement half court. You go shoot some buckets while your dad and I talk. Hey Randy, come out here and play some horse with Danny!"

Randy appeared instantly, proving he'd been listening behind the door. He wasn't much older than me. "We went to a Lakers game," he volunteered, "man, that George Mikan, I got a hook shot just like him." Randy wasn't so sassy when Urs was within grabbing distance.

Urs was pissed: "You got a basketball court and you can't afford to buy some nets to right a wrong done by your son?"

"It's the principle of the thing, Urs. By rights, you should pay me for the trouble of removing those nets from the paddlewheel. I had to pay three days' wages to two men to get those blame things unwound. I hope to heaven they got it fixed by now cuz I booked a special Fourth of July tour for this evening."

"They're in the office drinkin' beer," I said.

"Randy, get the ball and play some horse with Danny."

"I'm stayin' here," I said.

Jack's face turned red. I had the feeling he'da gone for my throat if Urs wasn't there.

"Did Larkin put you up to it—drivin' through my nets?" Urs blurted out.

Jack stopped carving and gestured with the knife: "Look here, Urs, times are changing. There's big plans for that island next to your place. There's going be a resort bringing in rich eggheads from as far away as Chicago. They got money and they like to spend it. The Queen's gonna run tours every day of the week and twice on Saturdays." Urs spat.

"You know what, Urs, I just had the best idea. I'll hire you to work on the Queen. You'll need to cut your hair and shave every day but heck, we all need to do that, don't we. We'll get you a uniform and everything." Jack put the stick of wood to his mouth and blew a whispy sound; turned out he was carving a whistle.

"I ain't workin' your boat," Urs said. He got up; I followed him off the porch.

"This is progress," Jack hollered at our backs, "and you're standing in the way of it! You're not getting any nets from me. And, by the way, are you an Indian, cuz you gotta be an Indian to net game fish or it's illegal! Did you hear me, Urs— you're illegal!"

"And you're an asshole," Urs muttered under his breath.

We skirted the crowd on the way back to the harbor and crossed over Main Street in back of the horses, which were the tail end of the parade for obvious reasons.

The trip back across the lake took twice as long as the trip over cuz the tar had chipped away and we both had to bail every so often. Urs took out his anger by attacking the waves with the oars. When we finally rounded the bend into our channel we saw Moonshine Monroe and Vivien sitting on our dock with big grins and a bottle between 'em.

6

If the hobos were on the one ten freighter they'd jump off a half mile past the cabin, when the train slowed for the curve. If they couldn't make the jump, they had to wait four miles till the stop to unload coal at the power plant, then either walk back on the tracks or hike up to the road and hitch a ride south. But who's gonna pick up ratty looking hobos, which made it important to make the jump.

There were five of 'em: Felix the Frenchman, who was too smart by half; Merle Monroe, but we called him "Moonshine" cuz of his line of work; Three Finger Eddie, who supposedly cut off the last two fingers on his right hand so it would slip more easily into a rich man's pocket (but we think he really lost 'em in an act of street justice after he slipped his hand into the wrong rich man's pocket; that man was foolish, though, to cut off the pinky and ring fingers and leave the grabbing fingers intact); Gaetan the Croonin' Cajun; and Viv, who was the glue that stuck 'em all together. This time she arrived with Moonshine, who lifted the bottle in a salute as we slid into the dock.

Moonshine was scanty and wobbly but he locked arms with Urs anyway and tried to pull the bear-human onto the dock. That was Moonshine's way—helping with things that didn't need to be done, especially helping Urs get drunk, which definitely didn't need to be done. Viv pulled me into a tight hug and wouldn't let go till the boat floated away and I had to wade in for it.

"Drag on this," said Moonshine, handing Urs the bottle. "It's a good vintage, made it last month." Urs dragged and squinched up his face like he'd sucked on lemon. "Smooth, huh," said Monroe. "What's for dinner; we ain't et today."

Urs welcomed the hobos for their help with summer chores like taking up the hay and working the nets but Merle thought supplying moonshine was the only contribution he needed to make. He would have us believe he was the genius behind a fine brew but we knew otherwise. He just knew a few places down south where he'd trade a half day's labor for a couple bottles of hooch, then sell 'em (but mostly drink 'em himself). His shoulder bag was heavy with bottles.

Urs turned to me: "What's for dinner?"

"I'll check the garden," I said.

"I need meat," demanded Moonshine.

"There's no fish," I said, "the nets got chewed up."

"You got chickens, doncha?"

"We need the eggs," I said.

"Well, how 'bout we eat donkey steaks," Merle grinned. Viv slapped him. She and Lettie McDonald were the only people who actually liked Dash.

"Get a squirrel," said Urs.

I walked to the cabin for my twenty two. "I'm comin' with you," said Viv.

"Leave that bottle!" shouted Moonshine.

"He'll be out cold by the time we're back," Viv said, "he's getting worse."

Viv and I and Woof walked south down the tracks and passed maybe a dozen squirrels in the first half mile. In summer I didn't take the ones close to the cabin so they'd be there in the winter when we really needed 'em.

"I brought you a book," Viv said. I looked forward to her books cuz she knew what I liked. Viv was pretty educated, even finished tenth grade. In my earliest memories I was tucked into her warm body while she read to me. Later on it was me reading to her after I knew how to sound the words. She got the books by hiding 'em under her shirt before they kicked her outta whatever library she was at. We had a box of books under the bed saying something like "Return to County Library, Jackson, Mississippi" inside the front cover. She brought me comics too, stolen from drug stores. I liked Spider the best.

We stopped at a trestle where the tracks pass over a bog that opens into a large backwater and waited for squirrel sounds and for Woof to catch up, slowed as she was by Borg's kick. In a few seconds she let out a low growl and a large gray squirrel clawed up a tree maybe fifty feet away, an easy shot. I propped my rifle on a limb and waited for a clear view. It was a Winchester twenty two at least fifty years old but it shot straight. Urs got it from Farmer Fred's Petting Farm in exchange for services performed by our goats and he bought a scope for it. When the squirrel poked his head around the trunk I clicked off the safety.

"That's not your squirrel!" We looked through the trees into the bog to see a lanky kid with a three pronged spear waist deep in the black water. "This is my dad's land and that's our squirrel," he said. The kid was bare chested except for a gold cross hanging from a thick neck chain. He was sunburn red all the way up except for his forehead, which was shaded by a floppy wide brim hat. His name's Winthrop, I found out a few months later, and he thought his daddy owned pretty much everything. He thrust the spear into the water and pulled up a wriggling carp. "Got another one," he said. He threaded it on a rope trailing behind him, fulla dead carp. "Oh, go ahead," he said, "shoot the squirrel, I don't need him."

"What do you do with the fish?" asked Viv.

"We throw 'em on the bank," said another voice, "they rot and smell worse'n a fat man's poop." Behind Winthrop was a chubby young man almost chest deep, wearing one of those hard helmets I seen in *National Geographic*.

"That's my little brother; I'm teaching him how to fish," grinned Winthrop. Fishing, as he called it, was easy when the water was low and a million carp were trapped in the slough.

"But you just throw 'em up on the bank." Viv was upset.

"Noboby's gonna eat these things. Go ahead and take the squirrel, I won't tell dad."

I fixed the crosshairs on the squirrel's eye and dropped him; Woof ambled after it. "Nice shot," little brother said. "Is that a twenty two? My daddy's got a thirty aught six; he lets me shoot it. Your dog smells skunky."

They watched as I gutted and skinned the squirrel.

"There's another one up that tree," said little brother.

"One's enough."

We headed back. "There were a hundred carp rotting on the bank," said Viv. She exaggerated but I got her point.

Monroe was laid out cold, as Viv predicted. Urs had potatoes, cabbage, onions, and peas on a stump and lard heated in a pot. I cut the squirrel into chunks and browned him, threw in well water and the vegetables. Viv watched with Moonshine's head in her lap. She was a good cook but all she did was smooth Moonshine's greasy hair and watch me with a look I didn't understand.

Moonshine woke up complaining. The ride up from Arkansas took a week and required five transfers. "All this jumpin' off one line to catch a different one is hard on a fellow. The railroads should get together and make it one straight shot. And put a tank of drinkin' water in each boxcar. And give those conductors a lesson in human kindness. Some are okay but every once in a while you run into an attitude like they think we're bums or something."

"We are bums," said Viv.

"We're frequent travelers," argued Monroe, "we work for a living and I got money in my pocket to prove it. I'm in distribution. If I didn't get hooch to lonesome men they'd have to kill themselves outta desperation. And now I'm here helping this poor man make a living on five acres and a mule."

"Donkey," I corrected, "and it's nine acres."

Moonshine ranted through dinner, then passed out on the beach. We covered him with a blanket. As dark closed in, Urs uncovered the morels hiding under a cloth on a stump and threw 'em on the griddle till the skunk smell burned off. We ate slow to make the taste last as we watched fireworks explode over Bluffton.

Viv slept in Urs's bed, the first time she'd felt a mattress and a sober man in weeks.

The morning was clear so Urs rolled me outta bed early to fix the trail leading up to the road. It was steep and the rains washed big gullies into it that were tough for Dash and the cart to pass. A couple times every summer we cut logs and stole a few big rocks from the berm along the tracks to hold the dirt in place and channel the water away. It was a god awful job and the hobos were supposed to help, but Moonshine was in no condition to do anything but mope around the beach. Viv matched Urs and me log for log, rock for rock.

After we ate leftover squirrel stew, hoping it hadn't turned overnight, Urs threw a bar of soap at Moonshine. "Clean yourself up," he said.

"You think I'm dirty?"

"I think you're disgusting," said Urs, "get in the lake or I'm gonna throw you in."

Monroe dawdled till Urs took a step toward him, then stripped down to naked and waded in. Viv sat on the dock with her feet dangling in the water and soaped Moonshine's hair over and over till the grease was out. Then she slipped off her dress and went in herself. We had similarities to a nudie camp. They made a point of that in the judge's office.

"Thanks for all the help," said Urs as Moonshine walked up from the lake.

Moonshine looked puzzled till he got the sarcasm. "You shoulda waited for the others," he said. "They'll be here, won't they?"

"Don't know," said Urs, "postman don't stop here and my phone's not workin'." More sarcasm. For a couple years I'd wondered when Urs'd tell Moonshine he wasn't welcome anymore. If Viv wasn't with him this mighta been the time.

"Eddie'll be here," said Moonshine. "We split up in Missouri cuz he had to go to Chicago for a convention. Five'll get you ten he's missing another finger."

Viv left the lake, wrapped herself in a blanket, and looked at the net fragments we'd pieced together. "What are you going to do about the nets?" Urs didn't answer. "You ever eat carp?"

That sent Urs into his carp rant: "garbage eatin' fish …" and so on.

After Urs ran out of swear words, Viv said softly: "I had smoked carp and it wasn't bad."

"In the bayou they cook 'em with so much spice it melts your ear wax," added Monroe.

I knew what Viv was thinking and the wheels in my head were spinning too, but we let it be. The afternoon was taken up with easy chores. I dragged a tub from the barn for washing clothes, which Merle did under protest, proclaiming it was women's work. Viv slapped him for it. She was of the opinion women's work and men's work were one and the same. Urs filed the scythe blade and replaced a rotten board on the dock. Viv and I gathered hay to make a bed in the barn, then we led Dash into the lake and washed him. She napped on the dock while I retrieved the skunky clothes we left down the trail and put 'em in the soapy water to soak. Dinner was cabbage boiled in leftover squirrel broth with a tomato on the side. "That's gonna make me fart," said Moonshine.

"Good thing you're sleeping in the barn by yourself," said Viv.

In the evening stillness, Viv and I sat on the dock with our feet in the water. She handed me the book from her bag. Inside the front cover it said "Property of Shelby County, Tennessee Library." I read: "You don't know about me without you have read a book by the name of *The Adventures of Tom Sawyer*; but that ain't no matter."

"I read the Tom Sawyer book, Viv, you brought it last year."

"This one's even better," she said.

I read to the end of chapter one, when Huckleberry slipped out the second floor window to meet Tom. I guess that's where I learned it.

7

Just before sunrise I got up to piss and saw Monroe naked, wet, and shivering. "Kinda chilly for a dip this early," I said.

"I'm a new man," he said, "just baptized myself."

"I'll get you a blanket."

"Nah, this is my penance. I done wrong and I need to suffer."

"How come you're up? You like to sleep late."

"Damn goats ate my bed," he said, "and they grind their teeth worse'n any woman I've ever been with." We assumed Moonshine knew to lock the goats in their stall for the night but we assumed wrong.

I spent most of the morning in the porch chair, reading the Huckleberry book till Viv grabbed the patched up fish net. "Get the other end," she said. We stretched it tight, making about eight feet. "Hey Urs," she yelled into the outhouse, "we'll be gone a while. You're comin' too, Monroe." She led me and Moonshine and Woof down the tracks to the backwater.

"It stinks here," said Moonshine.

"Like a fat man's poop?" Viv asked. Me and her chuckled.

"Strip down," she said.

"What the ..."

"We're catchin' some carp; take the net and stretch it between you."

So Moonshine and me stripped down to naked and waded barefoot into the slough. We dangled the net but nothing caught even though we could feel the fish against our legs.

"It needs to be anchored at the bottom," shouted Viv.

So we grabbed the bottom corner and scooped up three carp. We wrapped 'em in the net and hauled 'em back to the cabin. Viv set one on a stump: "I need a spoon and a sharp knife." Urs walked away muttering. Moonshine sat on a stump and eyed the half empty bottle he'd been working on the night before, when he wasn't a new man yet.

Viv ran the edge of the spoon over the fish, tail to head, sending the scales flying, slit open the belly, and scooped out the guts. She set the carcass on a stump and walked around it, waiting for an idea. "You got a steel pipe and some wire?"

Of course we had pipe and wire cuz Urs wouldn't let valuable stuff sit in anyone's trash. Viv wired the fish onto the pipe like he was riding it and balanced the pipe on rocks over the fire pit. She added oak splinters to the coals, which still smoked from the night before, blew the coals to red, and sat back.

"It's gonna take an eternity," said Moonshine.

Viv babied the fire, making it hot and smoky but not so hot it flamed up and burned the fish. I split some oak pieces down to slivers to add to the coals. She butchered another carp into skin-on filets and the last one into steaks, salted some of it, splashed a couple pieces with moonshine, left other pieces alone, and put 'em on the griddle.

"You're gonna ruin my griddle," said Urs.

"Shut up, Urs," she said. He went back to the porch chair.

In twilight we sampled Viv's creations, except for Urs. The meat flaked off the carp on the pipe. It was smoky and oily but a person could eat it. The steaks were burned on one side, which was good cuz the charring ate up the grease. There was too much salt on the filets and the moonshined pieces were disgusting but we ate it all, except Viv wrapped part of the smoked one in newspaper. The three of us spent time in the outhouse during the night.

Urs was up early. By the time the rest of us woke, he'd already turned the hay and was drying off from his morning dip. "I'm going to town," he said.

"We got no fish," I said, "and Penny's gonna kill us."

"I'm going," said Viv.

"What's in town?" asked Moonshine.

"Hardware store. I'm gonna see about nets."

"They'll cost," I said.

"There's over six bucks in Prince Albert."

"That'll buy what, about six feet of nets," said Viv.

"Jerry'll give me credit," said Urs.

"I'm comin'," I said, "I gotta see Jerry give you credit cuz that'll be a first." Besides, I wanted to see if Jerry's daughter was looking out the window.

I had to pull Dash outta the barn cuz the donkey was lazier'n usual due to his easy week. Moonshine pushed from behind, forgetting the donkey could kick. He used his injured leg as an excuse to stay behind (but it didn't look like Dash had actually connected). "How come you're takin' the cart when there's no fish to carry?" asked Moonshine.

"There's always stuff to bring back," I said.

"Well then, bring me a big titted woman with spunk," laughed Moonshine; "I ain't had one of them in a while." Viv shot him a look.

"That'd be Penny," Urs shot back, "and she's more'n you can handle. I know it for a fact." Viv shot Urs a look. We headed up to the road.

"He's gonna be drunk by the time we're back," said Urs.

"No he won't," I said, "he's a new man—baptized himself in the lake."

"Yes he will," said Urs, "he's baptized himself so many times God just looks the other way."

"No he won't," said Viv, "I hid the booze."

When we passed Penny's Kitchen, Jenkins saw us and ran out shouting "there they are! Penelope, they're out in the street!"

Penny rushed out and damn near assaulted us on Main Street: "Where the fuck are my fish? All week I've been serving fish head soup."

"That stuff's awful," whined Jenkins, "we damn near need buckets for people to puke in."

Penny yelled at Jenkins: "Get in there and peel potatoes!" Then she yelled at Urs: "You puny prick, shit spitting rat fucker! What in the goddamn hell am I gonna do?" If there was a cussin' contest between Penny and Urs, he'd come in second.

"Our nets got chewed up," mumbled Urs, "I'm seein' Jerry about some new ones."

By this time Syd was in front of his barber shop, scissors and comb in hand, laughing with Virgil Dickerson, who shouted "what happened to the nets, Urs? Did Alliconda chew 'em up?" I'm pretty sure Virgil was trying to impress Penny as well as humiliate Urs, but it's hard to impress a woman when you're wearing half a haircut.

Viv unwrapped the smoked carp and shoved it at Penny: "Try this."

"It smells awful," said Penny. She stomped into her restaurant.

Jerry was tipped back in a chair in front of his store, holding up the Bluffton Graphic with his spiky hair showing over the top. He pretended not to see us in spite of the fact we were conscrip... um, constripu ... what's that word?—everybody noticed us cuz we were unusual. He lowered the paper. "Morning, Urs."

"I need to buy some nets, Jerry."

"I got none in stock."

"But you can order some, can't you?"

"I suppose."

"Delivery's about two weeks, I'm guessing. Can I see a catalog?"

"Nets cost money, Urs. How much you got?"

"I can make a down payment."

"How much?"

"Six bucks. How much does a net cost?"

"Depends on the variety of net, but six bucks won't touch it."

"I'll pay the rest once the fishing picks up."

"You sure it's going to pick up, Urs? Word is the carp's driving out the walleyes."

"I need you to give me some credit, Jerry."

"You know what I need, Urs—what this whole town needs—is for you to make way for progress. Look over there," Jerry said, pointing at Bluffton across the lake, "that could be us with a little forward thinking. I'm sure you know what I mean."

I think I'm remembering that conversation pretty well but I admit I was distracted by Louise Christianson in the store window, staring straight at me. Her hair was in pigtails.

"And what about the possibility Captain Jack's gonna run his boat through that channel again? You need to think about that, Urs." That sounded almost like a threat but I can't be sure cuz I was looking at Louise but trying to make it seem like I wasn't. Jerry raised the paper. Urs stared at it a few seconds, then steered Dash into the alley behind the stores.

There was a mattress in the Mercantile's trash. Urs threw it on the cart along with a pair of wobbly crutches.

As we pulled away, Clyde Jackson ran outta the back door of the Mercantile. "That's the last time, Urs," he yelled. "From now on you leave my dumpster alone."

Viv went back and tried to be nice: "It's trash."

"It's my trash," said Clyde. "You tell Urs to stay away from it!" he yelled loud enough so Urs could hear from down the alley. "And tell him to wake up and smell the money!"

As far back as I could remember we took trash from that dumpster with no objection from Mr. Jackson. That wasn't the only thing that changed after Jack's boat ripped up our nets. After Urs stopped supplying Penny with walleyes, she stopped supplying him with affection and there was no reason for him to go to town on Saturday afternoons. You had to wonder if Penny and Clyde and Jerry and Syd and a few others formed a club that Urs couldn't join.

We hurried down the alley and looped back to Main Street. A black and white Pontiac with a red cop light was parked at the church. Father Matthias was on the curb laughing with Sheriff Hugo Pope. Deputy Linus Hooper was in the street, wagging his finger at cars if he thought they were speeding.

Noon on the first Friday of every month was when the sheriff stopped by Hertzville to enforce laws and collect votes for the next election. He and his deputy set up by the church for about an hour, which was the time some of the crew from the power plant took their lunch at Turlough's Tavern across the street. The father's theory, Urs told me, was that him standing there with the sheriff would turn the workers toward sobriety. The power plant management supported this practice since drunk workers tend to be less productive and more accident prone.

Urs tried to be gone by the time Pope and Hooper arrived but on this particular Friday they were early and it looked like they were waiting for us. We tried to be incon ... inconspicuous—there, I remembered that word—but how can a hairy, bear shaped man and sad donkey pulling a cart with a mattress on top be inconspicuous in a modern city with cars and a tarred road.

"Hold on there," said Pope. Urs stopped the cart. "You got a license for that donkey?" Pope and Father Matthias chuckled. "I'm joking with you, Urs," said the sheriff.

"Don't worry, Urs," said Matthias, "it's a minor sin; come to confession and I'll take care of it for you." There was another laugh from the sheriff, the reverend, and deputy Hooper, who waited to laugh till he knew it was supposed to be funny.

"I could write you up, though," said the sheriff, "because this is a public road and you do slow down the traffic. I've heard a complaint or two. I suppose the charge would be reckless endangerment, something like that. Maybe we should put a twenty mile an hour minimum speed on this road; can your donkey do that? Be a shame if you couldn't get to town for supplies."

"Care for some carp?" asked Viv, holding the fish to the sheriff's nose. His eyes shot darts, making it obvious he understood Viv's exact meaning, which was "fuck you."

"I tell you what, Urs," barked the sheriff, "I been hearing about goings on at your place and I bet I could issue a shitload of citations if I came down there and looked around. Some of it might even land you in jail. I'd think carefully about the future, if I was you."

"We'll be on our way, Sheriff," said Urs, slapping Dash in the rear.

"God be with you," said Father Matthias.

"And with you," said Viv, which of course meant "fuck you."

"I better not find donkey shit on the road," yelled the sheriff.

We crossed Prospect Road and in clear view of Pope and the Father, Urs steered the cart into Turlough's Tavern, his own version of "fuck you."

Urs bought himself a beer and Viv and me a soda, bringing our life savings down to five dollars and forty cents. Skeeter the barkeep said I had to go to the pool room if the sheriff drove up.

Viv laid the fish on the bar in front of Skeeter: "Smoked carp."

"Never had it," said Skeeter.

"First time for everything," she said.

He tasted it and made a face. "Hey Rudy, try this."

Rudy tried some. "Needs something," he said.

"Hot sauce," said Ambrose, "to help with the gamey taste."

"Barbecue rub," said Fritz.

"Pretty bad," said Zack, but nobody threw up.

"Hey Urs," said Viv, "give me the rest of the money."

Urs weighed his options, the worst one being, if he refused, Viv would lay him out cold and take the money anyway, so he gave her the five bucks and forty cents.

"We'll be back," she said, pulling me out the door.

Viv and I headed back into town, past the Father and the sheriff.

"God be with you," said Matthias.

"And with you," replied Viv.

At Old Man's store Viv bought large bags of brown sugar, chili powder, garlic powder, paprika, pepper, and salt, using up Urs's money plus sixty five cents from her own pocket.

As we passed the church again the sheriff and his deputy were getting into the Pontiac. Viv waved at 'em and said "God be with you." They stared; that may have been one too many "fuck you's."

Urs was on his fifth beer, paid for by Skeeter and a few of the rowdies who enjoyed a good story. When Viv and I walked in he was at the end of the skunk story, only his words had no relation to the actual events. In this version Eunice was a doe in heat, begging to be mounted, and Larkin was paralyzed with fear. I hoped none of this got back to them since they were already pissed beyond imagining. Or to Borg cuz it seemed like he'd have no trouble killing somebody over a trivial thing.

Urs drained his beer and stumbled into a chair. "He needs another beer," someone said.

"No he doesn't!" snapped Viv. Zack helped us walk Urs out the door and lever him on top of the mattress. I led Dash down the road with Urs singing "A lady from France had ten men in her pants," one of Gaetan's compositions not sung in church. Viv tried to shut him up when cars slowed down to gawk, the kids no doubt thinking "look at the cute donkey and what's that hairy lump on the mattress in the cart."

From the road we could see smoke rising from beyond the cabin so we thought Moonshine must be cooking something. We tipped Urs out and made him walk down the trail. As we rounded the cabin Urs called out "Hey Moonshine," but before he could finish whatever curse he was about to lay on the lazy bastard, we were looking at Felix the Frenchman and Gaetan the Croonin' Cajun.

"Where in the name of creation is my hooch?" yelled Moonshine.

8

Felix, Gaetan and Moonshine were friends after a fashion. There were agreeable moments, for sure, like when Felix tickled our brains and incited dispute with his ideas. Monroe would say they were stupid and Felix would take a long draw on his pipe and say some words in French, which we assumed were cusswords, but we didn't know for sure, which made us the stupid ones.

Gaetan was never without his guitar. He could make up songs on the spot like the first time he heard Felix's thoughts about the condition of the human race: "Just ask Mr. Truman, who he thinks is human; would he bomb white folks to kingdom come?" I won't sing the rest cuz there's some sad talk about people burning. Also cuz my singing's terrible; in fact they told me in church to just sing the hymns in my head so I'd get the benefit of the holy music without wrecking it for others. Gaetan sang naughty songs in bars for pennies thrown into his hat but also suckered church folks by singing religious songs outside houses of worship as they walked in. On occasion the preacher would invite him inside to serenade folks into a pious mood before the preacher himself would call for repentance and a generous donation to the offering basket. A dollar or two would go to Gaetan, more if the preacher wasn't looking. Gaetan usually had folding money in his pocket and often benefited from the generosity of wealthy white folks out to demonstrate their sympathy for down and outs.

The problem with those two was akin to the problem with Merle Monroe, who thought the only contribution he needed to make was providing the brew and pissing on our compost pile. Felix thought he earned his keep by passing on the insight he learned in college and Gaetan thought sitting around the fire sending songs across the moonlit water was his gift to humanity. Getting those three to help with the things that actually kept us alive, like working the fish nets or taking care of crops, was almost as hard as making Dash stop being an asshole. Of course at that point the nets were gone, giving Urs even more reason to wonder if the three hobos had any practical value.

Without Viv we'd never see any of 'em. Back in the worst times she appeared outta nowhere and stayed till winter hit, then took off for warmer weather. I got this from Urs and didn't find out the whole story till I was seventeen. As far back as I can remember the hobos always appeared with Viv or shortly after. Gaetan started traveling with the group after they found him beat up in an alley and convinced him the north would be a better place to spend the summers.

"You missing your hooch, Monroe?" Viv was toying with him.

"You hid it, I know you did, now where is it?" Moonshine wasn't toying back.

"I heard you were a new man, Moonshine, so you don't need that stuff," she said.

"I was a new man yesterday. It didn't carry over. Now where is it, woman?"

"You call me woman again, mister, and you'll be missing some of your parts."

The rest of us wondered which parts he'd be missing. "I bet it's his nuts," giggled Felix.

Moonshine took a step toward Viv and raised his fist. You'd expect a person to back off in that situation but Viv took a step toward him and said quietly: "You lower that fist on the count of three or I will rip out your heart." His fist went down on the count of one.

Viv walked to the end of the dock and sat. Moonshine walked aimlessly about, then sat against the barn. They stayed that way in the waiting game that'd played out at least a dozen times.

Urs staggered to the porch chair and dozed off. Felix and Gaetan poked at the fire. They were trying to cook something cuz there was a pile of veg on a stump. "I'm going to make soup," said Felix. He looked at the veg for a few seconds, then asked: "How do you make soup?" For a smart guy he wasn't very smart.

"Heat grease in the pot, then put in the onion," I said.

"Did we get onion?" asked Felix.

"Nope," said Gaetan.

"Go get one, would you," said Felix. It's not that Felix was lazy. It was more like it was a real chore to get his large body off the ground. He called himself broadly structured where a lot of people would call him fat.

"Nope," said Gaetan, "I already done my field work for the day."

I got the onion, chopped it up, threw it in the hot grease and coached 'em through the soup making process: Add the garlic, carrots, green beans and potatoes, well water after a bit, then peas, cabbage, salt and pepper. Too bad we hadn't soaked the dry beans from the store.

The smell got Viv in from the dock. Moonshine walked slowly to her and dropped to his knees, pleading: "Viv, I went a whole day without a drop."

Viv let out a long sigh: "It's behind the hay bales in the donkey stall."

"You're an angel, Viv," shouted Moonshine, running for the barn.

It took Gaetan exactly a minute to compose the ballad of Merle Monroe. It went like this:

> "A desp'rate man named Merle Monroe,
> he needed booze to live.
> Alas his hooch was hidden
> by a sober gal named Viv.
> That disrespectful scalawag,
> that boozy little putz,
> he sassed that gal named Vivien
> and almost lost his nuts.
> And then the angel Vivien,
> that kind and decent soul,
> took pity on the hopeless drunk,
> that lovable arsehole.
> The hooch was hidden in the barn
> behind a bale of hay.
> So Moonshine got to drinkin' -
> he'd been sober one whole day."

Then Gaetan stood up and threw his voice to the sky and the rest of us started clapping and stomping to his beat, even Urs, who stumbled down from the porch.

> "We drink moonshine here on planet earth
> cuz heaven's strictly dry.
> Just give me booze and heaps of love
> and somehow I'll get by.
> I'll satisfy my appetites before the day I die,
> cuz there ain't no earthly pleasure
> in the everlasting sky."

There was another verse about Viv's generous nature but I won't sing that one cuz Viv didn't like it.

Gaetan had maybe a dozen different ballads devoted to Merle Monroe. I don't remember all of 'em but I know one was about his run-in with the law over stealing a chicken and another about how he was beat up at a whorehouse for not paying the bill.

We settled into the evening with full bellies and light spirits. The bottle passed from Monroe to Felix to Monroe to Gaetan to Monroe to Felix—you get the idea. Urs already had his drink for the day and was trying to get his head back to normal. Viv had been off the booze for months (and was reminded that a reformed drunk was the most irritating person in the world), and I hadn't warmed up to the devil's brew yet.

Next day Urs was all business. He had a work list in his head and made the hobos sweat. Felix and Monroe went to the garden to hill potatoes, tie up tomatoes, pull weeds and pick veg for lunch. Gaetan and Viv cleaned up in the barn and wheeled shit to the compost pile. Urs gathered the dried hay one forkful at a time and mounded some under the rain roof we'd built in the field, where the goats could pull at it. The rest he baled with the box he'd made from two by fours and plywood. It had a lever—or maybe you'd call it a plunger—that packed the hay into a tight square. Or "piston" might be the right word. Then he went down the trail to dig clay. He didn't give me a job so I climbed up to my ledge to read about Huckleberry. It was better than Danny and the Irish setter.

I leaned against the cliff and slept to make up for the late night and woke to little dramas playing out below. Felix and Moonshine had left the garden gate open so the goats were in there trampling plants and refusing to be caught. Monroe lassoed Tyrone with twine and yelled 'yahoo' as he tried to ride him like a cowboy. Tyrone planted his feet and threw Moonshine into the fence. I was more worried about the fence than Moonshine cuz chicken wire ain't sturdy. Neither is Monroe but he'd deserve a little pain. Gaetan was on the dock with a stick and fish line. I'm guessing there was a hook and a worm on the end but it didn't matter cuz he wasn't gonna catch a thing. I'm pretty sure he knew that and was just pretending to be useful. Viv was pulling pipes from the pile of valuable trash by the barn. She dragged three of 'em to the fire pit, then rolled some of the fire rocks to make a long bed instead of a round one.

Urs mixed the red clay with water till it was gooey and threw in paper scraps for binder. He used a flat knife to force the glop into the cracks in the cabin walls. It was one of those all day projects due to the big gaps between the logs, some of which needed wood chunks shoved into 'em to hold the clay in place till it dried, so I was surprised I wasn't called on to help. I think Urs wanted to be alone, working to sweat frustration out of his body.

I was happy to read another chapter. There was never a moment of affection between Huckleberry and his old man, just orneriness and threats. Huck's pap could learn a lesson from Urs, who was hard on the outside but let his soft inside show through once in a while with gentle hugs and forgiving words when I did something wrong. Once I ruined a tub fulla walleyes by letting it sit out in the sun. He yelled at me first but broke down crying and gave me a hug, saying stuff like that happens to everyone. Urs may or may not be my old man, I found out later.

Viv looked up toward my rock, which told me I was needed. I knew what she was doing with the pipe and the fire pit. Felix and Gaetan didn't have a clue so they were curious when Viv told 'em to grab the net and walk down the tracks with us to the backwater. Monroe tried to hide in the barn but Viv found him.

We snuck up to the backwater to be sure the two kids weren't there. All we found was a line of rotten, smelly fish. "Smells like a fat man's poop," said Moonshine. The water was down even more and there were places with carp stranded half outta water. We picked up a few of 'em, then Moonshine and me showed the others how to dip the net for fish. We took turns dipping, ending up with twenty nine fish. Musta been a weird sight—four men covered with so much mud you couldn't tell they were naked. We slogged over to the main channel to wash off.

Viv broke off a ten foot branch and threaded twine through the net and around the branch to make a carry sack for the fish. We took turns suspending the pole between us and marched down the tracks like we were on one of those safaris I saw in *National Geographic*.

"We need a hardwood fire," said Viv, "coals, not flames," so, while the others (not Urs of course) used spoons to strip off fish scales, I split oak chunks down to thin pieces, lined the long pit with 'em, and started a fire. We scaled and gutted twenty four fish cuz we could lay three pipes across the fire and each one held eight fish.

Viv mixed up a bowl of spices and rubbed it on the fish, inside and out, and we wired 'em onto the pipes like they were on parade. She set the poles on rocks so the fish roasted about three feet over the fire. "Turn 'em every half hour and keep those coals glowing," she said. We had five fish left over. Viv left the heads on those and hung 'em from wires on the clothes line to dry in the sun.

Part way into the evening Viv declared the fish done and slid one onto a stump. We waited for her to take the first bite.

She flaked off some flesh, smelled it, and shoved it into her mouth. "Good," she said, but like it was a question.

Gaetan wasn't too concerned since he'd eaten rough fish down south. He took a bite and said "better with beer," which inspired Moonshine to hit his bottle before he hit the fish.

Felix held a piece on his fork: "He was a bold man that first ate an oyster. Here we go then—boldness be my friend." He closed his eyes and thrust the fish into his mouth.

I tried it and gave Viv a small nod. We pecked away at that fish, then another and another. Urs ambled down and stared at us satisfying our hunger on the thing he hated most. He took a bite and made a face but kept eating.

Gaetan thought that called for another song which he made up quicker'n a hungry dog grabs a drumstick.

Oh the carp's on the fire a-whettin' our desire
for a belly full o' grease and grit.
It's unappetizin' but our hunger is arisin'
so we're really gonna eat that shit.
"The man named Urs let out a curse
when he saw that greasy sucker.
He formed a scowl, let out a growl
and ate that oily motherfucker.

As darkness closed us in, we sang it a few times, then broke into "We drink moonshine here on planet earth cuz heaven's strictly dry ..." We got louder and louder, and stomped around the fire with bodies gyrating to the beat. Gaetan jumped onto a stump and beat the guitar strings. Viv grabbed hold of Felix's blubbery body and swung it back and forth. They crashed into each other like waves against cliffs. Moonshine contorted himself into bends and lunges, pumping his bottle up and down. Urs danced from his shoulders up, then knelt down by Woof and those two howled like crazed wolves. I shuffled around the fire till Viv broke free from Felix and twirled me in and away. She put her arm around my waist and hurled me through circles and dips.

We were so keyed up with our whooping and gyrating we didn't hear the Delacroix Queen till its earsplitting horn stopped us in our tracks.

Captain Jack had drifted the boat into our channel. As it passed, Jack got on the loudspeaker and pointed out the scene on the beach, which had already been discovered by everyone on the boat. Proper ladies and gentlemen out for a Saturday night winging stopped jabbering and gawked at us. We gawked back but I'm sure we weren't thinking the same thing. They mighta been imagining things they'd seen in *National Geographic* like savage tribes and human sacrifices. Felix spoke for us: "Wish I had a cannon to blow a hole in that boat."

"What you're seeing on the beach," declared Jack through the speaker, "is a man named Urs and his son Danny and some hobos who drifted in from the south. They live in that cabin with no electricity and that's their outhouse over there. Interesting way to live, wouldn't you agree. Now take a look at the island on the other side of the boat," he continued, "it's going to have the ritziest hotel and resort north of Chicago." Nobody shifted to the other side. Their heads turned toward us in unison as the boat snaked past and disappeared around the island. Only Jack's voice remained: "If you want more information I have brochures here in the wheelhouse."

We sank to the ground. Finally Moonshine said "I didn't know your name was Danny."

9

The morning promised a scorcher of a day, and there were still nineteen carp riding the pipe. Moonshine studied the situation: "What are we doin' with that many fish?"

"Take 'em to the tavern," said Viv.

"Turlough's ain't open, nothing is," said Urs.

Viv forgot people in that neck of the woods are virtuous on Sundays cuz that's when God's watching. She was gonna march into the bar and persuade Skeeter Turlough to buy the fish at fifty cents each.

"Pretty soon they'll smell like a fat's man's ..."

"Shut up, Moonshine," said Viv. She stared at the fish. "Where's Turlough live?"

"In town but this time of year he'd be at his cabin up north. His son Skeeter's in charge."

"Well, then, where does he live?"

"In town. What are you plannin'?" Urs asked what everyone was thinking.

"We go to his house, talk him into buying the fish, he opens the tavern and puts it in his icebox. We give it to him on credit. If his customers eat it and he sells more beer cuz of the salt and grease, then he pays us."

"That'd be a first," said Felix, "hobos extending credit."

"Come on, Urs," said Viv, "let's go see him."

If anyone else had asked, Urs woulda laughed in their face, but it was Viv. "Felix has to go too."

"Well then, into the breach," sighed Felix.

"I'm going," I said, "I'll carry some fish."

"I'll go if I have to," said Gaetan.

"I'll stay here and guard the place," said Monroe.

"They also serve who only stand and wait," said Felix. I think some of the things he said had already been said by someone else.

We wrapped the fish in newspaper, stuffed it in shoulder bags, and headed toward Hertzville in the heat of the day.

Skeeter Turlough's house was five blocks up the hill, adding more misery to our trip. We listened around the side as Viv knocked. A young girl opened the door. "Is your dad home?" Viv asked.

"Nope, he's playin' baseball."

"How about your mom, is she home?"

"Nope."

"Is anyone else here?"

"Stanley."

"Do you think I could talk to Stanley?"

"Nope."

"Really, why not?"

"Cuz he's a dog."

We had to laugh and hope Skeeter's daughter didn't know enough to call the police cuz she heard strange men lurking around the corner. Viv came back laughing too in spite of her frustration.

"Now what?" asked Felix.

"You're a regular at Turlough's, Urs," said Viv.

"So what?"

"They wouldn't mind if you broke in, would they?" That reminded me what Sheriff Pope said regarding Urs going to jail. "We'll leave a note saying we're sorry and the fish in the icebox is a business opportunity."

Once again it was Viv doing the asking and Urs had a hard time refusing so we ended up at Turlough's back door. "Which one of us knows how to jimmy a lock?"

"I could do it," said Gaetan, "but if they caught me they'd have to open up the hardware store."

"Why's that?" a couple of us asked at the same time.

"To get a rope," he said. We all laughed and were immediately ashamed.

"The lock on the bathroom window's broke." Urs'd been withholding information. "You get started for home, Gaetan, we'll do the rest."

"So you think a lone black man walking down the road's safer than one breaking into a bar?" said Gaetan.

Felix went with him.

I was the only one who'd fit through the bathroom window so that's when I committed my first offense against the law if you don't count possession of stolen library books. I opened the back door and we quickly rearranged the beer in the icebox to make way for the fish. Viv found paper and pencil to write a note saying "sorry but we had to do it, will explain tomorrow." We left in a hurry and caught up to Felix and Gaetan.

The next morning Urs and Viv and me tried to get to the tavern before Skeeter arrived but he was already there. Good thing he wasn't too excitable and good thing his dad wasn't there (because he was excitable) and good thing Viv was a good talker and good thing Skeeter knew Urs to be a partly honest man. When Skeeter saw us he said "Glad you left a note cuz I'da called the sheriff to say my icebox was vandalized by fishmongers. Now tell me what I'm supposed to do with these things and by the way I'm getting the bathroom window fixed."

Viv explained how eating fish'd sell more beer and we'd found exactly the right combination of spices to make it irresistible and make people thirsty. "It's better than the one you tried the other day," she said.

Skeeter flaked off a piece and popped it in his mouth. He was a comedian, which comes with bartending, I gather, and he made a funny face before saying "I suppose a person could get used to it. But carp's got a bad reputation around here; who's gonna buy it?"

"You give it away," said Viv, "and raise the price of beer by a nickel."

"Leon!" Skeeter yelled, "come here a minute." Leon came in from the bathroom, mop in hand. "Taste this." Skeeter forked off a big piece and shoved it in Leon's mouth. "What do you think?"

"Can I have a beer to wash it down?" Skeeter poured him a beer. Leon picked off another piece and drained the beer. Viv smiled. "I gotta finish the bathroom," he said, and left.

"We can supply twenty four fish a week," said Viv, "and we need seventy five cents a fish."

"Where you getting these fish, Urs, I heard your nets got tore up," said Skeeter.

"We get 'em out of the lake just like everyone else," said Urs.

"Tell you what, I'll set some out tonight when the regulars come in and we'll see if we sell more beer. I'll give you forty five cents for every fish they eat."

"We got overhead," said Viv, "spices and labor. We need the seventy five cents."

"Sixty cents," said Skeeter, "final offer."

"The man drives a hard bargain, Viv, we should consider it." That was Urs, concealing his pleasure over the fact we were getting ten cents more than we thought.

Viv sighed: "Oh, I guess."

"But if pops comes back and doesn't want carp polluting his bar, the deal's off. He's funny that way," Skeeter shouted as we left.

That evening we made our third trip to Turlough's in two days to see what the regulars did with our fish. We begged Gaetan to join us, which he did with some concern. He brought his guitar, which, he said, tended to defuse racial tension. That and the fact Urs could bear hug the crap outta anyone who started a fuss. This time Monroe decided to go along in hopes there might be free beer for the people who supplied the tasty fish. Turned out he was a prophet.

We sat at a corner table away from the door. Around five o'clock people wandered in and by six there were a dozen folks drinking and joking and noticing the black man in the corner and the smoky smell coming from the bar. This was the crowd that drank their supper, owing to their hard day at the power plant, or maybe they didn't wanna go home to a ramshackle house and screaming kids. They needed a little nourishment and were quick to pick at the fish, even quicker after Skeeter explained it was free but sorry he had to raise beer to thirty cents.

By seven there were fifteen new folks to more than make up for the five who left. Skeeter had to set out more fish. Zack came over and sat reverse style: "So you're the ones who smoked this carp?"

"Yes, sir," replied Felix.

"Can't say it's good but I can't say it's bad either. Better'n the one a couple days ago. Hey Ambrose, come over here. This here's the gang did the fish."

"So you're the jokers."

"We are indeed," said Felix, "we are the masterminds who orchestrated this delicacy." I don't know why he decided to speak for us, but Viv kicked him under the table for it, cuz Turlough's wasn't the place for fancy talk.

"Hey Skeeter," yelled Ambrose, "a round for the table over here; put it on mine."

"What are you drinkin'?" yelled Skeeter.

"Beer!" yelled Moonshine.

"Good," yelled Skeeter, "cuz that's all we got."

"And a couple grape Nehis," yelled Viv.

Zack bought another round, which got the drinkers real relaxed, 'specially Gaetan, who strummed his guitar.

"Let's hear somethin', black man" someone yelled.

"His name's 'Gaetan'," shouted Viv.

A large man strode over to shake hands: "Glad to meet you, Gaetan. Play somethin'."

Gaetan didn't need urging. "Well, let's see," he said, "you like naughty songs?"

"Hey fellas," the large man yelled, "do we like naughty songs?"

"Hell yeah" came from someone, amidst encouragement from the fellas and the few ladies present.

"Well then, here goes." Gaetan had songs about making out in cars, skinny dipping and peeing in the bushes. The crowd cheered.

Skeeter showed up with a tray of beers and set one in front of each of us, including me. "Cops don't come around on Mondays," he winked. Viv rolled her eyes. I drank my beer and hers too.

Gaetan drained his beer and put his hand on Moonshine's shoulder. "Ladies and gentlemen," he said, "this man right here brings happiness to sad and lonely people. Give him some corn, a few pounds of sugar, a pinch of yeast and some equipment, and he'll whip up a brew that'll curl your toes and smooth your blues. They don't call him 'Moonshine Monroe' for nothin'." Gaetan launched into the song he'd made up a couple nights earlier and had people laughing and clapping to the beat. Moonshine was the butt of the joke but he'd drunk enough beer not to care.

Gaetan changed a couple words and invited the crowd to sing the chorus with him. They sang so loud Father Matthias could probably hear it inside the church across the road.

"We drink at Turlough's here on earth
cuz heaven's strictly dry.
Just give me beer and heaps of love
and somehow I'll get by.
I'll satisfy my appetites before the day I die,
cuz there ain't no earthly pleasure
in the everlasting sky."

Gaetan sank into his chair exhausted but every so often someone would start the chorus again and the folks'd join in and order another round. Skeeter had to press Leon into waiter duty even though Leon could barely handle a mop let alone a tray.

It took us twice as long to get home that night cuz we couldn't walk straight.

10

The next day started late cuz hangovers do that. It was afternoon before Viv finally got us on the porch to talk about fish: "What happens when the water rises and the carp can swim out of the backwater?"

Urs was about to answer when around the corner popped Gerald E. Norton, also known as Three Finger Eddie. He'd snuck down the trail from the road like only he can do; the goats didn't even notice.

Eddie was windy. He crowed about his transactions at the private detective convention in Chicago, and by "transactions" he meant "thefts." The bragging rights he earned were just as important as the loot he collected, so picking the pockets of a street smart group like detectives was a big deal. Eddie was good at his profession but he was also capable of some blunders. If he held up his right hand to order five beers the waiter would bring three.

Felix tried to stop Eddie's stories cuz it wasn't in a criminal's best interest to talk about his crimes and knowing about his deeds made us all accomplices. "If we have to testify in court," said Felix, "we'd have to choose between perjuring ourselves or sending you to prison."

"Well then, you'd perjure yourself," said Eddie, "nothing to that, I've told hundreds of lies."

I'd have to give that round to Eddie. Lying's no big deal unless you do it to someone you like. To be clear, though, everything I've told you is the honest truth. If I stretched anything it was for fun and I admitted it.

Eddie didn't carry a shoulder bag like the other bums. He had a regular suitcase with three different styles of clothes so he could fit in with whatever class of people he was robbing. He was wearing pants with an actual cuff at the bottom and a long sleeve white shirt and vest with a red bow tie and a hat like Laurence Larkin's. And his hair was trimmed and combed like a salesman. Eddie got off the train at the power plant and went to the bushes to change from his boxcar clothes to the peddler outfit, which made him look decent enough to hitch a ride. The driver was a businessman, he said, who didn't notice his cigarette case was missing when he dropped Eddie at the top of our hill. Eddie grinned and held up the gold case. "Oh my god, don't show me that," said Felix, covering his eyes.

"Wait!" said Eddie, "you won't believe what I scored." Before anyone could stop him, he turned over the suitcase and spilled out four wallets along with his clothes. "These private dicks are morons," he said. "Usually I'd heist one wallet and head for the hills, but these guys were so drunk it was like taking candy from babies—which I'd never do, by the way, because a man has to have principles. How about that, I outsmarted a bunch of detectives. Let 'em put that in their advertisements."

We were used to Eddie bragging and hogging the conversation, but he went on so long we made excuses and went our separate ways. Later around the fire, it was time to break out the stories we'd been stretching into epics in our heads. Felix lit his pipe and took over: "Did I ever tell you how Urs got his name?"

Of course he had, once every summer, but we loved to hear it cuz Felix made it bigger and funnier every year.

"Well," he began, "during the Coolidge administration, when Urs was still in diapers—he was twenty years old, mind you, but still in diapers—he was digging in a dumpster, looking for valuable trash, which to some would be an oxymoron, but Urs didn't know an oxymoron from a regular moron, so he went from one dumpster to the next, recovering stuff only he would find useful. It was toward the end of June, which is an important detail as you will see. It so happens there was a large female black bear also foraging near that particular dumpster. She wasn't the most beautiful bear in the forest; in fact, she was hard to look at since one of her eyeballs was hanging out of its socket and her jaw was bent sideways from the brain rattling swat she received when she tried to move in on another sow's boar. Even so, it was probably her whiny nagging and poor me attitude that made the male bears run the other way whenever she stumbled into the neighborhood. Now Urs was focused on a beat up book of old photographs looking for one that might incriminate someone into a blackmail payoff, so he had no idea there was a huge bear on the other side of the dumpster. And the bear had her nose to the ground, slurping up ants and running her tongue inside soup cans that had spilled onto the ground. She worked her way around and ended up face to face with Urs, who promptly shit his pants, which wasn't a big deal since, as I said, he was wearing diapers. Mama bear licked her chops and thick saliva mixed with Campbell's mushroom soup drooled down her crooked jowl. In a split second, Urs hoisted himself into the dumpster and congratulated himself on his quick thinking, forgetting bears have no problem pulling themselves into open dumpsters, which is exactly what this bear did. So there they were, face to face, in an eight foot long steel bucket. The bear snorted and drooled and Urs dug into the garbage, submerging himself in rotten cabbage from

Pedro's Mexican Restaurant, where the homemade sauerkraut never caught on. The bear pawed away the cabbage, eating as much as she cast aside, until she and Urs were nose to nose, causing him to gag on the stench of rotten cabbage bear breath. Then something unexpected happened—the bear stuck out her slimy tongue and licked Urs from the base of his neck to the top of his head. It was an affectionate lick, which Urs imitated in later years when making whoopee with human females. What in the name of Winnie the Pooh was going on, you might ask."

Felix re-loaded his pipe with Prince Albert tobacco and re-lighted it, leaving us in suspense for at least a minute. "Let's look at this from the bear's perspective," he continued. "She's had no male companionship for years due to her whiny nature, and the dangling eyeball doesn't help. She stumbles upon a burly beast covered in black hair, which her damaged eyesight takes to be another bear or at least close enough. Her nose still works, though, and she smells a raunchy, earthy odor, which we all know Urs emits. Remember I mentioned it was late June, which is the end of the mating season for bears. If they haven't got any nookie by then, they'll spend the whole next year frustrated and angry. So what does this bear do? She turns end for end and backs into Urs, who, at age twenty, was just reaching puberty and wasn't sure yet what to do with his boomstick. He vaulted out of the dumpster and ran for home, leaving behind a frustrated bear peering out the bin. A few years later I met Urs for the first time and he told me about his encounter with the bear so I told him to look at the night sky and there she was—Ursa Major, his unrequited love, known by some as the Big Dipper—making this man sitting here Ursa Infectus or Urs for short."

Even though we'd heard the story at least ten times, we let Felix tell it uninterrupted to see what details he would add.

This time the diapers, the Mexican sauerkraut and the Campbell's soup were all new and got hearty laughs. He also had a new word for the male organ every year; this time it was "boomstick" but in the past it's been "plonker," "tent pole," "general with two colonels" and ... I can't remember the rest. All this grew out of Urs saying that bears would come to our beach to take a bath. The thing about incriminating photos wasn't so funny and I hoped Felix would leave it out next year. Urs might acquire some small things not rightly his, but he'd never really hurt somebody—unless they kicked his dog, which I already mentioned.

It seemed like it was Viv's turn to spin a yarn. I had the feeling she was hiding some crazy stories but she never said a word so Urs took over. "Up on the bluff there's this colony of morel mushrooms," he began, and he spun the tale about Claude Pease, only he enlarged it with shotgun blasts as the farmer chased us on his tractor. Then Urs moved on to the skunks: "But a far more dangerous adversary lay in wait for us on the trail back to ..."

"Skunks!" I interrupted, "a hundred at least, and they'd been waitin' there to ambush us and our dog. Urs grabbed a stick and swung it wildly, yellin' 'take that, you motherfuckers' and brave old Woof jumped in to grab a few of 'em by the neck and fling 'em away but she got soaked with the spray ..."

Urs butted in again: "We stripped down naked and ran back to the cabin but there was a lonesome lady admiring my manhood and wishin' we were alone cuz ..."

"... cuz she'd give him a lecture on common decency," I yelled. "Her husband was there ..."

"He kicked the dog so I beat the shit outta him and the three of them hightailed it up the hill."

"Three of them?" asked Felix.

"Oh yeah," I said, "another guy tore up a buncha thousand dollar checks."

It was the most I'd ever conjured up a tale other than a quick lie. There was laughter and applause which gave me confidence like if I was ever on the witness stand I could be trusted to shape the facts into something agreeable to one person or another.

The fire crackled and settled into coals, turning our thoughts inward. Felix started in again: "How many stars do you suppose there are?"

We looked up. Moonshine guessed "thousands."

"More than that," said Eddie. The rest of us agreed.

"Would you believe billions," said Felix, "or even trillions? And would you believe that, at the beginning of time, they were all packed together in one tiny ball the size of a finger tip?"

"Who says so?" asked Eddie.

"A friend of mine."

"How can a whole universe be as big as this?" Eddie held up a pinky. "Your friend's not that smart."

"His friend used to be a professor at Oxbow College," said Viv. "Antoine Thomas. I read his book."

"Used to be? What's he do now?" You could tell Eddie was looking for a fight.

"He lives on the street," said Viv.

"So he ain't that smart." Eddie didn't care much about hurting people's feelings cuz he knew full well Felix'd been a professor at Oxbow and he was also living on the street. Him and Mr. Thomas got kicked outta Oxbow cuz of their unusual friendship.

Felix shook it off. "What if I told you that billions of years ago that pinky size ball exploded into all those stars and those stars will keep racing outward until they run out of energy?"

"What happens then?" I asked.

"They snap back," said Felix, "like they were on a giant rubber band."

We got lost in quiet thoughts.

Gaetan broke the silence. "Granddad played with Jean-Baptiste Bideau, the Louisiana bluesman. Gramps wasn't a real drummer—that was Silky Savoy's job—but he could keep a beat and he played some odd things like spoons on lively numbers or a rainstick in back of Bideau's blues. The real instrumentalist was Christian Fontenot, the fiddle player who could inspire an audience to dance and shout 'hallelujah' with his explosive riffs or bring 'em to tears with his counterpoint to Jean-Baptiste's raspy ballads of heartache and suffering. Granddad's real job was to line up dates for the group. Every month or so he'd hitch a ride to a new city and talk the owners of low class bars and sometimes whorehouses into allowing Bideau to perform in return for whatever money folks would throw into his hat. The group would follow in a Model T Ford and play from sunset to closing, the songs getting more and more soulful as the audience got more and more drunk. Their circuit passed through backwater towns in Louisiana, Mississippi, and sometimes Arkansas. It usually took six months to get around it, depending on how profitable any particular location was at any particular time. When they got back home, which was Dundee, Louisiana, granddad would sometimes take me with him to hear 'em play, my mom giving me up grudgingly to a late night in a worrisome environment. One time Bideau was off by himself trying chords and I was glued to his fingers as they hit the strings. He said "can you sing this, son? 'Ain't no use to cryin' if your honey bunch is lyin' 'bout a thing she done that just ain't right.'"

"I sang it and he said 'you got it, the pitch is perfect. Now sing it again and make me feel sad.' I sang it again and made him feel sad, along with Gramps and Silky and Fontenot, who applauded. I stayed for all four sets that night, way past my ten year old bedtime. Bideau's singing would stir the souls of humans and varmints alike. I was hooked. After the lights went out and the drunks had left the building, Bideau said to me: 'Come back tomorrow and tell Gramps to get you here an hour early.' When I got there, Bideau sat me down and put this very guitar in my hands. 'This instrument was played by my daddy,' said Bideau. 'It's got the nicks and bruises of a sad and forlorn life. It's the one I learned on. If you can play and sing 'Black Dog Blues' by the time we leave town next week, you can have it.' He showed me how to play a C chord and an A chord. I practiced till my finger tips were raw and a week later I could play and sing 'Black Dog Blues' so he gave me the guitar."

Gaetan strummed a few chords, then continued. "I loved Jean-Baptiste Bideau's music and so did everyone who heard him sing. That included the women who crowded close to the stage, hoping to catch his eye. He was a tall, handsome man and it was common for him to leave the bar with a different woman every night. On the night of July 4, 1933, a white woman named Jolene sat close to the stage at Fortress Bar, along with a couple lady friends. The crowd was particularly rowdy because patriotism and booze go well together. That's usually a good thing because an inebriated audience tends to be free with its money, especially if it's mostly white folks pretending to like black folks, as it was on this particular night. During the breaks after the first two sets, the ladies invited Bideau to sit with them for a beer, which he did. During the break after the third set, Jolene followed Bideau to the alley for a cigarette. Her husband, Cooter, was bar hopping that night. He and three friends staggered in to see Bideau and Jolene come in through the back door. After closing they waited for Jean-Baptiste outside and pushed him around some. 'We didn't do nothin' out back,' shouted Jolene and Cooter slapped her hard enough to make her fall. Gramps tried to help her up but Cooter shoved him to the ground. I saw all this through the window because Gramps told me to stay inside. Savoy and Fontenot had already left. Cooter and his friends kept pushing Bideau around and finally Cooter punched him in the stomach, then the mouth, sending him to the ground. Cooter went to kick him but one of his friends pulled him back saying that was enough cuz he knows how to sing. Gramps started to pull Jean-Baptiste to his feet and Cooter said 'leave him down there' but Granddad didn't pay attention. 'You do what I say, shithead!' Cooter screamed but Gramps pulled Bideau to his feet and dusted him off. Cooter decked Granddad and dragged him to a Chevrolet, all the while Jolene screaming 'leave him alone, he didn't do nothin'!' They forced Jolene into the Chevy too and the six of them drove off, leaving me and Bideau wondering what to do. We got in his Ford and drove to the police station, woke up the deputy, who said he'd have a cop investigate in the morning. Bideau drove me home to an hysterical mom and a sleepless night. The next morning a cop came by to say Granddad was found hanging from a sycamore tree. They needed to hang a black man and Jean-Baptiste Bideau was too good a singer so they did it to Gramps instead."

    Nobody spoke. Viv cozied up to Gaetan. He sang without the guitar, just his deep, rich voice reaching out to all who would listen.

    The song was about a black dog slouchin' down the road on a moonless night, trying to stay outta sight. I'm guessing the black dog was really Gaetan or his gramps and it probably called up Gaetan's memory of getting beaten before Viv and

Felix found him. I wish I could sing it for you but I can't sing and I ain't black so there's two reasons I wouldn't do it justice. The words floated over the glassy lake and anyone who heard 'em had to stop whatever they were doing and become a better person if only for a minute. We separated quietly. Gaetan and Viv went to the hay bed in the barn. I lay by the fire with my head on a rolled up blanket and wondered when the stars would snap back and crush us all.

11

Through the summer into September we settled into a routine that earned enough cash to keep a bear size man, a sixteen year old, and five hobos alive. The backwater was getting shallow due to the hot, dry summer, so we could spear most of the carp with the garden fork. We managed to get at least twenty on every trip, which we made on Fridays. We smoked 'em overnight Friday and all day Saturday and delivered 'em to the tavern by the time the regulars arrived in the late afternoon. Gaetan went along cuz people liked his songs and threw coins into the guitar case. Skeeter even started hanging a cardboard sign out front saying "Black man sings tonight." Once in a while he'd sneak some beer profits into Gaetan's pocket. If I ever figured out how to break Big Baasha loose to crush the town, I'd want to spare Skeeter. Him and his daughter. And Stanley.

Sometimes Felix or Moonshine would come along but we kept Eddie away owing to the trouble he would cause if his hand got caught in someone's pocket. He couldn't stop himself from stealing the same way Moonshine couldn't stop himself from drinking.

There was other work, mostly garden stuff like drying and pickling vegetables for the winter. And there was another cutting of hay, which was godawful work in the heat. Moonshine said once we worked him like a slave. Gaetan glared at him and walked away. Viv said "shut the fuck up, Monroe," which she said at least once a day.

Skeeter asked us to supply extra fish for his little party on Labor Day, so we did our catching and cleaning and smoking for Saturday night and did it again on Sunday for the Monday party.

That complicated Labor Day cuz we needed to get Otis and Tyrone to Farmer Fred's Petting Farm up the road. From spring to the end of August Fred charged money for kids to pet baby animals. He wanted gentle pigs, calves and goats and he needed 'em born by spring so the adult animals had to get to work right after he shut down the petting part of his operation for the season. Fred didn't keep the male animals around cuz they'd be jumping the females in front of the little kids. He coulda kept 'em in separate pens but then he'd have to feed 'em and besides they fetched a good price as meat, so he paid Otis and Tyrone five bucks each to visit his farm and service the mama goats. Fred paid someone else to supply pig and cow sperm. They also arrived on Labor Day so there was quite a spectacle in the barnyard.

Urs and me and Viv and Gaetan leashed up the goats and walked the two miles to Farmer Fred's. The other three stayed behind to tend the fish for Skeeter's party that night.

When we arrived, Angus was already there and his bull was playing piggyback with the cows. We let our goats into the barnyard and watched 'em work. Mr. Fatback drove his truck through the gate, opened a cage, and ran like hell cuz a mean boar jumped out. I don't know how they were gonna get him back in the cage when his work was done; maybe they'd just shoot him and haul him to the butcher.

We didn't know the man's name to be Angus, that's just what Urs called him cuz he was a cow man. Same with Fatback.

This was Gaetan's first time to see the show and a song about animal romance percolated through his brain. He laughed to himself every few minutes but wouldn't tell us what he'd come up with.

Farmer Fred hung his belly over the fence rail: "Wish I could get the missus to do some of that. She gave out a couple years ago." Fred gave Urs ten bucks with the promise of one more for each baby goat. Otis and Tyrone earned us fifteen to twenty bucks a year but I'm not sure it was enough to make up for the trouble they caused, like when they broke into the garden or stood on the railroad tracks, causing the train to blow its hellish horn. I think Urs kept 'em around for company; better to have assholes for friends than no friends at all.

On the way back we ran across a dead raccoon with a tire track across its head so the meaty parts were untouched. We dragged him back. Urs and Viv cleaned him and ran two rebar through him. They couldn't put him over the fire cuz the fish occupied that space so they propped him up on the shady side of the cabin and hoped he wouldn't spoil overnight. The goats were spent and went happily to their stalls; we locked 'em in cuz all of us were going to Skeeter's little party, even Eddie, who said we shouldn't worry cuz he didn't conduct transactions on holidays. The liar.

We got to town about five o'clock and found Skeeter's little party wasn't little at all since half the town was there, including people you wouldn't expect to be at a tavern.

Father Matthias had told his parishioners it was okay to attend as long as they parked their cars in the church lot across the street and as long as they didn't go inside the tavern and left before dark. It was good to be neighborly, he said, in an effort to influence the unrighteous toward God. Deacon Timothy passed around lemonade to the decent people, which included library ladies Gertrude and Frances, Hotel Harriet, the ladies from Lavinia's salon, and maybe twenty other god-fearing men and straight-backed women. They all pretended to enjoy their sinful neighbors.

Old man Turlough stood at a big barbecue rack, sucking on a cigar and slapping chicken legs and breasts and potato salad on paper plates for a dollar each. Leon carried the food to folks who mostly stood but some of the older and less stable ones sat on benches. When Leon couldn't keep up, Skeeter pressed me into service. I took around food and beer and brought the money to Skeeter, who pushed a buck into my pocket when his dad wasn't looking. Like I said, Skeeter was okay. I hoped Big Baasha would miss him. And his daughter. And Stanley.

I looked around for Louise but her and her mom weren't there. Her dad was, though; him and Virgil Dickerson were whispering. Maybe they had business to discuss but I caught 'em looking over at Urs a couple times so I had to wonder.

Later on Sheriff Pope and Linus stopped by in civilian clothes and ate for free in return for not noticing beer was being served by an underage boy. Urs was careful not to mingle with folks other than the Turlough Tavern regulars cuz of the tension between him and folks who didn't see eye to eye with him, which included anybody who would have profited by Urs giving up his property in favor of a road to the island resort—in other words everybody except for the few so deep in neglectfulness they were destined to live in poverty no matter what was going on around 'em. When the sheriff arrived, Urs withdrew even further and played horseshoes around the corner where most of the crowd couldn't see. Our fish was set out for people to nibble, which caused 'em to drink more beer at thirty five cents a glass (the price went up again).

As I delivered plates I heard Father Matthias saying how Big Baasha got its name. Back in the twenties the first priest named the rock after an insignificant guy in the Bible. The priest sermonized how the rock was gonna roll down and bash the sinners, for example those who took the lord's name in vain and those who killed people unless it was to protect the country in wartime.

Gaetan kept to himself, guitar in hand, still putting together the words for the barnyard romance song he would sing later. Viv kept a protective eye on him and ignored Jenkins when he sat beside her. It woulda been fun if he said the wrong thing and Viv decked him.

Eddie was dressed in respectable clothes and combed his hair every time the breeze ruffled it. He roamed through the crowd and gave no indication of criminal intent. For extra measure Felix stayed five steps behind. Eddie told Penelope she was a "vision," like he told all the women. She was wearing her usual floppy blouse and I'm sure he wanted to slide his left hand—the one with all five fingers attached— down it to feel around. Penelope probably woulda let him except Felix was watching like a hawk.

When the party was at its busiest we heard a car pull up and Laurence Larkin the Third appeared around the corner. Turlough dished him a plate and refused payment but Larkin peeled off a five dollar bill and stuck it in Turlough's shirt pocket. Then he shook hands with everybody who would be helpful in the pursuit of progress, ending up with Jerry Christianson and Virgil Dickerson, who were still whispering.

When he was done shaking hands and eating chicken, Larkin went around front, along with Jerry and Virgil. I peeked around the corner and saw Borg waiting in the Mercedes. He drove the three of 'em through town and stopped at Jerry's hardware store. I didn't know why but I figured it out later.

When the sun set, a lota folks wandered home. Old Man Turlough threw the last chicken pieces to Stanley and a couple other dogs and sank into a chair beside Sheriff Pope and Deputy Hooper. Skeeter wheeled the beer keg into the building and looked at Gaetan: "You got somethin' to play for us, black man?" Gaetan jumped at the chance.

The mood inside took a turn to the rough side maybe cuz Father Matthias and the decent people had left and Sheriff Pope was outside. Also cuz Skeeter let people pour their own beer for free. Gaetan plucked the guitar strings and people gathered round. Skeeter made Gaetan sit on the bar. "Who wants to hear some singin'?" shouted Skeeter. He set Gaetan's guitar case on the bar and threw in a buck; others threw coins.

"Play the drinkin' song!" someone shouted, so Gaetan launched into "We drink at Turlough's here on earth cuz heaven's strictly dry" and the crowd sang along. He followed with a couple naughty songs folks had heard before. Then Gaetan broke out the song he'd been working on all day: "Here's a little thing that occurred to me today as I was watchin' some barnyard romance," he said, and he sang out some verses that were wicked naughty and funny at the same time. There was one about a rooster pursuing a hen that went like this:

> "The chicky he was chasin',
> in a panic was a racin'
> around and around the yard.
> She was runnin' from he rooster
> who was tryin' to seduce 'er
> cuz his pecker was a gettin' real hard."

Gaetan used his poetic license on that one cuz roosters don't have peckers.

I'm a terrible singer as you just found out so I'm not going to sing any more but Gaetan had the animals engaging in all kinds of carnal mischief like bulls bangin' and stallions layin' pipe and pigs oinking while they were boinking.

One of the ladies who had a few beers, called out to Gaetan: "Hey, black man, you got a song to cheer up a man with a small pecker cuz that's what Tucker here's got and he's feelin' kinda sad." Tucker was a large man with a red face that got redder when it became obvious he had left the lady unsatisfied. Gaetan threw caution to the wind, maybe cuz he was eager to use the obvious rhyme with Tucker's name, and within a few seconds sang out: "There was a big man with a big red face—I think his name was Tucker. The man was tall but his dick so small his woman said he couldn't fuck her."

Tucker was crazy mad about a black man making fun of his white man dick. He hurled himself through the crowd, pulled Gaetan onto the floor, and kicked him in the face and ribs. Before he could kick anywhere else, Urs was on him from behind, squeezing till he turned from red to ... well, bright red ... and it seemed like his ribs should crack. Viv bloodied his face with three good punches and woulda done more except Felix yelled "hold her back or she'll kill him!"

Urs threw Tucker to the floor and sat on him while Viv bent over Gaetan, whose face was covered with blood. "Get the sheriff!" someone yelled and a minute later Hugo Pope walked in.

Linus was behind him: "I'll call the ambulance."

"Wait a minute, Linus, it's a black man." Pope cleared the crowd away and hunched over Gaetan. "How bad you hurt?"

"Where's my guitar?" moaned Gaetan.

"I got your guitar," I said.

"Put it in the case; keep it safe," whispered Gaetan.

"He will," said Viv, "but tell us where you're hurt."

"All over," whispered Gaetan, spitting blood. "My arm might be broke."

Who the hell started this?" demanded Pope.

"The black man was singin' about Tucker's manhood," came from the crowd.

"What manhood?" giggled the lady. I'm pretty sure she only meant for her friends to hear it, but she was drunk and it came out so loud that Tucker heard it and got up to leave.

"Where you going, Tucker, and who bloodied your nose?" asked the sheriff.

"She did!" Tucker pointed at Viv.

"Go on home, Tucker; tell your mama you got beat up by a woman," said Pope. Tucker slammed the door behind him. "Now what are we going to do with this guy?"

"The hospital in Virmeer!" someone shouted.

"It's a holiday," said Pope, "they're short staffed." I think that was a lie.

"He needs a bed and a doctor," said Viv.

Voices came from the crowd: "Over to the hotel." "Wake up Harriet." "What can she do for him?" "Give him a bed." "And some ice cream." People laughed at that last remark but some of 'em didn't think it was funny till Gaetan whispered "Ice cream sounds pretty good."

"Old Man McDonald was a medic in the war," said Skeeter.

"Linus, go wake up Harriet," commanded the sheriff, "we're bringing him over. Go out and get one of those benches for a stretcher."

"I can walk," said Gaetan, wobbling to his feet. Skeeter supplied bar towels for his face. Old Man Turlough made Leon wipe the blood off the floor, then pulled his son aside for a finger wagging lecture. I think it was about letting a black man into the bar. Or maybe it was about free beer.

Gaetan staggered to the sheriff's Pontiac. Viv stretched him out in the back seat and they headed into town with Urs and Felix and Monroe and me running behind. As we left the building I heard someone say "my wallet's missing."

Harriet was waiting with Linus at the hotel. "You didn't tell me he was black," she said. Viv shot her a sharp look. "But that doesn't matter," corrected Harriet. She led us to a room and watched while Viv and Urs eased Gaetan onto the mattress. "That blood's going to ruin my sheets," said Harriet.

"Send me a bill," said Sheriff Pope. "Linus, go get Old Man McDonald."

Linus headed out the door, then turned back: "Where is he?"

"Probably at home," said Harriet.

Linus turned back again: "Where is that?"

"He lives above his store," said Harriet, "but he's deaf so he won't hear you knocking."

"I'll throw stones at the window," said Linus.

"Not big ones," said his boss.

Skeeter was right—Old Man McDonald was a medic in the war, but not the last war. Or the one before that. He knew about aspirin and iodine. He hurried into the hotel in his pajamas with Lettie close behind and lifted the towel off Gaetan's face. "There's iodine in the store, bottom shelf in the drug section," he said.

Off went Linus. "And aspirin," McDonald shouted after him. Lettie mumbled a prayer and stroked Gaetan's good arm the same way she stroked Dash's neck. I decided I couldn't Baasha the town unless the McDonalds were away.

The iodine stung like crazy and Gaetan let out a scream. Nobody thought to dull his senses with whiskey. Harriet hurried to get ice cream.

When Gaetan was resting easier, which took a half hour, Sheriff Pope and Deputy Hooper headed off. Urs and me and three hobos wanted to stay but Harriet said there were rules. The doctor could stay but everybody else had to leave. "I'm stayin'," said Viv, her voice so fierce Hotel Harriet could only shrug her shoulders and walk away.

"Take care of my guitar," said Gaetan as we left.

"I got it," I said, "it's safe, Gaetan."

It was well after midnight when we got to the cabin and the four of us collapsed into sleep. After the moon had set, Woof barked to scare off a coyote. Or so I thought.

12

I woke to screaming and flames licking out the gaps in the barn. "Urs! Urs! Wake up! The barn!"

Urs ran out, rubbing his eyes: "Barn's on fire! Get the animals!" He ran barefoot to the barn door and pulled but it held fast. "It's jammed! Help me with this door!" Felix and Moonshine ran up. "Pull it off the hinges!"

We shoved our fingers into the crack between the door and the jamb and heaved backwards. The door ripped off the rotted part of the jamb and hung there till Dash barged through and tore it completely off. "Get him in the lake!" yelled Urs. Felix and Moonshine pushed and dragged Dash till he was neck deep in water and steam hissed off his hide.

Urs charged into the flames. I tried to follow but he pushed me back. He heaved himself against the goat stall, smashing it in, and dragged out one of the goats by the hind legs, then hauled himself into the lake, stripping off his smoldering clothes as he went. I ran a bucket of water to the goat. He was quivering in agony and I couldn't tell if it was Otis or Tyrone for the charring. I headed to the lake for more water but Urs shouted "Wait, get the gun."

I ran to the house and pulled the twenty two from the rack over the chest, grabbed shells, and loaded while I ran back: "Are you sure?"

"He's gone," said Urs, "do it quick."

I shot the goat through the brain to end his misery the fastest. The screaming from inside the barn stopped so we knew the other goat was gone and there was no hope for the chickens.

Moonshine ran up with a bucket of water but the flames were through the roof. "Let it go," said Urs, "it's too late." We watched the flames eat the building, which collapsed on itself in a few minutes. Dash dragged himself outta the lake and fell next to Urs, who cradled the donkey's head and wept. So did I.

Thick black smoke was still rising when the sun came up. People stopped their cars to watch through the breach and apparently one of 'em went to town to call the sheriff cuz a Pontiac with a red whirly light on top stopped and two officers walked down the trail.

"Looks like the barn's a goner," said one.

"That was bound to happen," said the other one under his breath. He didn't mean for me to hear it. "I'm Deputy Logan," he said, "this is Deputy Webster. Got a call a half hour ago; someone saw smoke."

"What's with that?" Webster was looking at Dash, who'd pulled himself onto the grass, probably cuz the beach sand grated on his burns.

"He's a donkey," I said. I can see how they thought that was a smartass thing to say, but I honestly didn't mean it that way. Their look said "cut it out."

"Anybody hurt?" said Logan.

"The goats are dead," said Felix, "and the chickens."

"I meant are any people hurt?" Now Logan thought Felix was a smartass.

"Urs here's got burns on his feet," said Moonshine, "and his hair's all burned off." Urs had his feet in a bucket of water and it was true, the massive thicket of chest hair was gone, leaving a red glow. His eyebrows were burnt off and the hair on his head was short and crinkly.

"Let's see the feet," said Logan. Urs lifted 'em outta the bucket, revealing red blisters so ugly you knew he couldn't walk. "Who's your doctor?"

"Don't have one."

"Should we take you to the hospital in Virmeer?"

"Heard they're under staffed."

"You're Urs, huh? Your name's been mentioned at the office. Sheriff Pope'll want to check into this fire. He's not on duty till noon. Unless there's an emergency somewhere, he'll probably stop by."

"If I were you," said Webster, "I'd do something about the donkey. If you want to save him, I'd hide him. The sheriff's kind of a shoot first and get the facts later guy and if he see's an animal in pain, you don't know what could happen."

The deputies left. Urs kept his feet in the bucket while we spread mud on Dash's burned patches so the air wouldn't get at 'em. I led him to a shady spot down the trail, tied him to a tree, and brought water and hay. Felix and Monroe picked vegetables. It seemed like a silly thing to do in the midst of such big events, but we had to eat. I set some overripe tomatoes in Woof's dish and only then did we realize she wasn't around.

"She wasn't in the barn, was she?" asked Monroe.

"I heard her bark. I think she chased off a coyote," I said.

We all knew any dispute with a coyote wasn't gonna end well for our old dog. A number of other concerns were left unsaid, such as Gaetan's health and how would we survive with no chickens, no nets, no barn, a crippled Urs and would Old Man Turlough put an end to the Saturday night fish cuz of the ruckus. And where the hell was Eddie? We slumped into exhaustion on the porch, till Sheriff Pope banged his nightstick against the cabin wall.

"What the hell went on here?" The sheriff had bloodshot eyes and was in a mood. Deputy Hooper was behind him with a notepad.

Felix answered: "We had a fire, sir."

"I can see that, numbskull. What the hell's wrong with your feet, Urs?"

"He ran into the fire," said Moonshine.

"I ain't talkin' to you," glared Pope. Urs held up his blistered feet. "And your hair's gone; guess the fire got that too. Who's that hairy guy in the Bible, Linus?"

"Samson," said Linus.

"Yeah, him; he wasn't so strong after his hair was gone." When the sheriff said that, I decided I would dynamite Big Baasha loose at noon on a Friday when he was talking to Father Matthias. "What in the name of creation is this?"

Pope was looking at the skinned raccoon propped against the cabin wall.

"Raccoon, sir," I said, "we was gonna cook it."

"Is it raccoon hunting season, Linus?"

"I don't believe so, sheriff."

"We got it off the road," I said, "it was already dead."

"Hmpph. Make a note, Linus—dead raccoon, out of season, rotting in the sun. Suspect claims it was already dead. Two metal rods sticking though it, looks like rebar. You stealin' from the highway department, Urs?"

"Don't answer that," said Felix.

"Hmpph. Barn's still hot so we're gonna wait till tomorrow to take a look. Linus, get that red rope." Linus left up the hill and Pope started rummaging inside the cabin. We heard things being moved about; drawers got opened, utensils stirred around. We held our breath when we heard the snaps on Eddie's suitcase unlock. "You going someplace, Urs, because it looks like you got some fancy clothes here. Not your size though."

The snaps closed and we breathed again. We heard the box slide out from under the bed and Pope walked out with two books. "This one says 'property of Shelby County, Tennessee Library.' That's Memphis, right? What are you doing with these books?"

"Readin' 'em," I said.

"I meant what the hell are books from Tennessee and Louisiana doin' way up here, you little asshole. And there's more in the box. What's your name, shithead?"

"Tom," I said, cuz I knew he wouldn't believe "Huckleberry."

"Well, then, Tom, tell me where the books came from."

"I found 'em in a dumpster up by the power plant. Guy musta stole 'em from down south and got tired of carryin' 'em around. I've read 'em all, sir, so I reckon they served their purpose. I was gonna return 'em if I ever get down south."

The sheriff studied my face for five seconds and laughed. "That's the funniest lie I ever heard, I'll give you that." He was right, it was a pretty good one if you were going for comedy, but if you were going for believability it was too clever by half. Linus returned with the red rope. "Put it around the barn, Linus. You have any reason to burn down your barn, Urs? Collect some insurance maybe?" We all gave the sheriff a squinty look. "Relax, guys, it was a joke. Say, Urs, you're a little short of furniture on this porch."

I ran to the fire for a stump. Sheriff Pope sat, pulled out a pack of gum, and offered it: "Care for a hit of this?"

"I'll take one," said Moonshine.

"How about you, Tom, might relax you, take off the edge."

"No thanks."

Once This River Ran Clear 91

As Deputy Hooper struggled to circle the red rope around the smoking rubble that used to be the barn, Sheriff Pope struck up a conversation like we were old friends passing the time. "Saw your rifle in there; it's an old one. You find it in a dumpster?" He looked at me and winked.

"No sir."

"Tough to kill anything with a twenty two. You'd have to hit it just so."

"Mostly target practice," I lied.

"Hmpph. Rough time last night, huh. Tucker's a handful—caused a ruckus up in Onawah too, had to pry him off an Indian woman. I hope your black friend's okay. Anybody check on him today?"

"No sir," said Felix, "but Viv's with him."

"Old Man McDonald's a hoot, huh? Probably drank some warm milk and went to bed at sundown, then we get him up in the middle of his dream about naked island women to tend to a black man who shoulda stayed down south. That bathrobe and those slippers, they're right out of the depression. A person can get stuck in his ways, don't ya think? I wonder if he used leeches back in the army. And he's sellin' dry beans out of a barrel; they've got those in cans now—you don't have to soak 'em. But he's happy, I guess, him and Lettie, bless her soul. Do you suppose they still have carnal relations? What the hell's that?" He'd just seen the lump on the beach.

"A goat," I said.

"Damn, Urs, that's some bad luck." I crossed my fingers, hoping he didn't think to ask about the donkey. He didn't, so maybe crossing fingers helps. "Hey Linus, what's taking so long?"

"The rope's too short, boss."

"Leave a gap—they get the idea. I don't want anyone near that barn before we check it out tomorrow, you understand? You can bury the goat, though; I'd do it soon."

Pope and Hooper left. Urs kept his feet in the bucket while the rest of us buried the goat and raccoon in the woods. After we mounded up the dirt, Moonshine said "should we put up a cross?"

"I don't think they were Christians," said Felix. The two of 'em led Dash back and I walked south on the tracks looking for Woof, thinking that was the direction of her bark. A hundred yards down I found a blood trail leading to Woof's body in the woods.

We knew her days were numbered; she was almost as old as me and sixteen's a lota years for a dog. Having it come on so sudden, though, was a stunner. I ran my hand down her side, and my throat swelled up. I lay down beside her, remembering hot nights when she and Viv would lie on the beach, cradling me between 'em. Viv'd tell stories and howl at the moon and Woof'd echo, telling her own story. That was before I could talk or even understand many words but I can remember the melodies in Viv's voice and the warmth of Woof's body.

It was curious she was stretched out like she'd been dragged into the woods. A coyote wouldn'ta done that. And her head was smashed in.

The losses were mounting and I didn't know how to make this last one any easier for Urs so I simply walked up and said "Woof's dead; something hit her head."

"Same something that started the fire," said Urs.

"Son of a bitch Tucker," said Moonshine. He uncorked a bottle of moonshine and was drunk before we thought to tell him he had to help bury a dog. So Felix and I did it. Actually I did most of it cuz Felix wheezed if he dug more'n five shovelfuls in a minute. In private, the hobos complained about traveling with him cuz he had a hard time hopping trains since it takes a certain amount of foot speed and timing to catch up to a moving boxcar. Up to this point I had no experience hopping trains.

We spent the rest of the day not knowing what to do, which resulted in doing nothing. The biggest concern was how would Gaetan and Viv get back to the cabin. Gaetan was in no condition to walk and Dash was in no condition to pull the cart. And what if he needed to go to the hospital? Old Man McDonald had an old Ford so maybe he'd give 'em a ride to one place or the other. Our minds eased a bit cuz Viv had the grit to manage things.

The only thing we accomplished was wrapping Urs's feet in rags so he could walk. The hair on his chest and legs was gone, revealing painful red flesh. He didn't look like Urs any more and we woulda laughed if it wasn't a tragedy. We ate raw vegetables and talked about how much we'd miss the eggs and how much one small thing—like losing three chickens—can change your life. Moonshine launched a drunken rant about Tucker and what he'd do if Tucker came near us again. Felix cautioned us not to jump to conclusions. I slept on the porch with my twenty two propped against the wall and got up five times during the night to circle the cabin with the rifle under my arm.

We slept past sunup and still had red eyes and grouchy voices cuz of Dash's painful brays during the night and the hellish dreams that kept waking us. Three of us roused ourselves with a wash in the lake and brought buckets of water to wash Urs on the edge of the porch. We heard voices coming down the hill and realized too late we'd forgot to hide Dash.

Sheriff Pope came round the corner: "Your donkey's lookin' shaky, Urs. You think he'll survive? I hate to see an animal in pain." No surprise the sheriff was accompanied by Linus but there was another man in a blue uniform. "This here's Porter from the fire marshall's," said Pope. "How you feeling, Urs?"

"You know anything about Gaetan and Viv?" asked Urs.

"Stopped at Harriet's on the way here," said the Sheriff. "She said Doc McDonald took 'em someplace in the middle of the night, the hospital I guess. He'll be fine, stitches maybe. Oh my god, I called him Doc, the old coot." Porter and Linus went to the barn and poked around. "You got your rifle sitting there," he said. "You planning on shooting something?"

"Tucker!" said Moonshine.

Sheriff Pope worked his gum. "Tucker's my business," he said, "all he did is beat up a black man." Pope unloaded the twenty two and put the shells in his pocket. "Don't make me take your rifle, son; put it back inside. What happened to the raccoon? You eat him?"

"Buried him," said Moonshine, "and the dog too."

"The dog? What happened to the dog?"

"Tucker got her too, hit her over the head with something." Moonshine stepped up as our spokesman, unappointed.

"I told you Tucker's my business; you leave it alone."

Deputy Hooper came trucking back from the barn with a charred, bent lantern: "Found this, boss. Fire marshall says it coulda started the blaze."

"Hmpph," said Pope, "anyone recognize this?"

"Not ours," said Urs.

"That's a railroad lantern," said Felix.

Hooper left it on the porch and went back to the barn.

Pope loosened his collar: "Some kinda heat wave we're havin', huh. The wife's agitating for one of those air conditioners; says if we don't get one, she'll run around naked. God, nobody wants to see that." He picked up the lantern: "Was the hay loose or in a bale?"

"Mostly bales," I said.

"Hmm," he said. I know he was thinking how kerosene on bales wouldn't burn so easy.

Deputy Hooper came running toward us on the porch, this time yelling "Sheriff! Sheriff!"

"What, Linus?"

"You gotta see this! Hurry!"

"Calm down, Linus, I'm on my way."

Sheriff Pope trotted to the ash heap, with us behind. Porter was standing amidst some half burned timbers near the rear of the building. He pulled one aside and pointed to a human foot. There is no word for the sounds coming out of us—shriek, scream, wail—none of those words are awful enough. My chest pounded.

Sheriff Pope collected himself: "Linus, go up to the car and radio the coroner. We need him now. The rest of you back to the cabin, I got questions."

"Who the hell is that in the barn?" demanded the sheriff, "and if you tell me Tucker, you're all going to jail!"

"Don't know," said Urs.

It's true we didn't know for a fact who it was, but logic would make it Eddie, hiding there after he stole a wallet at the bar.

"So there's someone living in your barn and you don't know a thing about it?"

During the next hour we paced and sweated and looked at each other with frantic eyes. I wanted to walk down the tracks to collect my thoughts but the sheriff made us stay where he could see us. He even pissed off the side of the porch to keep an eye on us. Linus had to do more than piss and was upset he had to use our outhouse. The coroner finally arrived with an assistant. They moved timbers and stirred around in the ashes, the coroner saying things we couldn't catch and the assistant writing notes. The wait was unbearable but finally they came over and the coroner said "There's two bodies. One's a Negro male, the other's a woman."

13

"Get an ambulance for these bodies!" the sheriff yelled at Hooper, who hightailed it up to the squad car. "And get Logan and Webster here!" The fire marshall, coroner and his assistant went back to the barn. Pope stayed with us: "I'm assuming those bodies belong to your friends we left at Harriet's hotel. What are their names?"

We could barely answer.

"Viv and Gaetan," choked out Felix.

"Viv and Gaetan who?"

"They were hobos, they didn't have a use for a last name," said Felix.

"What's his last name?" the sheriff asked, pointing at Monroe.

"Monroe," said Felix.

"Why do you know his name but not the others?"

"It's alliterative, sir—Merle Moonshine Monroe—easy to remember."

Pope turned to Monroe: "Moonshine? Are you selling hootch?"

Moonshine pretended to be parched so he could drink while he thought up a lie. "I was born under a full moon, sir." He gave Felix a nasty look.

"Hmpph," said Pope. "Someone tell me what they were doin' in the barn." We shook our heads. "Any chance the fire was started on purpose? I mean it was a black man with a white woman and lord knows there could be some jealousy over that. Maybe they were dead before the fire started. When's the last time that rifle was fired, son?"

"I killed a squirrel a few weeks ago," I said.

Pope got my rifle and smelled the barrel. "Smells like it's been fired recently."

"I forgot, sir, I had to kill a goat during the fire." I don't think the sheriff could really smell if the rifle was fired two nights ago or two years ago. If he was bluffing, it was a pretty good one. I really did forget about the goat cuz Viv and Gaetan weighed on me.

"The goat that was lying down there?"

"Yes, sir."

"Where's he now?"

"We buried him."

"We may have to unbury him and take a look."

The sheriff took us one by one down to the beach and sat us on a stump so he could question us without the others hearing. I was last. He asked me if anybody had a grudge against Gaetan or Viv. Did I think the two of 'em were keeping company, as they say, and was she keeping company with anybody else. Did I think Urs or any of the others would be capable of setting the fire? Did I notice anybody lurking around before the fire started? Who noticed the fire first? Why didn't the animals come running out? I gave him straight answers for a change.

When Logan and Webster arrived, the sheriff and three deputies inspected the whole area. They went through the cabin, checking places the sheriff missed before. We heard the bed being moved, mattresses flipped over, drawers removed and emptied, the cast iron stove opened and ashes stirred around. We weren't allowed to watch but through the door crack I saw Linus page through my books, making notes.

The sheriff came out: "Where'd that chest of drawers come from, Urs? It's a pretty good one except for the leg."

I answered for Urs: "It fell off somebody's truck, sir. They left it on the road cuz of the broken leg." Pope squinted at me. "That one wasn't a lie, sir."

The ambulance arrived with two men and a woman in uniforms. I choked down sobs as they lifted the burned bodies onto stretchers. They weren't happy about the two long hauls up the hill.

Logan and Webster reported to the sheriff. They'd gone through the junk pile to uncover two by fours with the price sticker still on 'em, twisted sheet metal, sections of pipe, tires and inner tubes, and pieces of garden tools, along with other stuff looking like it shouldn't belong to Urs.

"You're quite a collector," Pope said to Urs, then looked at me: "You said you buried the dog."

"Yes, sir."

"And the head was smashed in?"

"Yes, sir."

Pope eyed me for a moment, I assume to judge if it was another lie. "Well, then, we have to dig up the dog. Where is he? We need to use your shovel."

I showed 'em where Woof was and the deputies dug her up. The coroner studied her skull and told the ambulance people to load her up. "What?!" one said, but the coroner shot him a look. They did what he said and drove off. We looked around for an object that coulda been used as a club, like a pipe or a piece of hardwood, but found nothing.

Sheriff Pope made us sit on the porch and had Linus watch us while he talked with the coroner out of our earshot. Then he talked to us: "Here's what we have, gentlemen—two dead bodies and we're pretty sure they're the black man and the lady who stayed with him at Harriet's and ... by the way, Linus, did you look under the porch?"

"No sir," said Linus, "it's a tight squeeze."

"Well squeeze yourself under there and take a look."

Moonshine stiffened: "Pretty dirty under there; that's where the dog liked to lay; could be possums too."

Linus unhooked the flashlight from his belt and slid under the porch. We heard him bump his head on the beams and curse under his breath as Pope continued: "and we have a lantern that mighta started the fire but you're saying it's a railroad lantern. I suppose the deceased could've borrowed it from the railroad and used it to find their way into the barn in the middle of the night, another possibility being that you're lying and you stole it, Urs. We got a dead dog down the tracks and how that plays in I don't know, probably not at all. But here's something the coroner found ..."

"Holy shit," Linus interrupted from under the porch.

"Whatcha got, Linus?"

"A bag with bottles in it." Linus's arm reached out with Moonshine's bag, the bottles clanking.

Sheriff Pope picked up the bag and pulled out six bottles, uncorked one and smelled it. "Hoooeeee!" he shouted, "we got moonshine! Not a good batch, though, by the smell of it. Where's your still, Urs?"

"I got no still," said Urs.

"Well then, where'd this come from?"

We were silent, expecting Moonshine to confess, but he was frozen with his eyes on the bag.

"You all pleading the fifth, are you?" said the sheriff. As he said that his hand rested on the bag, which had lumps. He turned the bag over, spilling out four wallets. "What the hell, Urs, you got wallets stashed under your porch." Idiot Eddie had left the drivers licenses inside and Pope read 'em off:

"Cleveland, Joliet, Kansas City. My god, somebody gets around. Who would that be?"

Pope took a card from the fourth wallet and read: "We catch cheaters. Sam the Detective, Chicago, Illinois." He rifled through a wad of bills: "Looks like there's a lot of cheaters in Chicago." He handed the wallet to Linus, who took out the bills and whistled. "Careful with that, Linus, it's evidence. I'm expecting an answer to my question."

"The bag is mine," Moonshine finally said.

"So you've been to all these places and I'm guessin' people didn't just give you these wallets."

"The bag and the moonshine belong to me," said Monroe, "I don't know about the wallets."

"So you weren't born under a full moon," said Pope.

"I don't know, sir, I don't remember that far back."

"Linus," said the sheriff, "run up to the car and get some handcuffs."

"How many are we going to arrest?"

"I haven't decided so bring a bunch." Linus ran up the hill for the fifth time I could remember. Logan and Webster took up positions on each side of the porch so they could shoot us if anybody ran. "Anybody see this before; show 'em, Henry."

Henry the coroner held up a piece of wood: "It's charred but it didn't burn completely because it's hardwood, not the kind you build into a barn, specially a barn like this. We found it where the door used to be. Interesting it's a wedge shape."

"You said the door was stuck and you had to rip it off the hinges," said the sheriff. "Any possibility it was stuck because this was wedged underneath?"

I started thinking the devil was at work and I could tell Felix and Monroe and Urs felt it too cuz their breathing was heavy and their eyes intense.

Sheriff Pope worked his gum, then spit it out. "We're taking the skinny guy in for possessing moonshine and we're holding him until we figure out what he's doing with these wallets."

"Should I cuff him, boss?" Linus was back and outta breath.

"No, Linus, if he runs we'll just shoot him. The rest of you are staying right here unless you need to get to town for supplies, 'specially you, Urs. I got you on stolen two by fours and overdue library books and lord knows what else. If I come looking for you and you ain't around, I will personally hunt you down. I'm taking your rifle, son, in case we need to match it to bullet holes somewhere."

Sheriff Pope, his three deputies, the coroner, his assistant, and the fire marshall left with Monroe and the bag of moonshine. Deputy Hooper complained quietly to the coroner's assistant about having to run up the hill to get unneeded handcuffs. When they were outta earshot Urs broke into tortured sobbing such as I'd never seen from him. His hairless red body trembled. I gave way to tears too, mostly for Viv and Gaetan, but also for the Urs who didn't seem to exist anymore. I wanted to hit him and hug him both but I just sat there. Felix wandered away to give us privacy, I'm sure.

Urs finally stopped shaking and we were silent for a while, watching waves eat at the shore. Finally I said "I never liked anyone more than I liked Viv."

"She was your mother," said Urs.

14

Up on my ledge I dreamed of riding the river away from the misery. I picked Ursa Major out of the night sky and wondered if Urs would ever be the bear of a man I used to know or if he'd be the hopeless man I suddenly hated for not protecting Viv and Gaetan and for not telling me till now that Viv was my mother.

There was another question: Who was my father? I always assumed it was Urs, but Viv was generous with her affection so what if one of the hobos was my dad? It couldn't be Felix cuz I had no resemblence to his lumpy body and besides it was an unspoken understanding that Felix didn't yearn for women. That left Eddie and Moonshine and I hoped to hell it wasn't either of them, especially Moonshine. Or Eddie.

I stayed the night on the ledge. When the sun reached over the bluff and lit the western shore I climbed down and went to Urs, who was on the porch chair, head in his hands. "Are you my father?" I asked.

"I don't know, it might be Noodin," and in a slow voice he told me the story Viv had told him about the Ojibwa man she was with before she showed up at the cabin seventeen years before.

I took a long walk down the tracks, standing so close to the rails when the one ten freighter flew by the engineer blew his whistle and yelled at me. I climbed up the bluff to the cornfield, where the stalks were head high, and walked along the edge of the field, hoping to run into Claude Pease, wanting him to raise his shotgun to me cuz I would stare him down till he turned tail and drove off in his stupid rusty tractor. When I got back to the cabin I was done in. I collapsed on the beach at sundown and slept like the dead till the middle of the night, when I woke with a start: What did Deputy Webster mean when he whispered "it was bound to happen?"

Around noon a black Model A Ford coughed and stopped at the top of the hill. Old Man McDonald and Lettie got out and worked their way down the muddy trail with their canes. Felix and I went to help. Lettie and Old Man broke into tears, which caused me to choke up. Felix took Old Man's shoulder bag and I got between to steady 'em. When we rounded the corner of the cabin, Lettie dropped her cane and hugged Urs.

"Sheriff Pope was by yesterday," said Old Man. "He said what happened here. It hurt us to the core. We told them they could stay with us but they insisted on coming here."

"What?" said Urs, "who insisted?"

"The black man and the lady ... um ..."

"Viv," I said.

"Yes, Vivian," said Lettie, "we wanted them to stay with us for the night but they said, if we didn't mind, could we drive them here."

"They couldn't stay at the hotel," said Old Man, "because Harriet found them lying in bed together—fully clothed, mind you—and she threw a fit. A black man and a white woman in bed together, she said, what would the people at church say. I told her I was right there looking after the man's wounds and nothing scandalous was going on and in fact I was tempted to get in bed with them because the chair was uncomfortable. I've got this rheumatism, you know. I take cod liver oil for it, but once in a while it acts up something fierce and there's nothing to be done. Folks say rhubarb helps and I've tried that but it tastes sour so I dip it in sugar but that's not good for my diabetes ..."

"Oliver, you're straying again," said Lettie. She usually called him "Old Man" like the rest of us, but used his real name when it was important.

"Oh, sorry," said Old Man. "I thanked Harriet for her hospitality but I was thinking what a nasty old ..."

"Oliver," interrupted Lettie.

"Okay, dear, I won't say it, but I thought it. Anyway, I walked them over to our store and Lettie and I both thought they should stay with us ..."

Lettie interrupted: "... but Vivian asked if we could drive them here instead. We let them out at the top of the hill and watched to be sure they could get down the trail."

"Did they have a lantern?" asked Felix.

"No, the moon hadn't set yet, and it was pretty bright. We had no idea ..." Lettie put a hankie to her eyes, then changed the subject: "We brought some things you might want."

Old Man pulled paper bags out of his shoulder bag: "Beans. Apples."

"One of those is for the donkey," said Lettie.

"Coffee. Jelly beans, but I picked out the black ones, sorry. Noodles. Jar of honey—that's for your burns, Urs—aspirin, and iodine. Wish I'd thought to put in some salts for your feet. It's on the house," he winked.

Old Man went silent for a moment and had a faraway look. "This river used to run clear," he said. "When I was a kid you could drink the water right from the lake. Now it's full of stuff. I wade in up to my waist and I can't see my toes."

Old Man's mind seemed to run in two directions at once. We let him ramble. "There's a new A and P up in Onawah.

They let people pick groceries right off the shelf. They got no idea what they're buying, some of them, just grab stuff."

That wasn't how Old Man and Lettie did it. They'd pick coffee or candy off the shelf for you or scoop flour or beans out of a barrel into a paper bag and tell folks about it—how to cook it, why it was top quality, things like that. They'd weigh it, mark the price on the bag, then throw in a little bit more with a wink, saying "there's an Old Man discount for you." If there wasn't a customer waiting, Old Man would challenge you to checkers and if you beat him, you'd get a lemon drop. If you didn't beat him, you'd still get a lemon drop.

"Another damn war," Old Man switched tracks again.

"Oliver," Lettie interrupted again, but it was too late. Old Man's slight frame shook up and down as he sobbed into his hands. Lettie put an arm around his shoulders but he fought her off and walked toward the beach.

"We lost our son in the war," Lettie told us. We knew that, of course, everybody did. Their son Arthur died in France and you didn't mention it in the store or Old Man would break into tears. The amount of dying he saw as a medic in the war fifty years back wasn't enough to dull the pain when it was close to home. I wonder if I'll be able to shut out the pain of people dying when I'm Old Man's age.

After Lettie hugged Dash and fed him the apple, Felix and I helped her and Old Man up to their car.

"They didn't have a lantern," said Felix.

* * *

People need to survive, even in the thick of misery, so the next day the three of us pickled and dried vegetables for the winter. We ate the jelly beans Old Man left us but woulda traded 'em in a flash for vinegar, since we were down to our last two gallons for pickling green beans, squash, tomatoes, beets, and peppers. Even Old Man, fixed as he was on the old ways, probably valued jelly beans over vinegar.

When the sun was straight up, we took a break and waited for the one ten freighter to wake us from a nap. What woke us instead was loud moans. It was Eddie stumbling toward us on the tracks. He was messed up something fierce, like a bear got ahold of him, but with Eddie you knew it had to be pissed off humans beat him up. He stopped to look at the ash heap that used to be the barn, then collapsed onto the track. I had a notion to leave him there and let the train run him over but I forced it outta my brain. Me and Felix dragged him to the porch, laid him on the mattress in front of Urs and doused him with water. When he woke up the first thing he saw was Urs staring down at him like a red devil come to take him to hell. Eddie screamed and tried to run but collapsed again and rolled off the porch.

We forced cold soup down his throat, then stripped him naked and walked him into the lake with a bar of soap. He had cuts and bruises all over his body and a gash over his eye probably needing stitches but Eddie wasn't about to see a doctor cuz that would lead to questions from the police. We dabbed some of Old Man's iodine on the wounds and enjoyed his screaming. He was still naked when we sat him in front of Urs, who stared the truth right outta him. "I took a guy's wallet," he confessed. "When Gaetan was on the floor, guys were bending over him with their billfolds bulging out. I coulda taken three or four but I only took the one out of respect for Gaetan."

"How'd you get beat up?" asked Felix.

"The guy saw me outside the bar. I don't know why he thought I took his wallet, probably my accent. He bounced me around a little but I pushed him aside and ran for it. Some of these bruises are from the tumble I took down the hill. He chased me down the tracks but I outran him. I hid in the woods for a couple days with nothing to eat or drink except the backwater. But I got the wallet," he grinned, pulling it out of his discarded pants and holding it up like it was a gold medal. "I should give some of this to Gaetan since I couldn't have done it without him. How is he, by the way, and what the hell happened to the barn?"

We stared in disbelief. Finally Felix said "Viv and Gaetan were in it—they're dead. Sheriff took Monroe because he found the moonshine under the porch."

"Oh my god," moaned Eddie, "did he get my wallets?"

I swear, if the sheriff hadn't taken my rifle I'da shot Eddie through the eye right then.

"What kind of an idiot leaves the identification cards in stolen wallets?" asked Felix. "What kind of an idiot doesn't take out the money and burn the wallets?"

Eddie had no answer but I think I know what kind of idiot does that. Eddie bested private detectives from four big cities and every once in a while I bet he took out those wallets and looked at the names on the drivers licenses and felt like he could beat anybody the same way Sugar Ray Robinson beat Jake LaMotta and Rocky Graziano. I don't know this for a fact, I'm just guessing.

"Give me the wallet," I said.

"It's mine," said Eddie.

Urs lifted himself off the chair, which is all it took for Eddie to toss me the wallet.

"Good chance that wallet actually belongs to a Mr. Nathan Elliot." Sheriff Pope's foot was resting on the porch like he was there to pass the time of day. He scared the shit out of us and, in Eddie's case, I think that wasn't just an expression; three days of drinking swamp water plus a good scare can

Once This River Ran Clear

empty a person's bowels in a flash. "Let's see the wallet, son." I gave it to him. "Yep," he said, "this is it. Hold up your hand." Eddie held up his left hand. "Your other hand, shithead," said the sheriff. "So this Mr. Elliot reports his wallet was stole by a man with two fingers missing off his right hand and what I'm looking at is a man with two fingers missing off his right hand who's claiming this here wallet with Mr. Elliot's drivers license in it is actually his. This might be the dictionary definition of getting caught red handed. We gotta tell this one at the Sheriff's Convention in Omaha, what do you think, Linus?"

Deputy Hooper was standing in back of the sheriff as usual, holding my rifle. "It's a good one, boss."

"Too bad you were the one holding the wallet, son. That makes you guilty of possessing stolen property. You heard him say 'give me the wallet,' right, Linus?"

"Right, boss."

"Now what the hell are we going to do? Any ideas, Deputy Hooper?" Linus took off his police hat to scratch his head. "Don't give yourself a headache," the sheriff chuckled. "Tell me, son, what were you going to do with the wallet?"

"I was gonna take it to Turlough's and see if they knew how I could get it back to Mr. Elliot."

Pope let out a huge laugh, followed by one from Deputy Hooper, who always waited to see which direction the boss's mood was pointed. "You do come up with some good ones, son."

"You're right, I just said that for a laugh. I was gonna take out the cash and burn the wallet."

"That's better. You know, I came here to return your rifle because the coroner couldn't find any bullet holes in the deceased. But now we have a more complicated situation. Damn if I want to arrest you all but what choice do I have?

Linus, run up to the radio and tell 'em we're bringing four prisoners to Onawah jail, which I hate to do cuz the food's not so good there. Bring back some cuffs."

"Are we going to use the cuffs this time?" asked Hooper.

"What'd you say, Linus?"

"I'll bring the cuffs." Linus was off.

"Shame," said Pope, "it's Judge Fitzgerald now and he's a tough son of a bitch; took over for Judge Copeland cuz Copeland was too easy on the Indians. Fitzgerald's in Bluffton on Mondays and Onawah the rest of the week cuz most of the trouble's on this side of the river. Damn, Urs, just think—if you'd taken that thousand bucks and cleared off this piece of land like we wanted, you'd be sitting pretty with all your hair intact. You could be working at the power plant and Tom here'd be in school, maybe even a football star. Look at the build on this kid, bet you can run, huh. And your two friends wouldn't be lying on a slab in the morgue. They're going to be cremated, by the way, since they're already halfway there."

The sheriff looked around the corner of the cabin: "It's gonna take Linus a while and I need him to write down the charges. Tell you what—you just help me remember and we'll write it down later. Mr. three fingers—what's your name, by the way."

"Eddie."

"Eddie, I'm charging you—stand up and take it like a man." Eddie stood up, still naked. "Damn, those are some ugly bruises and put some clothes on." We got Eddie into pants while the sheriff continued. "I'm charging you with stealing a wallet belonging to Mr. Nathan Elliot and don't be surprised if there's four more counts of wallet thievery in your near future. Urs, let's see, there's some petty thievery in evidence all around your place but I'm not sure what's going to hold up in court. I'd love to charge you with standing in the way of progress but there's no statute to cover that. How about we go with accessory to some kind of felony or maybe housing criminals. And we'll have to do something with your boy, can't leave him here for the coyotes to chew on."

"I can take of myself," I said, "leave me the rifle."

"This could go a couple different ways for you, son. Best thing is to play it safe and you'll end up with a slap on the wrist and maybe a place in a decent home. Fitzgerald loves to sentence juvies to live with good families. And you're not getting the rifle back. And you ..."

"Felix, sir."

"Hmm. Damn, I'm coming up blank. Help me out here, what crimes have you committed?"

"He rides boxcars. The railroad guys don't like that," said Eddie. Apparently he thought since he was going down, we should all go with him.

"Let's go with that," said Pope, "we'll call it vagrancy. You got any valuables to lock up, Urs, not sure when you're coming back." I grabbed Gaetan's guitar. "What are we going to do about that donkey? I could shoot him right now and put him out of his misery."

There were a million times I'da shot Dash myself but suddenly he was the best donkey that ever lived. "That's my donkey and he better be safe."

"If you say so," said Pope. "Linus can drive by Farmer Fred's tomorrow to see if he'll take him. And how are we going to get you up the hill, Urs? Do I need to call the stretcher crew?"

"I'll walk," said Urs. He grabbed the crutches we resurrected from the mercantile dumpster a while back and hid his pain going up to the road to wait for the wagon. Halfway up we met Linus carrying the cuffs.

15

I spent the next two weeks in the Onawah jail among petty criminals and homeless people. Some of them make vagrancy a survival skill, exchanging a few days of freedom for a safe cell and three meals a day. They can get there by pissing on the sidewalk, but if they want a longer stay they'll do something to a rich man, like painting a dirty word on his house. It usually takes three or four days to get to court, where the judge normally throws out the charge cuz the jails are full but that's three or four days to enjoy the government's generosity. I got two whole weeks of free food, miserable as it was, and a shower every other day.

The original jail, known as the Cottage, was built in the last century, when posses on horseback waved pistols at bad guys. It had stone walls turning to dust and iron bars so loose in the cement a strong person could bash 'em out. The criminals in that building were the ones wanting to be there. That's where I stayed, along with a few regulars. The guards weren't as mean as those in the other buildings, especially Okemos, who slipped me gum every so often.

There were two additions to the original building, each one more secure than the last, to control bigger and meaner humans. Urs was put in the most secure addition, called the Tank, making it less likely he could kick down bars once his feet healed. Felix was there too, but I don't know why; if he threw himself against the bars, he'd just bounce. I never saw Urs but I ran into Felix when our twenty minutes in the yard overlapped. He told me to read books, which I did whenever I had sunlight.

I asked Okemos if he could scare up some books by the fellow who wrote the Huckleberry book. He found some good ones about pirates and musketeers, but the only others were about stupid people falling in love and doing nothing related to staying alive, so I read the Bible. I found the part about Baasha but I wish I hadn't cuz it turns out he wasn't a good man and God had to tell him to cut out the shit. Damn, cuz I wanted Big Baasha to be a rock full of righteousness that rolled down and wiped out the bad people in Hertzville. I told this to Father Matthias once and he wasn't amused. And he didn't believe I read the Bible.

Okemos got Gaetan's guitar from the evidence lockup for me and was sorry he did, cuz he and everybody else covered their ears when I tried to sing 'Black Dog Blues'. After that I only practiced the chords Gaetan showed me.

After a couple days a lawyer named Harvey Moss showed up. He was skinny, not more'n twenty five years old. He said he was gonna do his best for me but I had to tell him everything I did wrong so I told him about sliding through the tavern window, stealing carp outta someone's backwater, and looking down Penny's blouse. "Didn't you receive stolen property?" he asked. He was talking about the library books and the fact I was holding the wallet when Sheriff Pope showed up.

"I guess I did," I said, "but I didn't know readin' and holdin' a wallet was wrong."

"Well," laughed Mr. Moss, "I don't think you'll do hard time for that." He stuttered as he said these things but I'm not going to say it that way cuz it would be mean. "Is there anything else? We don't like surprises in court."

I searched my brain for all the things I ever did wrong. "I drank two beers and I stole a sip of Moonshine's brew," I said. "Does thinkin' about doin' bad things count, cuz I've had some wicked thoughts, but I never did 'em."

"No, you're okay there," he said, so I didn't tell him about Big Baasha or wanting to see Louise Christianson naked. "Judge Fitzgerald's going to see you in a couple days."

A couple days stretched into the two weeks I mentioned. I passed the time with the books and guitar and idle conversation with the drunks who left after they sobered up.

There was one who didn't leave, though, a barefoot old man with white hair flowing out from his weathered Indian Joe hat. It woulda made sense for him to trade that hat for some shoes cuz the stone floor was cold but he seemed just fine with cold feet and a warm head. If I had extra shoes his size I woulda made that trade cuz I liked the look of the hat. I'm ashamed to admit that cuz it's stupid to care how things look.

Okemos left the man's cell door open so he could wander around and talk to us inmates. "This here's Joshua Proudfoot," said Okemos, while the old man was looking into my cell. "He's here off and on cuz street corner philosophers don't earn that much. Careful what you tell this man cuz he remembers everything. Just ask him what happened on May twelve, nineteen thirty one."

I played along: "Hey Joshua, what happened on May twelve, nineteen thirty one?"

"Bonnie Big Bear had a baby boy and named him Barney." He pronounced every syllable in a slow gravelly voice, looking up as if the words came from above. "It rained in the morning but the afternoon was clear. Lorna Snickerdoodle had a toothache. Cyrus Ridgeway's dog was barkin' so loud at midnight the neighbors called the cops."

"You remember all that?" I asked.

"Hell no," he said, "but I know plenty other shit."

Okemos got a chuckle at my expense. I laughed too cuz making stuff up is impressive. I shoulda known I was being suckered, cuz who'd name their kid Barney Big Bear. And Snickerdoodle's a cookie for shit sake. He was eating one when he said that.

Joshua would sit on a stool in the aisle between the cell rows and say stuff that stretched your mind like "The peace which is the most important is that which comes within the souls of people when they realize their oneness with the universe and all its powers."

"That's lofty," said a man two cells down. "You made that up?"

"Nope. Black Elk. But I know plenty other shit."

Okemos brought in a couple Indian kids and put 'em in side by side cells across from me: "Say hello to Kohana and Mato. This ain't their first visit. They're the ones scribbling all over town."

"That's not us," grinned Mato.

"We're innocent," said Kohana, "and it's not scribbling, it's art."

Okemos slammed their cells shut and handed 'em gum.

"Hey, Cowboy, what are you in for?" asked Kohana. He and Mato used stones to carve pictures on the wall between 'em.

"Don't know," I said. "What're you in for?"

"Like I said, we're artists," said Kohana. "They don't like it when we paint pictures around town."

"Did you paint the horse on the hardware store?"

"One of our best," said Mato.

"I liked it."

"That asshole Jerry painted over it," said Kohana. "He'd shit his pants if he knew his daughter snuck us the paint."

"You mean Louise?" I asked.

"Yup."

"You know her?"

"She goes to school in Onawah. So did we but we dropped out."

Suddenly I wanted to go to school in Onawah. I needed to know more but I didn't know what question to ask: "Is she ... I mean, how come ..."

"How come she sneaks us the paint?" Mato read my mind.

"Cuz she likes good art," said Kohana.

"And she hates her dad," said Mato. "He used to whup her but now she's old enough to whup back. There's still marks on her legs."

Mato stepped back to look at his work: "I got a hawk."

"Oh yeah, well I got an eagle and he's gonna eat your hawk," said Kohana.

"Well I'm carvin' a rifle to shoot your eagle," said Mato.

"And I'm carvin' a police guy to arrest your sorry ass for killin' the symbol of our great country," said Kohana. They laughed.

Kohana looked over at me: "What's yer name, Cowboy?"

"I go by Tom."

"I'm Kohana. I can run fast."

"Not fast enough," said Mato, "cuz they caught you."

"I can run pretty fast," I said.

"How fast?"

"Faster'n the freight train for a quarter mile."

"So why do they call you Tom? You need a better name, kid. You run like the wind so they should call you 'Noodin'."

When Mato said that my chest tightened up and I froze with my mouth open. I was awake all night, staring into the dark.

* * *

On Friday Okemos raked his keys across my cell bars: "Hey, pardner, you're gonna meet the judge." He walked me a block away into the courthouse and knocked on a door that said "Judge Patrick Fitzgerald—private." The door opened to smoke and the smell of cigars, which were sucked on by two men in chairs, those being Sheriff Pope and a man behind a desk, who turned out to be the judge. In another chair sat a shiny man wearing a suit and tie and holding a tiny suitcase in his lap. Standing in a row were Felix and Moonshine and Eddie, all in handcuffs. They were between two men in brown uniforms, one with muscles bulging out of a short sleeve shirt and the other so skinny he'd blow away in a stiff wind. He twirled his night stick like the girl in front of the band twirled her baton. Urs was there too, not cuffed, though, cuz he needed his hands to keep himself propped against crutches. Harvey Moss was close by and that's the first I knew he was the lawyer for all five of us. The judge and sheriff puffed away, talking about fishing.

Finally the judge looked at me: "I see the young man's here. What's your name, son?"

"Tom."

"Make yourself comfortable, Tom." I didn't know how I was supposed to do that since there were no more chairs so I slid my back down the wall and sat on the floor underneath the smoke.

Okemos looked down and shook his head: "Watch yourself, kid, he's Irish."

The judge turned to the man in the suit: "Tell me why we're here, Price, and make it short cuz it's Friday."

"There's strong evidence, your honor, that there's a criminal gang operating out of the residence of a Mr. Anton Magnusson, who goes by the name of Urs. He's the large man on crutches. On his property the sheriff found wallets from four different midwest cities and one from down the road in Hertzville. There with Mr. Magnusson are Mr. Merle Monroe, Mr. Gerald Norton and Mr. Felix Levasseur. They do their thievery in the south and midwest during the winter and spring, then meet at Mr. Magnusson's in the summer to divide the spoils. This has been going on for some time so it's a good guess those five wallets are just the tip of the iceberg. We also found library books from as far away as Louisiana. It's likely we'll uncover a stash of stolen goods once we search the whole property. And to boot, your honor, we found six bottles of this. Show him, Sheriff."

Sheriff Pope pulled one of the moonshine bottles from his coat pocket and set it in front of the judge, who uncorked it and smelled: "Whoooeeee, I'd have to be pretty desperate to drink that. Who cooked up this shit?" Moonshine flinched and his cuffs rattled. "I think I flushed him out. Is this yours, Mr. Monroe?"

Harvey Moss stepped forward and stuttered: "My client refuses to answer, your honor, on grounds ..."

"Shut up, junior," ordered the judge, "did you make this stuff, Monroe?"

"He's already confessed to it," said the sheriff.

"But I didn't do the wallets!" shouted Moonshine before Moss could stop him.

"We're going to search the property for the still, your honor. If we can find that, we'll have enough to put this gang away for a while. And the sheriff's office has received other complaints regarding Mr. Magnusson."

Sheriff Pope cut in: "There's a shitload of 'em, your honor: nudity, petty theft, illegal netting of game fish because the guy's not an Indian, a raccoon killed out of season, stolen two by fours and rebar, an expensive chest of drawers ..."

I jumped up: "I told you that fell off a truck and they left it." Okemos pulled me back.

"Tell your client to shut his mouth," the judge directed Moss, who gave me an angry look.

I swear they left that chest on the road cuz of the broken leg. The trouble with getting caught lying is people don't believe you when you're telling the truth. So the trick is not to get caught.

"Tom gets a bee in his bonnet once in a while, judge, but he's a good kid," said Sheriff Pope, winking at me, "and he can run like the dickens."

"Hmmph," grunted the judge. He turned to the man in the suit: "This is a highly unusual meeting you called, Price, what are you trying to do?"

"Your honor, our office is jammed up with a backlog of cases and so's the public defender. You can see they could spare only one attorney for these five criminals. If we could handle this as one case and get some guilty pleas to petty theft, I could recommend lenient sentences. They'd be harsher, of course, if we find a still."

"You ain't gonna find it," shouted Moonshine, "it's down south." Felix elbowed Moonshine so hard you knew it had to hurt.

"And that's it?" asked the judge. "What about that fire? Two people got burned up, right?"

"There's a good chance that was an accident, judge."

"And a good chance it was murder," said the judge. "Are you telling me you're just going to let it be?"

"It was a black man and a hobo woman, sir. Like I said, we're really jammed up."

Fitzgerald started screaming: "I'll show you jammed up. You let a murderer get away under my jurisdiction and you won't be district attorney any more. This side of the river is rotten with scum and some of the worst of it was right there when that barn burned. The people elected you to clean it up and by God you better do your job. Look at these four men. Do they look like honest citizens who wouldn't slit your throat for a buck? I'll give you ten to one it was one of them lit that fire or maybe it was all of 'em!"

By this time the judge was standing up, jabbing the air with his finger. Moonshine jumped forward, yelling and shaking his cuffed hands: "It was Tucker set the fire, you asshole, go get that son of a bitch and throw him in jail!"

Then all hell broke loose. Skinny guard punched Moonshine in the stomach with the end of his stick, sending him reeling toward muscle guard, who banged him on the head with his fist. Urs threw off his crutches, grabbed muscle guard from behind and squeezed. Skinny guard knocked Urs a weak one on the head with the stick but Urs kept squeezing. I took a step forward but Okemos caught me. "Let the white men fight," he said.

Skinny guard raised his stick again but held up and turned around to find his wallet in Eddie's cuffed hands so he slammed his stick on Eddie's fingers, making him howl like a hellcat. Felix was at Urs's back trying to pull him off muscle guard but that's hard to do in cuffs. He was yelling "Urs, stop it, you're making it worse, Urs! Urs!" Skinny guard had his wallet back in his pocket and turned toward Urs but Felix was between 'em. He grabbed Felix around the neck and climbed his back to get another shot at Urs but Felix turned and threw him forward like a bucking bronco onto the judge's desk.

There was a gunshot. Sheriff Pope stood on his chair with his pistol pointed up and bits of ceiling floating down around him. Everyone froze. Except for Urs, who had his man gasping and didn't let up till the sheriff jumped off the chair and whacked him on the head with his pistol. Urs and muscle guard sank to the floor.

Two more guards barged into the room with pistols out. "Everybody face down on the floor!" one yelled. "I said everybody!"

"I'm the judge!" shouted Fitzgerald.

"On the floor, judge! It's procedure! Who fired that shot?!"

"I did," yelled the sheriff, who refused to lie down. "You can get up judge. Everybody take a breath."

I crawled over to Urs, who was bleeding from the back of his skull: "You killed him!"

Urs opened his eyes: "No, but I got a headache."

"He'll be okay, we'll take him in for stitches," said Pope. "Get the kid out of here."

Okemos led me back to my cell, where I paced all afternoon and kicked the wall. Harvey Moss showed up to say Urs had thirteen stitches; he'd be okay but now he was looking at serious jail time. The scuffle was technically contempt of court and could even be attempted murder. "Eddie's going away too because snatching that guard's wallet was pretty much a confession regarding the other wallets. And Mr. Monroe..."

"He should be locked up for bein' an asshole," I said.

"I think everybody knows he's the one behind the moonshine and calling the judge names doesn't help so there's no use taking him to trial. Mr Levasseur didn't do much except he needs to stick around because he might be involved in the fire ..."

"He's not."

"All the same, the judge wants an accounting of what went on and all four of them are being looked into. And, to be honest, so are you, but you won't spend much time in jail if I can persuade the judge to let you stay with a good family. There's people who do that. Anything else you need to know?"

"Is my name 'Magnusson'?"

16

Over the weekend I eased my worries by trading stories and complaints with Kohana and Mato. In the yard one day they motioned for me to sit between 'em.

"Can you paint?" Mato asked.

"I painted the rowboat." They laughed.

"So you ain't an artist," said Kohana.

"I never tried."

"Can you keep a secret?" he asked.

"And I can tell lies."

"You know that rock they call Big Baasha?"

"Yup." They talked fast and I can't remember exactly which one said what cuz I was excited by the mention of Big Baasha.

"We're gonna paint a face on it."

"The Great Spirit."

"It's gonna look like the white man's god."

"Except it's a brown man with black hair and it's gonna scare the shit outta Hertzville."

"Gotta be white hair, Kohana; the white god has white hair."

"But he's really an Indian," said Kohana, "so he's gonna have black hair."

"You want him to scare people, right?" Mato tried to talk sense. "Black hair's just gonna make 'em laugh. They won't know it's God. If you wanna scare white people you sic their own god on 'em. Besides he'll have a brown skin cuz the rock's brown. That's enough to scare the ones who think the Great Spirit's come to get revenge."

"Okay, but angry, with fire in his eyes." Kohana wanted fire coming out of everything they painted.

"Like the horses?" I asked.

"Yeah, like the horses."

"And smoke comin' out his nose."

"Like hell, Kohana, he's not a dragon for shit sake." Mato wanted God to look real, if there is such a thing.

"Okay, but he'll be lookin' down on the town like he's gonna burn up the bad people."

"Who are the bad ones?" I asked, cuz I wanted to know if Kohana's bad people were the same as my bad people.

"The ones who call us Chunkers," he said. "The ones who tell me to go live on the rez. The ones who don't care that my great great grandfather was here before their great great grandfather planted a seed in their great great grandmother."

Kohana got up and ran a circle around the yard like he was a wild bronco. If he couldn't paint his pictures, he'd probably kill people. I'm just guessing. "And that asshole Jerry Christianson," yelled Kohana as he ran, "I'd burn him up too."

"Why?"

"Ask Louise," he yelled, "and her mother." He ran another circle around the yard, then sank beside us, outta breath.

"You don't really want God to burn people up, do you?" asked Mato.

"Okay then, but he has to smite 'em like in the Bible."

"How do you smite somebody?" asked Mato.

"I don't know—you whack 'em with a sword, you throw rocks at 'em, you kick 'em in the nuts."

"You pound 'em with your fist," I said. "That's what it means."

"So there has to be a fist," said Kohana.

"We said it was just a face."

"How is a face gonna smite someone?"

"Too complicated, we gotta do the whole thing in one night."

It had to be one night, they said, cuz if you come back to finish it, the cops'll be waiting to throw your ass in jail. That's how they got caught this time, cuz Mato's a perfectionist and he came back a week later to color in the yellow part of the wolf's eyes on the back of Harriet's hotel. She was watching all night with the cops on alert. Never mind that the wolf improved the looks of her ratty hotel. Part of their sentence was painting over the wolf and painting the walls of her two guest rooms. She gave 'em a lecture on how decent people behave. And a bowl of ice cream.

"So he'll have white hair, eyes, nose and mouth. And a fist."

"What's the fist attached to, Kohana? It can't be growing out of his face."

"It's just there, Mato. This is modern art; things don't need to be attached."

They argued about what the Great Spirit actually looked like and was he gonna have a chin and ears and what in hell the fist was attached to. It was the kind of argument Moonshine and Viv used to have, the kind where the people got even madder cuz deep down they like each other.

"So what do you think?" Mato asked, "you with us?"

The thing I've been saying about dynamiting Big Baasha loose to crush Hertzville was never an actual idea, just something I thought when I saw people acting mean and crazy. It was like God throwing a fit and wrecking things in the Bible. But painting the face of an angry God on the rock—that could make folks shit their pants. So I told Mato and

Kohana I was with 'em, but I didn't know how I could help. They needed me at the top of the rock to lower 'em on ropes and pass down buckets of paint.

Okemos came to get us back inside.

"You tell anybody about this and we'll cut out your tongue," said Mato.

"You got secrets?" asked Okemos.

"Big ones," said Kohana.

* * *

Harvey Moss was right: Judge Fitzgerald saw fit to give me to a decent family instead of sending me to prison for stealing library books or someone's carp or whatever I did. It was pretty curious, though, which family he gave me to.

Four days after the brawl in the judge's office, Harvey told me to gather my possessions, which amounted to Gaetan's guitar, and took me into the real courtroom this time. There was a line of criminals with their lawyers, and the judge spit out sentences like Claude Pease's rusty Allis Chalmers spit out black smoke: a year in jail for robbing the grocery store and you have to pay for the food; two years for bruising the old woman's arm and don't tell me it was her fault for hanging on to the purse; five years cuz there was a baby in the back when you stole the car. Judge Fitzgerald was unforgiving in his fight to civilize the Indian side of the river. When it was our turn he looked at me hard: "You've been bent in the wrong direction, young man, and we're not going to let you become a blight on the community. You need the influence of a decent family and that's exactly what I'm going to give you. See that woman in the back?" There was a woman with yellow hair and dangly earrings. "You're going to live with her family until you're old enough to join the army. You'll go to school and church and do chores. And I hear you can run so I expect you'll be on the football team."

"Your honor," said Moss.

The judge cut him off: "What in the name of Christ can you be objecting to, junior? I just gave your client the break of a lifetime. You better get him out the door before I change my mind. You can take him now, Gloria," said the judge.

The lady smiled and led me out the door to a little red car without a roof. "It's our fun car," she said. "We live in Hertzville but right now we're going to Bluffton. Have you been there?" I told her I was in their Fourth of July parade. We got to town in about twenty minutes cuz she drove fast and I have to admit, hopping the road humps gave my stomach a fun feeling.

"What sports do you like?" she asked.

I told her I liked fishing and I knew someone with a basketball court in their back yard. She looked at me funny.

"Ever play football?"

"I heard about it."

"Judge says you can run."

"I could beat Viv after I turned ten."

"Who's Viv?" I was quiet. "What songs can you play?"

"I know the chords to 'Black Dog Blues'."

"I don't know that one. You can sing it for us at home."

"I can't sing."

River Road ran down the west side of the lake into Bluffton. It was wider than the road through Hertzville, but on foot you risked your life all the same. The cars went faster, especially Gloria's, cuz she sped up when it seemed like you should slow down, and she drove up close behind slower cars and either passed 'em or honked. She stopped at Serge's hair place. I left without my long curls.

At Rose's men's furnishing store she bought five school outfits, a coat and tie for church, and jeans for roughing it. And I had to start wearing underwear, she said, so Mr. Rose threw in two five packs of white skivvies. (I don't know how she knew I was free balling unless Mr. Rose winked at her when he measured my leg.) My patched up britches went in the dumpster and I wore brown pants and a long sleeve yellow shirt outta the store.

Mr. Florine smiled us into his shoe store and I ended up with shiny black oxfords for church and sneakers for school. The oxfords hurt like crazy so it was a good thing I only had to wear 'em once a week. Gloria wanted to throw my running shoes in the trash but I put 'em back on my feet. At all these places she just waved and walked out the door without reaching in her purse.

Gloria took Lyon Avenue past the park and the statue of the guy on a horse: "That's Buster Pritchett," she said.

"He gave his life for our freedom," I said.

We turned onto Prairie Street and pulled up to a large red brick building with rows of windows. "That's Lincoln High. It's named after one of our presidents. He freed the slaves." I gave her a dumb look. "The boys go here. We'll get you in tomorrow."

"I thought the bus went to Onawah."

"That school's full of Indians," she said. We have a driver take the boys here." I didn't tell her I might be an Indian.

"Bluffton's got the best football team in the conference."

At the office inside a woman moved papers around a desk. "Hello, Gloria," she said, like it was her duty to say it. "He's in a ..."

"This'll just take a minute," Gloria said. The lady laughed but not cuz it was funny. Gloria opened the door into an office where three men in suits were talking. "Just wanted you to meet your new student, George; this is Tom." The three men put on thin smiles. "He can run so we're putting him on the team."

"The season's half over, Gloria," said George.

"The judge said he had to; I'll talk to Larry, it'll be fine." On the way past the two women she said "Tom'll be in the same classes as Winthrop." She drove around the building to a big field with kids in uniforms bashing into each other and a guy yelling like he was mad at 'em: "Hey, Larry, this is Tom, he'll be on the team."

"Hello, Gloria. What grade is he in?"

"He's sixteen, so tenth."

"You ever play football, son?"

"Nope."

"Maybe we'll have him watch and get him on next year."

"He can run, Larry, it'll be fine. He can get suited up tomorrow. Nice win last Friday."

We left before Larry could answer and flew back up the road, over the bridge, down past the power plant and Farmer Fred's, and past the trail to the cabin where I caught a peek at men in hard hats walking around.

Gloria turned up Prospect Road and took the curves so fast I thought we'd fly off the edge and roll down onto the church. She stopped at the only house on the road, large and white with a hedge along the driveway. "We own a hundred and ten acres up here. It's going to be high class houses, none of that Indian stuff."

A cream colored four door Mercedes was parked next to a mailbox that said "Larkin."

17

Back in August, when we were all alive and free, Moonshine got burned by a spark and said Old Harry was throwing flames from hell. Felix drew on his pipe and asked what evidence Moonshine had about fires in hell. "Cuz that's what everybody says," Moonshine answered.

"Not everybody," said Felix, "there's some who think it's ice, some who think it's torture chambers, and others who think it's just darkness. And some people think we're actually living in hell right here on earth. Myself, I think hell is not knowing the reason the universe exists."

Gaetan had already told us about his experience in hell, which was a place where old black men could be hung cuz they helped another black man to his feet. Moonshine revised his opinion and decided hell was the quivering and shaking when you go three days without liquor. Eddie laughed till Viv ripped him: "He's right, Eddie, it's hell. I've been there, so shut up."

My own thought is hell's a place like the huge house Gloria led me into, a place where the spaces had no meaning other than being a place you could say was yours, a place so removed from the every day efforts a person needed to save his own life that there was no joy in it, just a kind of darkness even in a place fulla light.

"Take off your shoes," said Gloria, so I left my running shoes by the front door. "The boys are watching TV in the den. That's Winthrop and the fat one's Dominic. Say hi to Tom, boys, he's going to live here."

Dominic stared for a second: "He shot the squirrel."

"What, hon?" said Gloria.

"Never mind, Mom, it's nothing," said Winthrop, and she left. "Shut up, fatass."

"You like the Lone Ranger?" asked Dominic.

"I don't know him."

"You're funny," he laughed.

I sat on the floor and watched a man in a mask riding a white horse, with his Indian friend riding behind.

"Sit in a chair, Tom." Gloria was back with Laurence Larkin—the same one who tore up a thousand dollar check the last time I saw him. "This is Mr. Larkin, Tom."

"Hello, Tom, how do you like the house? Your room's upstairs. It's got a desk for schoolwork and a view like you won't believe. Take a look out the back window, there's a pool out there, and further back's going to be houses—classy ones with big green lawns and a ball field in there somewhere. And when we get the top of this bluff developed, we're going to work on the town below. Whoever laid it out ought to be shot. And we're changing the name too: Hertzville—sounds like a town in pain."

Larkin flipped Winthrop two sets of keys. "Show Tom how you can drive."

"C'mon," said Winthrop, heading out the door.

"I get shotgun," said Dominic.

"No you don't, fatass, that's for the new kid. Get in front, Tom. It's a Mercedes One Seventy V with a 1.8 liter engine," Winthrop said. He revved it and squealed the tires, lurching the car into the garage. He did the same with the little red car. "This one's a Jaguar XK120." There was another car in the garage, dark green and ordinary looking. "That's a Ford Crestliner. I get to drive it around town even though I'm only sixteen. Sheriff said it's okay."

"I get to drive 'em when I'm sixteen," said Dominic. "Dad let's me shoot the thirty aught six."

At dinner we sat around a table so large you couldn't reach the next person if you wanted to slap his back for telling a good joke. I had to fold my hands and bow my head as Mr. Larkin thanked God for the steak set in front of us by a short woman named "Noki." Larkin watched her walk out of the room and whispered with a grin: "She's an Indian, we civilized her."

After dinner we watched television. It was stupid but the guy with the cigar wasn't bad. Gloria told Winthrop to instruct me how to use the flush toilet. They were stupid for assuming I couldn't figure it out. Larkin certainly remembered I was with Urs, but he gave no sign of it till I was in bed wearing Winthrop's pajamas. He opened the door: "Hey buddy, just want you to know I'm going to let bygones be bygones. Breakfast at seven. Sleep tight."

My room was big enough for Urs and me and all five hobos spread out so far on the floor there was no chance of rolling into each other. The wallpaper was cowboys on horses and Indians hiding behind rocks. Dominic musta picked it out. The bed was too comfortable by half. I sank into it and slept so sound I wouldn'ta heard a bear clawing at the door. The people who make those mattresses must not know what can happen during the night.

"Rise and shine," said Noki, knocking on my door. I was already up, looking out the window at a bulldozer growling in the distance, knocking over trees. Us three boys polished off Noki's bacon, eggs and toast. "Driver's here," said Noki when a gray Nash pulled around back of the garage.

Winthrop hoisted the garage door and we climbed into the Crestliner. The driver's door opened and in slid a tall man. He looked at me in the rear view mirror and narrowed his eyes. "That's Borg," said Dominic.

Now I knew I was in hell cuz the devil was driving the car.

18

"Go fast on the curves," said Dominic.

Borg said nothing till he dropped us at the school door: "Five O'clock."

"What do you mean, five o'clock!" shouted Dominic.

"He's got football."

"I'll miss Hopalong Cassidy!" but Borg drove away.

"Shut up, fatass," said Winthrop, "Mom said we have to stay and watch him play football."

I followed Winthrop through hallways, which was like walking through the backwater with carp brushing against you. "Don't look the big kids in the eyes," said Winthrop, "or they'll smack you." It was like bears, I guess, cuz looking them in the eyes was daring 'em to fight.

Mr. Trondson was upset to see me in his history class cuz he didn't have an extra book. "You can look at mine," said a girl whose real face was hidden behind makeup. "My name's Tammy." There was an "oooooo" from the boys and Mr. Trondson frowned cuz you're not supposed to say flirty stuff at school.

"You won't need a book today," said Mr. Trondson, "just take notes on my lecture. What's your name, son?"

"Tom."

"And your last name."

"I'm not sure," I said. The room exploded with laughter and Trondson turned red cuz he thought I was sassing him. That was the truth though.

"You got him good," whispered a red haired kid, "but don't do that to Sershen."

Trondson lectured us on the revolution. After class he said he could catch me up on the pilgrims and the Indians.

"Thanks, but Felix already told me about 'em and I got football," I said. I walked outta the room and a big kid with fat rolls on his forehead pushed me into a locker: "Hands off Tammy."

I went to push him back but Winthrop caught me: "Don't mess with Harlan. He's put kids in the hospital."

Miss Severson in the next class was warned about me cuz she had a desk and English book ready. "You must be my new student," she said, "what's your name?"

"He don't know it," someone shouted.

"He doesn't know it," Miss Severson corrected, "and that wasn't very nice, Arnold."

"I go by Tom," I said.

We talked about a book by Charles Dickens that I'd already read, thanks to Viv. The class was just past the part where Oliver gets mixed up with criminals. "Does anybody think it's okay to steal food if you're hungry?" Miss Severson looked into everyone's eyes to see who would answer. She paused when she got to me, which made me think I was supposed to say something.

"Starving people ain't got much of a choice," I said.

"'Ain't' is not a word," chirped Arnold.

"Sure it is, lots of people say it."

Miss Severson didn't turn red like Trondson did when he heard sass. When she talked to the class she sat on the front of her desk and leaned forward, even further if she was saying something important or funny, and when you had something to say, she looked you in the eyes like she really wanted to hear it. It didn't hurt that she was dead on gorgeous with hair falling down to her shoulders. She caught me looking once and smiled.

"Tom's made an interesting point," she said. "It's about how words become words. We'll talk about that sometime." When class was over Miss Severson stopped me: "I gather you've read *Oliver Twist*."

"Yes, Viv got it for me."

"Who's Viv?"

"She's ... a hobo." I have to stop mentioning Viv, I thought.

"Tom," she said, "one of the assignments I gave the class was to talk about something that happened last summer. We've been hearing one or two of these every week, depending on who thinks they're ready, and Principal Walker comes in to listen to make it more interesting. It's a way to use your creativity and conquer your nerves when talking to people. Do you think you can do it?"

"Yes, mam." I already knew I was gonna talk about the skunks.

"Good for you. It should be about five minutes. Let me know when you're ready, maybe next week."

Winthrop was waiting in the hall and made me run to the next class. "It's Sershen and he yells and makes you do pushups if you're late." We barely made it before the bell. Mr. Sershen scowled and yelled at me: "Why aren't you in your seat?"

"Because I don't have one."

Sershen was wearing a short sleeve shirt, I'm guessing to show off his muscles. "Son, you mouth off to me again and you'll get a dose of military discipline." His stare wasn't half as fierce as Urs's and I stared him right back. He was so close if I brought up my knee I'd crush his nuts. If I did that, I probably woulda been the school hero. "Look around, son, do you see an empty desk?"

I saw the one he meant: "I'll sit there."

We did math problems all hour and I didn't understand none of it. And damned if I was gonna let him tutor me after school.

Lunch was worse than bad. I made a face when a woman in a hairnet slapped a stiff piece of meat on my plate as I walked through the line: "Flying saucer." The lady made a face back at me that said she didn't care if it was cardboard and I better not mess with her. There was also a mound of runny mashed potatoes and soggy carrots; the only thing that looked okay to eat was the banana. Kids paid at the end of the line but Winthrop said "he's with me" so I didn't have to pay, which was good since I didn't have money.

We sat with tenth graders who guarded their plates. I looked away once and when I looked back there were three more flying saucers on my plate and the banana was gone. "It's puties and takies," said Winthrop, "anything you don't want you put on someone's plate when they're not looking and you can grab something you want." I tried grabbing my banana back but got slapped with the flat part of a knife. "And if you catch someone going after your food, you can slap 'em with your knife." To top it off, one of the hairnet women chewed me out for scraping all the flying saucers into the garbage. There's starving children in Africa, she said, and here I was wasting food. How was I gonna grow up strong and healthy? "By not eatin' this food," I said. She swung at me with a spatula but I ducked. I was just being honest, which ain't always the best policy.

Phy ed was right after lunch, which ain't the best time to run races. I didn't have gym clothes yet so I got the evil eye from Mr. Moe, who said I had to run two laps tomorrow. So

I sat with Waldo Larson, who was in a wheelchair and got away with a lota shit cuz of his deformed leg and wide grin.

Study hall was a time when boys pestered girls to show they liked 'em and girls passed notes to other girls to get the other girls to tell one of the boys she likes him so he could pester her. Some of the girls looked at me and whispered.

In biology class Mrs. Schleuter gave us dead frogs that smelled like Moonshine's brew. We teamed up and cut 'em with little knives so we could see their insides. Some of the girls went "ewww," and the boys made fun of 'em for being squeamish, but I saw a couple boys flinch when frog guts spilled out. I've ripped the guts outta plenty dead animals but then I cooked the flesh and set the guts out for crows to pick at. Seemed like a waste of a good frog.

When I showed up for football, coach Larry had his assistant Stewie squeeze me into pants, a shirt, pads, and a helmet. "Next time wear a jock strap," Stewie said. He made me wear shoes with spikes to grip the ground better. I told him I could grip the ground just fine in my bare feet and he looked at me funny.

Football's a mean game. Kids who were otherwise peace loving banged into each other like Otis and Tyrone banged their heads together and the meaner and louder the banging, the more the coaches loved it. If a mean kid like Harlan banged into you, you could get hurt and if you got hurt, the coaches said "suck it up and get back in there." Every time someone tried to bang into me I dodged or backed off so he'd end up on the ground. "Damn it," coach Larry yelled, "get in there and hit somebody!"

"I ain't got a quarrel with anybody!" I yelled.

Coach started to yell back but he couldn't cuz the other coaches were laughing too loud and he couldn't help but laugh too. I said it as honest as I could.

At dinner that night, Larkin asked God to bless the food and help him turn Hertzville into a thriving community. And to help me through my transition into civilization. Like every night, the three of us boys had to tell about our day. Dominic said he was mad he had to miss Hopalong Cassidy. Winthrop told how I kept dodging at football and how the coaches yelled at me. "You gotta get in there and get dirty, son," said Larkin, "that's what men do."

"I don't like football," I said, "but Miss Severson is okay. And I need a jock strap."

Dominic giggled and Larkin froze for a moment: "We don't talk about private things in mixed company."

"Oh for heaven's sake, Larry, if he needs a jock strap, I'll get him a jock strap," said Gloria. "What do you think—I don't know about boys? And if the boy can dodge, why isn't he a running back? I'm talking to Larry."

"No you ain't, Mom," said Winthrop, "you need to quit butting in."

Gloria drew a breath: "Ain't is not a word!"

"It's gonna be, Mom, you wait and see. Huh, Tom?"

I kept quiet.

"You apologize to your mother!" said Larkin.

Winthrop lowered his head: "Sorry, Mom."

"What are you sorry for—saying 'ain't' or telling me to quit butting in?"

"Both, Mom."

"Well then, who wants ice cream? Noki! Ice Cream!" Noki knew what was next, cuz the second after Larkin said that, she burst through the kitchen door with a big smile and a platter of ice cream bowls. If I was her I'd want to spit in 'em but I'm sure she didn't.

In my room that night I stood at the window a long time. The moon was just past full, making the trees silver on one side and black on the other. I opened the window and stuck my head out to hear coyotes, but there was no sound save for the flapping of ivy on the trellis that climbed from the ground up to my window.

    I slept in the cool of the open window but woke from a nightmare and realized the screaming during the fire was Viv and Gaetan and not the goats.

19

Football amounted to me running laps around the track as punishment for not hitting people. Running was apparently the official punishment for every sin, which suited me since running was just about my favorite thing. Every lap made my legs stronger and my breathing deeper. And I lifted weights to bulk up. Coach and I agreed I should quit, but Gloria said the judge made me play so I wouldn't be a blight on the community, and Gloria seemed to be in charge. I never actually played in a game.

Sunday was waffles day and I admit they were good—an artistic version of pancakes, but I think the butter and syrup coulda made anything good, even Urs's chewy flapjacks. Sunday was also church day so I had to dress up and wear the painful black oxfords. Gloria was a vision, as slick Eddie would say, with her dangly earrings and wavy yellow hair under a large red hat.

The six of us sat in front. Apparently that bench was reserved for the Larkins cuz nobody sat with us even though there was space and even though the people in the rest of the church had to wiggle their asses down between other asses to hit the bench. Father Matthias glided around in a white robe with a long, fancy cloth around his neck, speaking a strange language. He was followed by a kid in a white robe who lit candles and handed Matthias things to wave around. After singing by people in black robes, Matthias launched into a long talk about how Jesus wanted Hertzville to grow and prosper. Us kids were surrounded by the adults so they could elbow us if we dozed off. Poor Dominic had Noki on one side and Gloria on the other and musta got a bruise on each side every time his head slipped down. I think he ate too many waffles.

On our way out Father Matthias shook everyone's hand. He held mine a long time and winked at Gloria. "A lost lamb now in the fold," he whispered. "We'll see you at bingo, won't we," he said.

A broadly structured lady leaned close enough so her wide hat covered both our heads and said "It's great fun, you'll love it."

The next week in Severson's class a pigtailed girl told about her first babysitting job, which was a disaster cuz the three year old was a brat. The girl was stiff and nervous and used note cards. She shoulda let the words fly outta her mouth like it was happening right then. Her arms shoulda been waving, her pigtails flapping, and she shoulda squinched up her face when she told about cleaning up the puke. Mr. Walker grinned like a monkey, but I could tell the kids thought it was boring cuz there was only lazy clapping. A good story grabs you and doesn't let loose. It leaves a feeling in your gut or an idea in your head. I was lucky to learn these things from Felix and Urs cuz it led to my storytelling career.

I was ready with my story and Miss Severson had me give it on Wednesday. Principal Walker walked in, neat and shiny in his blue suit and red tie, shook my hand, and squeezed into a desk in the back.

I told about morel mushrooms and how they were the best tasting thing after walleyes, 'specially if you fried 'em in an iron pan with butter and wild thyme. You chew 'em slow to fill your whole mouth with the taste and you let 'em slide down your throat to make the sensation last. Last summer, I said, when my friend and I went to our favorite mushroom patch there was a crusty old farmer protecting the morels. He had an eye patch and exactly one tooth in his mouth and a two barrel shotgun in his lap. (I stretched that one since Claude Pease didn't know a morel mushroom from his petrified pecker and didn't have an eye patch. He had just the one tooth, though.) I said my buddy created a diversion to lure the farmer away while I filled a bag with mushrooms (another stretcher).

But this was only the beginning of the story, I said. I told 'em how our faithful dog waited at the bottom of the hill to lead us home when she suddenly veered off the path and pawed at a pile of rotten logs.

"And what do you think was in that pile of logs?" Kids leaned forward expecting something unbelievable. "Skunks!" I shouted, and I talked at a furious pace. "There was a hundred at least, and they'd been waiting there to ambush us. They charged us with a vengeance, turning their rear ends, lifting their tails to drench us with their stink. My buddy grabbed a stick and swung wildly at 'em, yelling 'save the morels' and 'take that, you motherfuckers' and our brave old dog jumped in to grab a few of 'em by the neck and fling 'em away but she got soaked with the ..."

The room was quiet. The kids were either taken back in a wide eyed gasp or their cheeks were puffed out trying to stifle a laugh. Mr. Walker pried himself out of the desk and said "come with me, young man!"

Miss Severson tried to stop him: "Wait a minute, George," but he cut her off: "Not this time, Severson!"

I ended up in the principal's office getting a lecture on my unacceptable language. Turns out "motherfucker" or any word that has "fuck" in it ain't tolerated in school. "Or anywhere else!" shouted the principal. "What are we going to do with you?"

"I don't know, sir."

"That was a rhetorical question; you don't answer those. You're on the football team, right?" I didn't answer. "Well, you're not any more because I'm taking away that privilege. And next time you use inappropriate language I will suspend you for a week. Now I'm calling Mrs. Larkin to get you."

I thought how happy I was and how happy coach Larry would be to have me off the team. And I wondered what word I'd say to get a week off school.

Gloria drove me straight to church, screaming all the way, and marched into the office, surprising Father Matthias before he could get his feet off the desk: "We need to go to the confessional."

"What's this about, Gloria?"

"We need to go to the booth and I'll tell you what he did."

"Technically, Gloria, the person who committed the sin is supposed to do the confessing."

"Tell him what you said, Tom, then you can walk home and go to your room without supper. There's baseball on television tonight, for God's sake, and I've got a million people coming over. I don't need this shit!" She hoofed it outta there, clicking her heels against the stone floor. We heard the little red car zoom up Prospect Road.

"I said 'fuck', sir."

"Wait a minute, we have to go to the confessional, and wait for me to ask for your confession."

We got into a cramped booth and he pulled aside the little curtain between us: "Is there something you want to confess, son?"

"I said 'fuck'."

"Don't say that word. Just call it the 'F' word."

"Actually it was the 'M' word, sir."

"The 'M' word?"

"Motherfucker."

"Quit saying that word, damn it, we're in church!"

"I'm sorry, sir, but it's a good word. It comes in handy in a lota situations." Apparently "damn" is okay, I thought.

Father Matthias took a few seconds to calm himself: "Listen to me, son, there is no situation where the 'F' word ... or the 'M' word ... is appropriate. Can you imagine Jesus saying those words?"

Probably not, I thought, since Jesus didn't speak English. "No sir."

"Well then, let's try to be like Jesus and quit behaving like you were raised by monkeys. God didn't make us animals. Is there anything else you need to confess?"

"No," I said, even though there were things on my mind like eating too many waffles.

"What do you think your punishment should be?"

"Runnin' laps around the track?"

"No, we'll go easy this time. Apparently you'll be fasting tonight so why don't you just say one hail Mary; Mrs. Larkin can tell you what that is. And you need to apologize to the class for saying the 'F' word."

"The 'M' word?"

"The 'F' part of the 'M' word. Now go home."

I ran up Prospect Road and went straight to my room. Winthrop snuck me a hot dog and apple pie. I asked him what a hail Mary was.

"It's when you do something wrong, you can say one or two of those and it's like the bad thing you did never happened so you can do it again if you want."

I didn't have to stay in my room all night. Gloria sent Noki up to get me when those million people started arriving cuz she needed me to help bring 'round the hot dogs and beer.

20

I knew about baseball cuz I saw kids and even adults playing it, but it wasn't till I watched the World Series on Larkin's television that I saw it on a real field with real players running and diving and yelling at the umps. The Larkins were Yankees fans cuz of guys named Yogi and Joltin' Joe, and so was everyone who dropped by to see the games on the only television on the Indian side of the river. I think they figured they had to be Yankees fans, even the ones who preferred Philadelphia, cuz they ate Larkin's hot dogs and drank his beer. I'm guessing Gloria was happy the Yankees won four straight cuz she was done with having to act nice to ordinary people, including some who were part Indian.

Except she wasn't done. On Fridays people piled into Larkin's den to watch the fights. The room overflowed when Sugar Ray Robinson was boxing cuz he was on a winning streak. He's a black man beating up on white guys and the people of Hertzville loved him as long as he was confined to the television.

During these events Larkin slapped backs and shook hands like folks were his best buddies. He'd slip in talk about how Main Street was gonna look once the town set its mind to being modern, and how the resort on the island was the key to the whole thing cuz it would get people with money to notice the town. "And by the way," he'd say at least ten times a day, "we're changing that name—'Hertzville' sounds like a town in pain." Then he might whisper: "And we're going to bulldoze that eyesore north of town—you know what I mean."

He did that to me too—treating me like his best friend, putting his arm around my shoulder to whisper secrets in my ear, and calling me "buddy." I knew him and Gloria had disagreements about me cuz I'd hear 'em talking in low tones. Winthrop showed me how to listen with a glass pressed against the wall, which I did sometimes when I was in the bathroom next to their bedroom. That's how I knew Gloria was embarassed to have me around. She was pissed I got thrown off the football team and talked long and hard to the principal, but for once he stood his ground cuz there's not much worse than saying "motherfucker" in school. She put on a smile, though, and bought me stuff, like a watch and a chain with a cross on it, both of which were useless. But the new running shoes were good, I'll give her that.

I learned things from Winthrop and began to like him in spite of him thinking his daddy owned everything and in spite of him getting everything he wanted. There was a craftiness to the way he worked his dad with claps on the back for telling stupid jokes. Once in a while they'd argue like they were Sugar Ray and LaMotta dancing around the ring throwing quick jabs, but Winthrop knew when to back off so he didn't get hit too hard. His mom got pissed when he embarassed her with teenage behavior and he took her tongue lashings like a guilty dog, then wangled her with puffery, which often resulted in him getting something like a new baseball glove.

(I learned "wangled with puffery" from Felix, who talked about politicians wangling people with puffery while they stabbed 'em in the back. I said those words in Severson's class once and she looked at me like I was Charles Dickens.)

I taught Winthrop a few things too, like how to tell a lie. You look a person in the eyes and don't look away right afterward. And don't fidget your feet.

Larkin taught me to drive the Ford and I drove County 33 between Hertzville and Onawah, trading off with Winthrop, who was damn near an expert driver cuz he almost never ground the gears. Dominic sat in back yelling "go faster."

And we went to the gravel pit to shoot tin cans and pumpkins. The first time I shot the thirty aught six it kicked me over, causing the three of 'em to laugh. Larkin put it in Dominic's hands and said "pretend you're a sniper and that's the enemy."

Dominic sighted and shot, exploding a pumpkin: "Man, if the Lone Ranger had this …"

I didn't see any advantage to blowing things to bits. There'd be nothing left of a squirrel and it'd destroy a good chunk of meat on a raccoon. It might be okay for a charging bear but I don't expect to kill any of those. "I'd do better with my twenty two," I said.

Two days later Sheriff Pope was at the front door holding my rifle in a brand new case. "Looks like we don't need this for evidence, son, so here you go." He winked at Larkin. "Anything else you need?"

"I need to go see Urs."

"Well, that's for the judge to decide. Urs isn't allowed visitors right now."

"He's my dad; why can't I see him?"

"Why can't I see Rita Hayworth. Some things just never gonna happen. You're living high off the hog here, son. Be happy with that."

Larkin put the rifle in the gun cabinet. I watched how he locked it cuz I had a feeling I'd want to get in there some day without anyone knowing.

The next Saturday Larkin and me went shooting, just the two of us. My twenty two punched neat little holes through the tin cans and carved a smile on the pumpkin, then Larkin blew it to smithereens with the thirty aught six and sat us down for a chat: "You said you want to see Urs."

"Yes."

"We might be able to arrange that."

"Sheriff said the Judge had to okay it."

"Maybe we can convince Fitzgerald to go easy on Urs if we could show him Urs is a changed man and a good citizen. What if we talked Urs into taking that thousand dollars for his property?"

"You tore up that check."

"Well, I guess I could write another check."

I knew he could do that, of course. I was playing dumb cuz sometimes that makes people give away more than they want.

"If you could get Urs to sign over his property for the good of the community, we might get him a deal. I bet that attorney and Judge Fitzgerald wouldn't mind staying at my new resort for free. You know what I could do—I could slip you a hundred as a transaction fee."

I said nothing.

"Hey, guess what: I was thinking Winthrop would like one of those Harley Davidson motorcycles. What if I bought two of those things and you could go riding together?"

I admit I flinched at the motorcycle idea. I'd seen those things zoom by, the riders grinning at us and our donkey. I figured riding those machines round the bends and over the rises was like bouncing over the waves in a rowboat only ten times the fun.

Larkin saw the idea take hold: "Let's take a day off school on Tuesday and go talk to Urs." I nodded. "And don't say anything about motorcycles to Winthrop."

On Tuesday I skipped school and went running while Borg drove Larkin over to Pressworth to meet with Laurence Larkin the Second regarding their Cherry Grove houses. I think it was Larkin's daddy who taught him to build stuff. They got back after lunch and Borg drove us to Onawah. Larkin gave me a big envelope with papers inside. "This is a purchase agreement," he said, "there's some mumbo jumbo legal stuff but Urs doesn't need to read that. The idea is he's selling the property to me. All he has to do is sign on this line. And here's the thousand dollar check. I'll sign it after he signs the agreement." He handed me the envelope and pulled out his wallet: "You ever see one of these?" He dangled a hundred dollar bill in front of me. "That's Ben Franklin; you know who he is?"

"I've heard of him."

"You bring back that agreement with Urs's signature on it and Mr. Franklin's going to jump right into your pocket. Does Urs know how to write, by the way?"

Urs was in a room by himself. He pulled me into a hug but it wasn't like the hugs I remembered. Those were back slapping squeezes that made me feel like him and me together could tackle a grizzly bear. This was more like he wanted something from me. He hung on for a long time, then sat down and looked across the table at me. "I heard you're at Larkin's place." I nodded. "What's in the envelope?"

"He wants you to sign a paper."

"Is it the deed?"

"He wants to give you the thousand dollars."

Urs stared at the envelope for a long time: "Tear it up."

"Are you sure? The check's in there, just needs to be signed."

"Tear it up."

I tore up the envelope without taking out the papers. I guessed I wasn't getting the extra hundred or the motorcycle.

"I need to know more about Viv," I said.

Before Urs could answer, the guard was through the door: "Time's up."

"It's only been a couple minutes," I said.

"It only takes a couple minutes to sign a paper." That was Larkin, right behind the guard, risking his life being in the same room with Urs uncuffed. When he saw the ripped up envelope, Larkin stormed out yelling "son of a bitch!" just like the last time a thousand dollar check got tore up. Only this time I was the one tore it up.

Nobody talked on the ride back. Larkin sat in front, staring straight ahead, as Borg tore like a demon over the potholes and wrinkles in the road. I wondered if I'd live through the ride or the night.

At the front door Gloria scared the shit out of me. She was wearing a black outfit and a pointy black hat and her face was painted green. Her hands were bent into claws and she reared up like a bear. She howled, then choked off a laugh when she saw her husband's face: "What's wrong?" They left the room.

Noki walked in wearing cat whiskers and a frown: "It's Halloween," she said, setting down a bowl of candy, "this is dinner."

That night there was a parade of goblins, witches, vampires, werewolves, and a couple Cinderellas at the door, yelling "trick or treat." Every time the door opened Gloria scared the goblins with her witch act, which got more and more spooky since she was drinking wine between door knocks. Dominic passed out candy in his skeleton outfit, which was comical cuz how many fat skeletons do you know.

Noki was the only one who talked to me the whole next day. Even Winthrop turned away and stared out the window on the way to school. At bedtime Larkin stood in my doorway. "Son," he said, "we're going to build that resort whether Anton Magnusson signs the papers or not. And we're going to run a road right through his property and his filthy shack." He closed the door behind him.

Winthrop warmed up after a couple days and we talked about girls and had I seen one naked yet. I said yes but didn't tell him it was a hobo taking a bath in the lake or that it was my mother. He was impressed and told me about some places we should go peek in windows. He got a kick outta my name being "Tom" cuz I'd be a peeping Tom. I didn't tell him I'd just picked that name from a book.

That Sunday Father Matthias talked about a mustard seed. Jesus told people things start small and they're supposed to grow, "just like that seed and just like Hertzville," Matthias said, looking in my direction, "and Jesus wants us to make it happen."

⇒ 21 ⇐

After school the next day there was a beat up Ford in the driveway and Larkin was talking to Harvey Moss in the den. Larkin left and Moss closed the door: "How's it going?"

"I need to see Urs."

"We might be able to arrange that."

"They wouldn't let me talk to him."

"You tore up the agreement."

"Cuz Urs told me to."

"Listen, Tom," he said gentle, "sometimes we have to take the best deal we can get, even though we don't like it. I think we can get a deal for Urs if he cooperates. If we got the judge to go for disorderly conduct, maybe even time served, would you talk to Urs?"

I nodded.

Moss and Larkin talked quietly by Moss's Ford. I wondered if Harvey was getting a Ben Franklin and a motorcycle. Probably not the motorcycle. Two days later Moss drove me to Onawah. Too bad I was missing another day of school, cuz Severson had us reading a Shakespeare play.

"Here's what we have going for us," said Moss. "They want to grade the road down the hill before the snow flies, so they can get the heavy equipment down to the island in March. And they need to build a pontoon bridge over to the island; the real bridge can come next summer. So they're ready to give Urs a deal, as long as he signs over the property."

I wasn't clear why Urs signing over his land meant he was less guilty of whatever crimes he committed but then I ain't a lawyer.

Attorney Price was waiting for us at the jail and began the talking: "Mr Magnusson, we've given your case some consideration and we might be willing to drop the investigation into those tragic deaths in your barn fire …"

"They were murdered," said Urs.

"Anton, please listen," said Moss.

"Mr. Magnusson, I'm trying to do you a favor. I'm saying you won't have that hanging over your head any more. Judge Fitzgerald's a tough customer but we might be able to make everything but that fracus in the judge's office go away. How about you plead guilty to aggravated assault and I'll recommend a year in jail?"

"A year in jail!" exploded Moss, "that's ridiculous!"

"For God's sake, Moss, he twisted that guard like a pretzel. And he threw the other guard on the judge's desk. Fizgerald's not going to forget that."

"Mr. Levasseur threw the guard off his back," said Moss, "I saw it."

"He didn't have to if Mr. Magnusson hadn't started the brawl in the first place."

"We're not agreeing to anything more than disturbing the peace," said Moss, who was acting like he suddenly grew some balls.

"And he gets outta jail now," I said, feeling my own balls drop.

Price knew how the conversation was gonna go right from the start and got to the important part: "If we agree to time served then Mr. Magnusson has to perform an act of contrition to demonstrate his sincere regret over his conduct."

"And what would that be?" asked Moss. Him and me and Urs all knew what was coming next.

"He needs to sign over his property to show he's a caring member of the community."

"And Larkin has to pay him for it," I blurted out, "two thousand dollars!" Harvey Moss and Leonard Price looked at me like I took a dump on the table.

"That would be for Mr. Larkin to decide," stammered Price.

Moss asked for some time with me and Urs so Price left the room. "Anton, this is a terrific deal. You plead to disturbing the peace and sell your property and Price might get the judge to let you go. Now's when we have leverage because Larkin needs to do some work before the ground freezes."

Urs stared at Moss: "Felix, Eddie and Monroe go too."

Moss gasped: "That's impossible."

"They go or there's no deal."

Moss turned red and stuttered: "Do you know what you're asking?! That's a thief and a moonshiner and a ... a ... queer! If those guys don't do at least a year in jail, Price'll look like a fool; so will the judge. They have to get something out of this!"

"Then we're done," said Urs and he got up to leave.

"Urs, wait," I said. He thought for a bit and sat down.

Moss fidgeted and finally said "I'll talk to Price." He took a big breath and walked out. There were low voices, then hollering from Price. He stormed into the room yelling how Urs was messing with dangerous people and why was he trying to help three hobos not worth a shit. Urs gave him one of his penetrating stares and the attorney stalked out.

That night through the bathroom wall I heard Larkin yelling into his bedroom phone that the bulldozer was already hired and the judge better play along. I wondered how many Ben Franklins were changing hands. And who was in charge of upholding the law.

The next day Gloria drove Winthrop and Dominic to school and left me behind. Larkin took me to the garage where Borg was waiting with his stick. "Two thousand dollars!" yelled Larkin, "who the hell do you think you are?!"

Larkin left and Borg grabbed me by the neck, forced me against the Ford, and whupped my ass. I lasted five strokes before I had to scream. He stopped and I sank into a heap by the tire, stayed there till noon, and went to my room for the rest of the day. Noki brought me dinner and witch hazel salve for my backside. She said nothing, but her expression said we were kin. When I kill Borg, I thought, it will be for her as well as for Viv and Gaetan.

As usual, Larkin poked his head in my room without knocking: "Son, you need to gain some respect for your elders, 'specially the ones who house and feed you."

I woulda said Urs was my elder and he housed and fed me just fine but I didn't think fast enough.

School was off the next day due to Armistice Day, which was to remember the soldiers in the third to the last war. I'd made up my mind I wasn't going to school anyway since my sore ass made it hard to sit down. I stayed in my room past breakfast, thinking of ways to kill Borg.

After a while Winthrop came up with pancakes: "Borg whupped you?"

"Uh huh."

"How bad did he get you; pull down your pants." I looked at him like he was crazy. "Come on," he said, "I ain't a queer or anything." So I showed him the welts on my butt. "Shit, man, how many times did he hit you?"

"Five."

"Idiot. You take one or two at the most, then you scream, that's what he wants. Once I screamed when he was just raising the stick and he never hit me at all."

"He whupped you too?"

"Yup."

"How come?"

"I farted in church."

I cracked up in spite of my blistered butt hurting like crazy. So did Winthrop: "You shoulda seen Matthias when the smell made it up to the pulpit. His face puckered up like this." Winthrop made a face that left me howling so loud I had to gasp for air. "I couldn't stop laughin' and Matthias looked at me like I was going straight to hell." That sent us both down to our knees, pounding the floor.

When we got control of ourselves, Winthrop said watching the priest and his mom turn bright red was worth the whupping. Right then it seemed me and Winthrop were something like brothers since we got beat up by the same guy.

22

Bingo's about the dumbest game ever, no offense to Noki. She was crazy for Saturday evenings when Father Matthias herded a few hundred people into the church basement, saying to some how he was glad they could make it to bingo even if they couldn't make it on Sunday mornings. A few folks thought breathing the church air was enough to purify 'em for the week. (I'm just guessing.)

Larkin and Gloria had left for an Armistice Day celebration in Pressworth, where there were some old army guys who remembered how Laurence Larkin the First gave his life like Buster Pritchett did. They'd be gone overnight so us kids needed to stick with Noki so we didn't do anything God wouldn't like, which meant we had to go to bingo. Noki was pretty excited Larkin left a twenty dollar bill for her to play with, but I'm guessing she was even happier the Larkins were gone for the night so she could drink Gloria's wine and laugh a little. Winthrop drove us to church in the Ford.

At a table inside sat the broadly structured lady I mentioned before, wearing the same wide hat, selling bingo cards. There was a sign saying "Children admitted only with parent."

"Are these your children?" the woman asked Noki.

"Yes, mam," said Noki.

The lady winked at Noki, cuz everyone knew us three kids were not Noki's, owing to our lack of resemblance. It was a little white lie, Noki told us, which was not the same as the big black lies told every time the Indians signed a treaty. She bought a card for each of us.

The object of bingo is ... oh shit, you know about bingo. Father Matthias was the honorary caller for the first round. He stepped up to a bowl of little white balls and put his hand up for silence. People bowed their heads as he asked the Lord to bless all of us with good fortune. I didn't know how that was possible cuz, according to Urs, in order for some to have good fortune others have to get the shit kicked out of 'em.

After Matthias called out a few numbers, an old lady in a wheelchair jumped up and yelled "bingo" as loud as you'd yell if there was a fire. People groaned but clapped when they realized the lady's legs had been healed. Noki said some Indian cuss words and bought more cards as an old man with an army hat and a shaky voice took over for Matthias. That slowed down the game, which was good for Noki, who played more and more cards herself.

Dominic was the first to get bored and made a few trips to the punch bowl in back. I went with him once to get my sore ass off the chair. After a couple more rounds Noki was playing my cards and Winthrop's too and saying more Indian words cuz the Lord wasn't giving her a bingo.

I looked around for people I knew. Hotel Harriet was sitting up straight like she probably read someplace in the Bible and marking her card with determination. Lavinia was with four other ladies I'd seen in her hair place. They all had poofed up hair like they were in a club. Penny was next to a tall guy with long, greasy hair. I bet he replaced Urs on Saturday afternoons and I bet Virgil Dickerson hated him for it, same as he hated Urs. I guessed Penny didn't like Virgil cuz he wasn't big and hairy like Urs and the greasy guy.

Deacon Timothy sat near the door with a silver collection plate and a sign that said "STEEPLE FUND DONATIONS."

It was an embarrassment that the church didn't have a steeple cuz the Catholic church in Bluffton had one and had probably saved more people because of it. Harriet kept a record of those who were saved and posted the list in her hotel window. Nobody I knew was on it.

Across the room was a lady wearing a scarf even though the church was warm. When she leaned forward I saw she was with Louise, who was staring straight at me. I looked back at her but she didn't flinch like most people do when they're caught spying. After a few seconds my face heated up and I had to look away. The lady in the scarf had to be her mom, who wasn't seen about town much due to poor health. At least that's what Jerry told people.

When the final round of bingo came up Noki spent the rest of the twenty on eight cards. She played five herself and made us kids concentrate on one each. She marked her cards like her life depended on it. When she almost had a bingo she kept whispering "G 49, G 49, G 49" and when the army hat man choked out "G 49" she jumped up and yelled "Bingo! Bingo! Bingo!" She beamed when they brought the twenty dollar prize.

On the way out Louise bumped into me: "You cut your hair."

"Uh huh."

"You shouldn't have," and she walked away. Her dark brown hair fell to her shoulders like a waterfall drops into a pool.

At home Noki uncorked a bottle of red wine and poured a glass. Winthrop wanted some but she said no, only he took a swig when she went to her room off the kitchen to hide the twenty and get the Monopoly game. I don't know why Noki didn't just keep Larkin's twenty instead of making us play bingo with it but I'm not an expert on religion.

Monopoly's better'n bingo cuz there's more going on. I tried to save my money instead of buying stuff but I guess that's the way a person goes broke in Monopoly and the real world too, which don't make sense. The easiest thing for me was to be in jail so I tried to spend as much time there as possible. Noki got a little drunk and yelled "bingo" every time someone visited one of her hotels.

Bingo and Monopoly aren't nearly as good as Felix's game. You had to say three true things and also tell one flat out lie, only you scrambled the order so nobody knew which one was the lie. Felix was the best at it, of course, cuz he knew so much. You got a point for each person who didn't guess your lie and another point for guessing someone else's lie. But the winner never got twenty bucks, just the last mushroom on the griddle.

* * *

The next week Harvey Moss was waiting for me after school to say they let Felix outta jail. "He's a bit under the weather," said Moss. That was his way of saying Felix got the crap beat outta him and they had to let him out before they had another murder on their hands. That and the fact he did nothing wrong to start with.

"Urs?"

"He'll get out April first and that's when he gets the thousand dollars. Mr. Monroe gets out then too unless they find his still. Mr. Norton has to stay in jail while they track down the owners of those wallets—could be a while."

"Thousand dollars?"

"He signed over the property."

"Not two thousand?"

"Mr. Magnusson is concerned about your safety, son. He wanted to settle it." My chest tightened cuz it was more clear than ever I was Larkin's hostage. I bet Urs heard about Borg beating me.

"Where's Felix?"

"Well, here's the thing." Moss cleared his throat and fidgeted. "There were conditions. He's supposed to get out of town as soon as he can travel."

"Where is he now?"

"A place in Onawah for a few days, then he has to go."

"What place, I have to see him."

"Well, here's the other thing." Harvey studied the hedge along the driveway. "He's not supposed to see anybody."

"But I can see him, right?"

"I'm afraid not." Harvey Moss was ashamed to say that, you could tell. "There's a possibility he's a bad influence."

"Like hell! He's the smartest person I know. I learned lots from him. Tell me where he is."

"I'm sorry, I'm not supposed to." Moss got in his beat up Ford and started the engine but couldn't move cuz I was standing in front of it. "I have to go," he said.

"Not till you tell me where Felix is."

Moss turned off the engine and leaned his head against the steering wheel. I went to his window. "He's at a motel on County 33 north of Onawah. It's drab green." He started the engine and left.

There was a surprise in church that Sunday. The message on the sign outside said "Special Guest: Our Future." People were probably thinking the special guest was Deacon Timothy reporting on the steeple fund, so they were surprised when Laurence Larken went to the pulpit to announce that construction was beginning on the resort right after Thanksgiving. The hotel would put Hertzville on the map, he said, and by the way, he was awarding a hundred dollars to the person who could come up with a better name for our wonderful town. I think that mighta been the hundred he saved on me. He was gonna put a suggestion box in the church lobby and the town would put it to a vote on Labor day. This was the first step, he said, in growing that mustard seed that Matthias talked about a couple weeks back. It's what Jesus wants, he said.

It's hard to tell exactly when the devil took control of my life. Maybe it happened bit by bit over the past few months, but I felt Old Harry's hand around my neck as Larkin came back to his seat with everyone clapping. Except me, cuz I was thinking about doing things Jesus wouldn't like.

23

The only way me and Urs ever knew it was Thanksgiving was cuz the church sign said "Special Thanksgiving Service; Turkey Dinner After" and on the other side of Prospect Road the cardboard sign in Turlough's Tavern window said "Closed for Thanksgiving." If the turkey dinner was at Turlough's we mighta gone.

That time of year was gloomy cuz it opened the door to winter and the only fish to be caught were stray walleyes or perch through thin ice. If we caught one we'd eat it ourselves. If we caught two we'd debate if it was worth trekking to Penny's for the fifty cents they'd bring and the little bit of coffee or fresh produce we could buy with the money. Penny liked it when we did show up with a fish or two so she had something to serve besides the fishhead soup that woulda made vultures puke. She had just a few customers in the winter cuz she wore a sweater.

When the snow flew Viv would jump a southbound train. It's not just that she hated the cold; she also hated being a drain on the provisions that wouldn't feed more'n a couple people. The potatoes, onions and carrots from the garden would keep till March in the cool space under the floor boards, but once those ran out, we depended on whatever eggs the chickens decided to donate, dried veg like peas, cabbage, and tomatoes, plus any road kill we could find or squirrels foolish enough to leave tracks in the snow.

This Thanksgiving was saddest of all cuz Viv was gone for good. I couldn't work up excitement about family and I was tired of stories about Pilgrims and Indians being friends cuz Felix told me otherwise. There was no school Thanksgiving week so the Larkins were driving clear to Chicago to spend a few days with Gloria's lawyer brother and his wife, the fashion model. I said I wasn't going and sensed relief from Gloria, who had a hard time concealing how I embarrassed her. Larkin probably didn't want me along either, but he didn't know what to do with me cuz he didn't want me alone in the house doing who knows what kinda damage. It'd be okay, he thought, if Noki was staying home, but this was her time with her kin in Onawah. Noki looked down while Larkin and Gloria argued but finally raised her head and said "He's coming with me."

On Monday morning Noki saw the family off and set about three days of "deep cleaning" the house to make it bright and shiny when they got back. I helped her clean out drawers, dust the tops of things, clean carpets, and move furniture to clean places nobody was ever gonna see. The worst was scrubbing and polishing the kitchen floor on our knees, which was terrible for Noki cuz of her age. I never heard how old she was but I'm guessing it was more than fifty. When I cleaned around the gun cabinet I jimmied the lock with my jackknife to be sure I could do it. In the evenings we drank Gloria's wine and tried to find something to watch on the television.

As soon as we finished cleaning on Wednesday afternoon Noki yelled "Get packed." I threw clothes in my bag and grabbed the guitar. She grabbed her pack and walking stick and we set off. After five cars passed us on County 33 I asked "Are we hitchin'?"

"Yep."

"Ain't you supposed to put out your thumb?"

"Don't have to."

Three cars later an Indian man with greasy hands pulled over and signaled us into his Hudson: "Indian Town?"

"Yep," said Noki, and the car sputtered north.

"Who's the half breed?" he wondered out loud.

The man turned right on Indian Town Road and dropped us off in a mile.

Indian Town is a suburb, so to speak, two miles east of Onawah. It's kinda like Ho Chunk Flats only the terrain is flat so the folks don't have to worry about a big storm washing their home down a hill. There's a circle of fifty trailers, give or take, so close together you could reach out the window and pass a peace pipe to the person in the window next door, except there's a gap for a huge pine tree. In the middle there's a big fire.

This was home to two hundred Indians, give or take, and maybe thirty of 'em were Noki's blood relatives. Even if they weren't, they acted like they were. Noki headed for a trailer with straw bales around the sides and walked in. Actually there were straw bales around all the trailers. "Doya!," she yelled, but the place was empty. "There's your couch," she said, "put your stuff there or someone else'll get it. There might be food in the icebox."

"Where do you live?"

"I'm going to try Koma's." Noki left and I stayed on the couch for fear of losing my sleeping spot. I wished I'd brought a book but I didn't think ahead, so I played the chords to 'Black Dog Blues' on Gaetan's guitar. Before I got to the A chord the door opened and in walked a woman in a shirt that said "Onawah Pearl Buttons" followed by the biggest Indian I've ever seen, wearing a wicked knife on his belt.

"A trespasser, Doya!" He put his hand on the knife, looked me square in the eye and boomed: "If you value your life, boy, you'll play me a song right now."

"But ... but ..." I don't remember how many "buts" I said but it was a bunch. "But I can't sing ... sir."

"By god, you'll sing or else!" the giant roared out.

"Oh, cut it out, you scared the crap out of him," said the woman as she pulled stuff from the icebox.

"Well then, just shake my hand. Name's Jim but they call me Big Jim for short. Who are you?"

"Um ... um ... " I also don't remember how many "ums" I said cuz I was focused on keeping my asshole tight.

"Doya, this is Um Um," said the man and he pulled me into a hug. If he and Urs ever get into a hugging match, I thought, that'd be something to see.

"I take it you'll be sleeping on our couch," said Jim.

"Noki said it might be okay."

"That damn Noki."

"Shut your face, Jim, and give the kid a beer."

He did and I drank it. Jim drank one himself while Doya chopped carrots.

The smell of burning wood leaked into the house. "Smells like somebody found some hickory logs," said Jim, "probably stole 'em. Damn Indians. Come on."

I followed Jim out to the fire, which was drawing the attention of maybe forty people, almost all with a Pabst Blue Ribbon in hand. Somebody musta robbed a PBR delivery truck, I thought, and was immediately ashamed I thought it.

There was a big kettle hanging over the fire, giving off sizzles and a greasy smell. Every few minutes a man poked in a big spoon to stir things around. After a while he poured in water and women threw in vegetables. There were onions and potatoes and tomatoes and Doya's carrots and other stuff, reminding me of my soup.

People stood in threes and fours, laughing between drags on their beer. Others arrived in weary posture, like they endured a day of rough work. No stares were directed at me, which was surprising. I sat on a stump and worked the burrs off a dog that musta had a motley assortment of ancesters, just like Woof.

After the pot bubbled for twenty minutes, the man cupped some of the steam to his nose, raised his arms, shouted "mockwa naboob!" and filled cups with stew. Jim set one beside me. The taste was earthy and familiar but I couldn't place it. I ate it pretty quick and Jim brought me another cup: "So you like bear stew." That made me laugh like a tickled hyena, partly cuz it triggered Felix's story about the horny bear and partly cuz I was a little drunk.

People kept arriving till there were at least eighty Indians drinking beer and dipping into the stew till the pot was empty. The fire was built up with four foot logs stacked teepee fashion. Some Indians sat cross legged, staring into the fire like it held the answer to every question. Others talked softly, turning one side of their body, then the other, to the heat. Eventually the logs caved in, sending people scrambling from the sparks.

That's when Jim decided to make it a party. He was the biggest man there by half so when he stepped into the light he was hard to miss. "How'd you Indians like to hear some music?"

The crowd clapped and hooted. I thought "good, I'm gonna hear some Indian music." Then tragedy struck.

Jim pulled me up and handed me the guitar: "This man's a friend of mine. His name's Um Um. He's gonna sing us a song." I was petrified and I had to tighten my butt cheeks again.

"What are you gonna sing?" someone shouted.

"Um, um ..." was all I could say.

"We know your name, just sing us a song."

"Well, I'm not a very good singer."

"Who gives a shit." Big laugh.

I even giggled a little cuz the beer had ahold of me. "Well, here's one that kinda fits the occasion." I couldn't believe I was doing it, but I sang Gaetan's drinking song with a few of the words changed, strumming the whole thing on a C chord, which, I've learned, works with just about every song but this one.

> "We drink Pabst Blue Ribbon here on earth
> cuz heaven's strictly dry.
> Just give me beer and heaps o' lovin'—
> somehow I'll get by.
> I'll satisfy my appetites
> before the day I die,
> cuz there ain't no earthly pleasure
> in the everlasting sky."

The Indians cheered. There was a voice I recognized: "He's right, he can't sing!" And another voice I knew: "And he can't play guitar either!" Mato and Kohana, fresh outta jail, pushed through the crowd: "Hey, Cowboy, sing it again," Mato yelled.

So I did and everybody joined in. They sang it again as they danced around the fire. And again only some of 'em sang "boom dada boom boom," like tom toms keeping the rhythm. And again, but softer, as some sank to the ground gasping.

The fire was a glowing heap when I stumbled in and collapsed on the couch. I hoped I was in the right trailer but it didn't matter. The last thing I remember is laughing to myself cuz "Big Jim" was short for "Jim."

There was no need for bear stew or any other kind of cooking the next day cuz three churches were serving free meals for "White Man's Thanksgiving." If you did it right, you could get to all of 'em, the best plan being lunch with the Baptists, a long nap before the Lutherans at four o'clock and then a skedaddle over to the Catholics before last call. The Baptists and Catholics made you listen to the preacher talk before you could eat. The Lutherans didn't cuz they were liberal, which was good, cuz we were more interested in filling our stomachs than our souls. Their mashed potatoes were the best too, cuz of the garlic. Transportation wasn't a problem since the Indians had eight or nine cars devoted to driving people around.

Kohana and Mato sat with me at the Catholics. "The wolf howls at midnight," whispered Mato.

"The rabbit runs for cover," whispered Kohana. "Remember that, Cowboy."

"So what do you think?" That was Kohana, I think, but I'm not sure cuz he and Mato seemed to think and talk the same.

"About what?"

"You know," whispered Mato, "Big Baasha."

"Oh yeah."

"The face of god!" said Kohana way too loud. That drew a smile from the preacher, who thought we were being religious.

"You're still in, right?"

I changed the subject: "I thought you guys lived in the Flats."

"Kinda, we get around."

"Full moon tomorrow."

"Shut up, Kohana, we can't do it tomorrow, we got no paint and she's gone for the weekend."

"Well then, next month," said Kohana, who was fixed on doing stuff under a full moon. "Full moon's the day before Christmas, what could be better."

I gotta admit that woulda been special—people waking up on Christmas to see God's face on Big Baasha. That could make the mean people in Hertzville bow down and repent. Or maybe the worst ones would kill themselves.

"You're in, right?"

I stammered: "Well, um …"

"We need you, man."

"You're stayin' up on Prospect Hill, right?"

"Yeah."

"You're just a half mile from the top of Big Baasha. Meet us there after everyone's asleep."

"They lock the door at night."

"So unlock it."

"A bell rings every time the door opens." I was looking for ways to get out of this so I didn't get beat up by Borg.

"Crawl out the window, stupid."

"My room's on the second floor." I didn't mention the trellis.

"You can't jump?"

"I'd leave tracks in the snow. And how would I get back in? Won't the paint be too thick in the cold?"

"You mix it with turpentine."

"Damn, the half breed's got lots of excuses." Kohana went for more turkey. That was the second time in two days I was called a half breed.

There was no fire that night cuz the church turkey put folks to sleep. The snooze lasted well into Friday morning so the only people up were those working at the power plant or some other essential place. A couple hours past sunrise Jim and Doya were still snoring, so I stole out to do the thing I really had in mind when I told the Larkins I wasn't going to Chicago—find Felix.

It was a while since I had a good run so my joints were stiff and the five pounds of food in my gut didn't help, but I managed to jog the mile to where Indian Town Road met County 33, then north on 33 past the Lutheran church.

About a mile up from the intersection I found a drab green motel called the "Wild Card." There was a guy at a desk, smoking a Lucky Strike and reading a newspaper.

"Is there a guy named Felix staying here?" I asked.

"Maybe, who wants to know?"

"I'm supposed to give him a message."

"What kinda message?"

"It's private."

"Well, so's his room. He's not supposed to see anybody, so bug off, kid."

I sized up the asshole, wondering if I could take him but guessed there was a pistol behind the desk, and I had a better idea. The motel was shaped like a horseshoe so I stood in the middle of it and shouted "Felix!" at the top of my lungs. I shouted three more times and folks peeked out their doors. Lucky Strike guy ran out, yelling "Get your ass out of here, you little shit!"

I'm not sure what got ahold of me, maybe it was remembering how Viv handled Moonshine when he raised his fist to her, but I didn't back away like a person would normally do. I took a couple steps toward the guy, which threw him off balance, and looked him square in the eye. "You get back in the office, asshole, or I'm gonna shove that cigarette down your throat."

His eyes widened and he backed up, then trotted to the office, looking over his shoulder. Holy shit, I thought, it works!

Then I heard a feeble voice calling "up here." Felix was standing in the doorway of room 226.

24

There's dirt that holds things in place, such as lakes and trees, and dirt that feeds gardens, and dirt that builds up on a person during a day's work, but the dirt in room 226 gave all that dirt a bad name. Felix saw my disgust at the sticky floor and stained bedding: "At least I can shower in peace."

At first I didn't have to ask questions. He rambled, jumping from one thought to the next, without much connection: "They gave me two weeks to get out of town or they'll put me back in jail for vagrancy. Food in jail made me sick. County attorney put me up in this shithole for two weeks—did I say that? They bring food once a day but it's all rice. I have to be gone by Wednesday. Damn, I can't keep the food down; they must cook it in swamp water."

"What are you going to do? You think you'll hop a train?"

"I couldn't hop a phone book in this condition." He gave a snort, so there was still some of the old Felix in there.

I changed the subject: "Urs'll get out in the spring. He sold the property to Larkin and they're gonna start wrecking the place next week." Felix didn't know that. "Do you know anything about Eddie and Moonshine?"

"Moonshine had a couple bad weeks with no booze. He'd shiver and sweat and he thought he saw Jesus floating above him. Eddie kept grabbing the air with his thumb and two fingers, I suppose to stay in practice."

I returned to the most important thing: "What will you do?"

"Thinking's not easy right now. I have to lie down."

I didn't know what to do. Felix was flat on his back, his chest going up and down with quick breaths.

"I'm gonna get you some food." It was a promise made outta necessity without knowing exactly how it would get carried out. I stood with my head against the door and finally: "Do you like garlic in your mashed potatoes?"

"Mmmmm," he groaned, and I left with a grin. I ran the mile back to the Lutheran church and tried the front, side and back doors. They were locked so maybe the Lutherans had a turkey hangover like the Indians. I pounded on the back door just in case. Nothing happened and I sat on the step to think.

The door creaked open and a young woman with a scarred face appeared, dragging a heaped up garbage can. She stopped short like I mighta scared her. "Oh, was it you poundin'? I thought it was the furnace. That damn thing. I mean that darn thing. What do you want?"

"I need some food."

"Oh."

"Do you have some left over from yesterday?"

"Um ..."

"It's for a friend and he's really hungry."

"Well, I could call somebody."

"What if they say no?"

"Hmm ..."

"Are you the only one here?"

"Well ..."

"I'm not gonna hurt you, I just need some food. Is there any turkey left in the icebox?"

"I'm not supposed to do stuff unless the preacher says. And he has today off church."

"You know, Jesus would say it's okay to help out a hungry person." I hate it when people say stuff like that but I had to.

"I gotta dump this." She started dragging the garbage to the dumpster but I jumped in and did it for her. She looked at me with sad eyes and said "The icebox is downstairs." There were five turkey carcasses. "They cook those up for soup. The ladies'll be here in a bit."

"Can I take one?" That panicked her. She damn near broke out in a sweat, trying to decide if I was the devil leading her into temptation or Jesus testing her goodness. "How about if I take this one?" I reached for one with meat on the thigh. "That'll leave four others for the soup. Believe me, I've made lots of soup and four turkey carcasses is gonna be more'n enough."

"Okay."

"I need somethin' to ..." She handed me newspaper to wrap around the carcass. She gave me a spoon and pointed to the mashed potatoes so I scooped some into the carcass. "Jesus loves you," I said; she smiled. As I left I said "I'll bring back the spoon."

I don't know if God exists, but I thanked him for Lutheran janitors, just in case.

I had to coax Felix awake, but when he saw the turkey he sat up and took interest. I ripped flesh off the carcass and spooned potatoes into his mouth. After a minute he did the ripping and spooning himself. He looked around for a drink, which I plumb forgot to get.

"They sell Coca Cola in the office," he said.

"Can't you drink the tap water?" I didn't want to go back to the office.

"It makes me throw up."

"Okay, I'll get a coke, give me some money."

"I don't have any. The jail's keeping it till I'm headed out of town. Don't you have some?"

"Nope," but out I went, hoping Lucky Strike man was done work early. There he was, though, barely visible through the smoke. I leaned on the counter: "I need a Coca Cola for the guy in two twenty six."

"Ten cents," he said.

"I can pay you later."

"Then you can have the Coke later."

"He needs it now."

"Sorry, pal."

"How would you like me to tell the police you're killing the guy. He's sick as a mad dog from your poison water and if he don't get a Coca Cola real soon, he's gonna die. I guarantee I'll pay you later."

"What's your name, kid?"

"Eddie Monroe." That's the best I could think of on the spot.

"Okay, Mr. Monroe, here's your Coca Cola." The words came out like spit.

"Open it for me please." So he opened it and I ran out before I broke out laughing.

I told Felix the guy really thought Coke could save a person from dying, which got a huge laugh. "I'm dying for a Coke," coughed Felix with a big gesture. "That's my Barrymore." Then in a high, girly, southern voice, waving an imaginary fan: "Ah'm dyun' for a Coca Cola. That's my Vivien Leigh."

"Vivien Leigh?"

"Frankly, my dear, I don't give a shit. That's my Clark Gable only I updated it." He laughed pretty loud so I guess turkey works quick. "You'll see that movie some day. They burned Atlanta to the ground. Do you see a pencil and paper anywhere?" There was none. "They'll have it in the office."

I took a breath for courage and marched to the office. This time what appeared through the smoke was a large, white faced woman reading *True Crime* magazine: "Yeah?"

"Can I have a pencil and paper?"

"Whatta you think, this is the Hilton?"

"I really need it for the guy in two twenty six."

"So you're the asshole." She leaned forward and spit out words and smoke: "You attack my son again and I'll scratch out yer eyeballs." She lifted the magazine and I left while I could still see.

"They didn't have pencil and paper," I told Felix.

"Well then, how's your memory?"

"Great, except it's a little short." I heard Moonshine say that once and I thought it was funny. Felix winced.

"Let's have a memory lesson." He gave me a string of words to repeat: "It was the best of times, it was ..."

"... the worst of times." I finished the sentence cuz I read that book. Then I said "Please sir, I want some more."

He laughed heartily: "I forgive you for the memory joke. Leave that one for Monroe to tell." He was telling me jokes ain't funny the second time around. Neither are stories, which is why he always threw surprises into his story about Urs and the bear. I was grateful for learning stuff like that from Felix, cuz it's handy for my storytelling career.

Felix turned serious: "Let's be honest—when they said I had two weeks to leave town, what they meant is two weeks to leave earth. They put me in this godforsaken motel and told them to feed me rotten food so I'd die here instead of in jail, which eliminates a fair amount of legal complication for them. Back to your memory. I'm going to tell you a city where you can find my friend Antoine Thomas and I'm going to give you the locations of two shelters, three parks and a library. If you ever have occasion to head south, chances are good you will find Mr. Thomas in one of these places."

Felix gave me all the information, which was pretty complicated. He drilled me till I had it perfect.

"Here is why I need you to know this. There is a serious doubt I will make it out of this town alive let alone survive cold, bumpy boxcars all the way to the south. Mr. Thomas is my dear friend and I need him to know if I've died. He's the kind who would wait up all night for a friend, but waiting up for a dead friend's a waste of time and lamp oil. If you ever happen to travel south perhaps you will find him and tell him whatever you know of my fate."

"I do think I'll head south someday, but I'm sure it won't be to give Mr. Thomas bad news."

"You're a life saver, kid. He's a large caucasian man, by the way, with a long white beard he fingers when he's deep in thought. He'll never shave it or he wouldn't be able to think. And he has a hickory walking stick taller than he is."

"Tell me about Viv." I had no idea I was gonna say that till the words were on my tongue. "I need to know."

The turkey and mashed potatoes gave Felix enough energy to spend the next hour telling me everything he knew about Viv, which was a lot. When he was done he said "you have grit in your marrow, kid, just like your mom. Now go have some fun."

I left, trying to feel the grit in my marrow. I know that's just an expression, but still. I said I'd return the spoon so I stopped at the church and told the two soup ladies I found it outside so I assumed it was theirs. They blessed me, which gave me a thought. "Ladies," I said, "I am in serious need of ten cents to help a sick friend."

"Be honest, young man," one said, "isn't it really you who wants the money?"

The other one: "Are you going to buy an alcoholic beverage with it?"

"Mams," I said in my most god fearing voice, "it's for a very sick man and it ain't for an alcoholic beverage. It wouldn't be enough anyway—beer costs thirty five cents."

Each of 'em pulled out a nickel. They bowed their heads and prayed: "Dear God, let these nickels be used in your service and not in the service of the devil and his brew. Amen."

"Amen," I said, and I caused 'em to smile when I said their mashed potatoes were the best.

"Young man," said the one who smelled like flowers, "how would you like a piece of apple pie?"

I said "you bet" and ate while they leaned on the table watching. "This is the best pie I ever had," I said, and I wasn't lying.

They grinned: "It's our own recipe," said flower smelling lady.

"There's a secret ingredient," said the other one, "but we can tell you—it's rum."

Flower smelling lady jumped in quick: "But it's okay—the alcohol cooks off."

I thanked 'em, ran back to the motel, slapped the nickels on the counter in front of True Crime Lady, then peeked in on Felix: "I paid for the Coke."

"Where'd you get the money?"

"God." I took off for Indian Town feeling my legs get stronger with every stride. It struck me that whatever could be done to help Urs and Felix and the other two hobos depended on me.

25

That night Indian Town woke up around dark as the turkey dinners wore off and workers came slogging home to join those already camped around a small fire. Cans of food with spoons sticking out were passed around. You took a mouthful of beans or peaches or corn and passed it on. When the can was empty you drained the juice onto a log for the dogs to lick.

Voices were hushed. Big Jim returned from the power plant and propped his sore feet up on a log for Doya to rub: "You get into any mischief today?"

"He was gone all day and he worked up a sweat," said Doya.

"Really," said Jim, "where'd you go?"

"Leave the kid alone," said Doya.

"I will not leave the kid alone. He's hidin' something. Is it a woman?"

"I stole a turkey. Actually I didn't steal it, a woman gave it to me."

Jim propped up on his elbows: "Now we're gettin' somewhere. Was she ripe and volupcheeous like Doya? Ow!" he yelled, when Doya pretended to slap him.

"She was just doin' her job, cleanin' the church."

"What I really want to know," said Jim, "is what you did for her that earned you a turkey."

"For god's sake, leave him alone." Doya again.

"But at least tell me where you put the turkey."

"It was a turkey carcass and I gave it to a hungry friend."

A wolf howl suddenly spooked us. It wasn't a real wolf, and it took only a second before everyone laughed at how they got suckered. I've heard plenty of wolf howls and this one was pretty good only Urs could do it better. People think it sounds like a siren but it usually sounds like a guy moaning cuz his girlfriend left him; that's what Urs told me. Once he howled a lonesome wolf right to the edge of the woods and you could see his yellow eyes glowing in the fire light. The wolf's eyes, I mean—Urs's eyes are blue.

"Damn you, Kohana," someone yelled. Kohana and Mato stepped into the light, soaking up attention. Some of the teens gathered around 'em, whispering about episodes of misbehavior, judging from the glances they gave their moms. Kohana and Mato were considered a bad influence. Kids weren't allowed to be with 'em out of sight of their moms for fear they would ruin their future. That probably explains why those two were after me to help with their mischief, since my future was already ruined with a criminal record and I didn't have a mom to rein me in.

They sat with me, one on each side like in the jail yard. It was like that cricket sitting on the kid's shoulder telling him to do good things only I had one on each shoulder telling me to do bad things. Across the fire Noki looked up from her knitting and narrowed her eyes at me.

Kohana said the obvious: "Full moon tonight." The orange moon had eased up from the bluff to sit on top of the huge pine tree.

"Are you gonna paint somethin'?"

"I told you, Cowboy, she's gone for the weekend."

"Who's gone?"

"Louise," said Mato, "weren't you listenin'? She gives us the paint."

"Oh yeah." I was listening, 'specially since Louise was brought up.

"Full moon tonight," Kohana said again, "and we got nothin'."

"We'll do somethin' tomorrow," said Mato.

"Full moon's tonight, not tomorrow, ain't you been listenin'?" The full moon pulled at Kohana like it pulled at the ocean. He said once a month the moon called Indians to do daring deeds. Mato said that was Indian talk—they just liked to see where they were going.

"How 'bout the Goodwin house?"

"We already painted that."

Kohana was referring to the ghost they painted on the back wall. Nobody's painted over it even to this day, far as I know, probably stemming from a fear of ghosts. There were all sorts of unfounded things the town of Hertzville believed in.

"Yeah, but we didn't go inside. If we did, we'd be the first since the old biddy died." Mato meant Mrs. Goodwin. I told you about her possibly poisoning Mr. Goodwin, then dying on the way out of church, which was five years before. There's been a "For Sale" sign in front ever since.

"So all you wanna do is break into an empty house?" Kohana wanted more.

"A house with a ghost," said Mato.

Kohana gave in: "Shit, let's do it. You're comin', right?"

I looked for Noki but she was gone so there was no good cricket around: "I suppose."

We snuck away and hitched a ride on Indian Town Road and then hitched with a guy and a woman going south on 33. The three of us squeezed into the back seat of the Chevy. As we passed Farmer Fred's something came over me. "Stop!" I yelled. The guy pulled over. "I need to see if my donkey's here."

"What donkey?" they all asked.

"I had a donkey. They said they took him here."

"If they took him here he's hamburger. Fred sells 'em for meat."

I lunged for Kohana's neck when he said that. Lucky that Mato was between us to break up a fight but that didn't stop the woman from screaming: "I told you not to pick 'em up! I told you they were Indians! I told you ..."

"Out!" the guy yelled. The car peeled away. Kohana and me were ready to throw punches but Mato stood between us. Finally Kohana said "I ain't gonna see no fuckin' donkey" and started walking. I followed but two miles down the road I stopped short when I saw a bulldozer gleaming yellow in the moonlight, parked opposite the trail to the cabin.

I knew Larkin was gonna start wrecking the place, but it was one of those things that sits in your brain and doesn't cause a tight feeling in your chest till you come face to face with it. I stood in front of the machine long enough for Mato to think there was something wrong with me. "You're actin' crazy," he said.

I started down the trail and heard 'em following after they figured I wasn't coming back. The cabin door was open but the moonlight wasn't reaching through the opening so it was hard to tell if there were varmints inside, or maybe hobos. "Hello," I said. Only answer was the clicking of mouse feet.

"Whose place is this?"

"Mine. And Urs's."

"You lived here?" Mato lit a match. Things were outta place like someone was looking for valuables. Both mattresses were tore apart, leaving feathers all over. They didn't discover the chink in the north wall, though. Mato lit another match and I pulled out the Prince Albert tin and put three dollars and twenty two cents in my pocket.

Kohana stepped onto the porch: "What burned down?"

I swallowed hard. "Our barn. The fire burned up two goats and three chickens ... and my mother. A black singer died too. The donkey's the only one made it out." I told 'em the whole story about how this property collected the residue of a heartless country, including hobos, road kill, and an Ojibwa dog.

Kohana burst out: "We're wreckin' that thing." He was over the tracks and up to the road in a rush with Mato and me trying to keep up. Kohana jumped on the bulldozer: "No keys. Light a match, Mato."

Kohana loosened screws with his knife and pried the cover off a buncha wires. He scraped the housing off some of 'em and rubbed 'em together till the machine started with a racket.

"You drive it over the edge." Kohana was looking at me. "Goose it but jump off or you'll end up flat as fry bread."

"I never drove a bulldozer."

"It's your rodeo, Cowboy, you gonna ride or what?"

"Hurry," said Mato, "car could come along."

I jumped into the seat. "How do you ..."

Kohana hoisted up a big rock: "Point it toward the bank, put this on the pedal, and jump." He slammed the gear lever into place and jumped off. I steered it toward the bank in a slow arc. When it was lined up with the gap, I put the rock on the pedal, causing the thing to lurch and throw me to my knees. I crawled to the side, kicked off, hit the tread hard, and rolled off. The machine pitched over the bank and through the gap, snapping small trees, and came to rest against a large oak. We ran like hell and hit the ditch to let a car pass, hoping the driver was too drunk to notice the dozer, which was still chugging.

"Oh my god," I said, "now I really am a criminal."

"Not until they catch you," said Kohana.

The moon was going down so we gave up on seeing the ghost and worked our way up the Ho Chunk Flats road to Mato's trailer. "It's just me, Mom," he whispered. He went to his bed, I got the sofa, and Kohana slept in a chair.

I didn't wake till Mato's mom banged pots together—on purpose, I'm sure—and stood over me. She yelled "Mato, you dog, wake up and tell me who's sleepin' on my couch! And why is Kohana here instead of his own trailer?!"

Kohana opened his right eye: "Cuz you make better breakfast than my mom."

Mato appeared in his underwear: "Cowboy, that's my mom, Maemaengwahn, but just call her Butterfly. What's for breakfast?"

"A smack on the ass for comin' in at three o'clock in the morning. What were you doin' all night?"

"The moon was so big and bright we had to stay out and watch till it set." Kohana's eye was open again to see if Butterfly bought Mato's story.

"And where've you been for three days?"

"It was Thanksgiving, Mom; we were up in Onawah giving thanks at church. And eatin' turkey."

"And how much turkey'd you bring me? None, I bet. And how much thanks did I get for the pain of pushin' you outta my body? None, I bet."

"Oh, Mom, you're the best." He hugged her.

"You dog. When are you gonna get a job? Put some clothes on, I'll make eggs and sausage."

We ate with Butterfly looking from one to the next. She knew we were doing more than moon watching.

I promised Felix more food so I left and ran the mile to Old Man's store. He and Lettie informed me there were some shenanigans with a bulldozer. I calculated the shenanigans happened only seven hours before so there's an example of how fast news travels these days. "Really," I said, "what happened?" They didn't know the details.

"I have three dollars and twenty two cents," I said, "what can I buy for a guy who's starvin'?"

Old Man pulled broccoli from the icebox. "You can eat it raw," he said, and he grabbed a quart of milk. Lettie added bread, peanut butter and strawberry jam. "What you do," she said, "is smear peanut butter on the bread, then jam on top. It's pure heaven."

"And here's some jelly beans," said Old Man, but I'm keeping the black ones." I put the money on the counter. "Comes to twenty two cents," he said, pushing back the three dollars. "Care for some checkers?"

I hesitated. "It's a slow day," said Lettie, "our only customer's the guy who told us about the bulldozer." She stuffed the food into a shoulder bag.

Old Man let me win so he had an excuse to give back the twenty two cents. I left with a day's worth of provisions plus all my money and hitched up 33 with a guy driving home from an all night drunk.

As we passed the scar where the bulldozer went down we saw pissed off men in hard hats and a couple deputies. "Injuns did that, you can bet your bottom dollar," said the guy, "they oughta get that dozer out and flatten every one of those shacks in Ho Chunk Flats." He drove me all the way to the Wild Card Motel.

I walked into room 226 to find Felix hanging from the rafter with a bedsheet around his neck.

≠ 26 ≠

I sank to the floor, sobbing, and stayed there for a dog's year, afraid to look up. It was hard to gather myself, but I finally quit trembling and took measures.

Felix had stood on the chair, tied the sheet to a rafter, and kicked over the chair. I tried to untie the knot around his neck but there was too much tension so I sawed the sheet with my jackknife till it split and Felix fell to the floor. I untied the sheet from his neck and the other part from the rafter and stuffed the two halves into Lettie's shoulder bag. Pulling Felix onto the bed wasn't easy but I managed to drag him under the armpits. I covered him with the blanket, making it look like he died in his sleep so nobody would have the satisfaction of knowing they drove him to suicide.

I left the room, hid the bag in some bushes, and walked through the smoke cloud in the office: "The man in 226 is dead."

True Crime lady picked up the phone: "You wait outside."

Lucky Strike Man was sprawled on a sofa blowing smoke rings: "Another one bites the dust."

Two officers showed up. Lucky they weren't involved in the police work at the cabin so they didn't recognize me. They took a quick look at Felix and asked my name. I had to say it was "Eddie Monroe" cuz that's what I told Lucky Strike Man and he was standing right there. They wanted to know how I discovered the body, what was my relation to the man, did he have any family, and did he owe me money for doing him any favors. I didn't understand the reason for that last question till this year when one of my hobo friends down south here explained it to me. The officers were suspicious when I said he was just a friend. They made me empty my pockets, finding only the jackknife and three dollars and twenty two cents.

"This guy," said Lucky Strike Man, "has been here a couple times, threatenin' me and beggin' for Coca Colas."

"Oh really, how did he threaten you?" asked Officer One.

"He looked at me funny." Officer One turned away to hide a laugh.

"Did you look at him funny?" Officer Two asked me.

"Yes sir, I did."

"There, you see," said the asshole.

"Why did you look at him funny?"

"Cuz he's an asshole." Now both One and Two had to turn away.

"What do you think," One asked Two, "should we run 'em in? We got that one for being an asshole and the kid here for lookin' at him funny."

In a different situation I woulda laughed, but they were cracking jokes over my friend's body. "Can I go now?"

"Hang on," said Two, "where do you live in case we need you?"

It was a good question: "I move around some. Indian Town for now."

"You can go but you need to quit bein' friends with older men like this one, you understand what I'm saying?"

I left but when I was out of sight I doubled back to pick up the bag. I ran down County 33 and stopped at the Lutheran's dumpster to ditch the sheet.

One and Two weren't great detectives, I figured, cuz they didn't notice a sheet was missing or see the red mark around Felix's neck. They woulda noticed those things if Felix was a respectable man who died in a respectable place. And I was a dumb cluck for saying my name was Eddie Monroe cuz they wrote that in their report and it wouldn't take much to work it back to Eddie Norton and Merle Monroe, who were right under their noses in jail. I didn't think ahead on that one.

I ran to where 33 hit Indian Town Road, trying to shake the feeling I was to blame for Felix dying cuz the food I brought gave him enough strength to stand on the chair. I didn't turn towards Indian Town, just kept running south, and ended up at Farmer Fred's.

"We're closed!" Fred yelled down from the hay loft.

"I know!" I yelled back. "I just want to see my donkey."

"I charge a nickel to pet the animals!"

"How about if I help you throw down some hay?"

"Deal," he shouted, "ladder's inside."

Fred was down to his union suit tops but still sweating in the November air. He sat on a bale while I threw down ten.

"You're Urs's kid," he said, "with the goats."

"They burned up."

"I know, with a couple hobos." Fred looked at me funny: "Are you safe, son?"

The question caught me off guard. Maybe Fred saw Felix's death written on my face. "Why are you askin'?"

"Just some stories around town."

"Stories?"

Fred looked at me a few seconds like he was holding back a secret. "Just idle talk. You know how things get exaggerated. But watch your back, just in case. Now, about that donkey..." ("Damn," I thought, he's gonna tell me he sold Dash for meat) ... "he's in the other barn."

Fred lowered himself down the ladder, which took some time cuz his belly dragged over the crosspieces, and led me to a smaller barn. Dash was there, getting along with a couple pigs. "This donkey look familiar?"

"That's him. Are you plannin' to get rid of him?"

"Hell no, he can pull a cart. We'll give kids a ride for a nickle each." I didn't tell him Dash could kick like a mule even though he was just a donkey.

"We patched up those burns with salve. Stay a while if you want. It's Saturday so the missus is washing her hair. This could be the night." Fred left.

I held out the broccoli for Dash. He was the only one I knew as family who wasn't dead or in jail. I made him lie down with his head in my lap while I cried. Sometime after sundown I got ahold of myself. "You be good, Dash," I said. He smiled, or so it seemed. I hitched a ride to Indian Town, where I fell onto Big Jim's sofa and slept in the grasp of nightmares.

When I woke, Noki and a couple others were in Doya's kitchen eating my peanut butter and jelly on toast. "Thanks for the feast," said Doya.

"You know about peanut butter and jelly sandwiches?"

"Old Indian recipe," said Doya. She brought me one and it was pure heaven, just like Lettie said.

Noki was trying not to look at me. If she was supposed to watch over me for the long weekend, she did a piss poor job. All she watched over was her knitting and she had no idea— rather, didn't want to know—that I wrecked a bulldozer, moved a dead body, destroyed evidence, and stole a turkey carcass and two nickels from God in the space of four days. She needed to get back to cook dinner for the Larkins, due home that night. I told her I had business in Onawah so I'd see her later.

When people die you gotta tell their friends about it as quick as possible. I don't remember seeing that in the Bible but I still think it's a rule, so I grabbed my bag and the guitar and headed for the jail downtown.

I brewed up a story about an urgent message for Urs, only it was Muscle Guard—the one Urs squeezed so hard in the judge's office. I guessed he wasn't about to let anyone see Urs, so I asked to see Mr. Monroe instead cuz he needed to know his mother died. It wasn't a total lie since Felix acted like everybody's mom.

"Who are you?" asked Muscle Guard. He didn't recognize me in my short hair.

"I'm Mr. Monroe's nephew. We got word today his mother died of pneumonia." I added the pneumonia part cuz there's satisfaction in crafting good stories, which are best if they're right on the edge of believability. I wish I'd said it was typhoid, though, cuz the word sounds evil.

Muscle Guard mighta argued if it was anything but a mother dying. I figured he had a mother and could put himself in Moonshine's shoes. "Leave your stuff here," he said, and led me down the aisle to Moonshine's cell. "Your nephew's here."

"I ain't got a ..."

"It's Tom, Uncle Merle," I yelled.

"You can have five minutes. I'm not supposed to do this without paperwork, but under the circumstances ..." Muscle Guard opened the cell and walked away.

Moonshine used up a minute hugging me and another one with non-stop talk about Jesus before I could get him to stop and listen. "Felix died," I said. Moonshine crumpled to his knees and listened to as much of the story as I could tell in three minutes. When we heard Muscle Guard coming back I said "Tell Urs and Eddie."

"Time's up," said Muscle Guard, so I left. "Sorry about your mother," he told Moonshine.

"Huh?" said Moonshine. I got out the door quick and hitched to Hertzville. The dozer was already pulled outta the woods and sitting on the road, proving a person needs to do a lot more than scuttle a bulldozer to stop progress.

I ran up Prospect to Larkin Way, where the Mercedes was already parked in the drive and Noki was hauling in suitcases.

The family was exhausted so dinner was quiet. I wasn't asked what I'd been doing so I didn't have to make up lies. There was no sign Larkin knew about the bulldozer yet. I went to my room early, saying I had homework, which was the truth since I had to read that Shakespeare play about two people falling in love but their families were assholes. I told Winthrop what happened in the story since he never read the assignments. He let me copy his math to make it fair.

I was never questioned about the bulldozer. When stuff like that happens on our side of the river, it's assumed the Indians did it, which seems unfair, even though in this case it was the truth. Larkin probably even made some hay over it cuz it was one more example of why we needed to do something about Indians standing in the way of progress.

At church the next Sunday Father Matthias let Larkin preach the sermon again. I figured Matthias was okay with that as long as Larkin mentioned Jesus, which he did ten times, give or take. He told how he was willing to pay the Ho Chunk Flats Indians two hundred dollars each for their trailers and land as long as every one of 'em agreed to it. "Then you know what I'll do," said Larkin, "with the help of Jesus, I'll haul away every one of those trailers and build a park for the kids of Hertzville to play in. Anybody here like to see a park?" he asked, and the congregation stood and clapped, even though Matthias didn't say it was time to stand or okay to clap and even though any park built on that land would go uphill at a thirty degree angle. "And by the way, progress has started on the resort. Some degenerates tried to wreck our bulldozer, but we'll still have the road to the island laid by Christmas." The congregation rose again and cheered. All but Old Man and Lettie McDonald. People probably assumed they stayed seated cuz of arthritis but I'm guessing that wasn't it.

What really made me mad was he said "tried to wreck," meaning the machine was still working and I almost killed myself for nothing.

On the way to school the next day Borg slowed down as we passed the trail to the cabin. He made sure I saw the dozer rip through the trees. "Couple days and that shanty'll be gone," and then under his breath: "Shoulda torched it with the barn." He wanted me to hear cuz he was looking at me in the mirror when he said it.

In my head I keep a list of things I'm willing to kill. Mosquitoes and the such are on it. So are fish and squirrels but only cuz they help keep us alive. I killed a deer once and felt bad cuz we could usually get our deer meat off road kill. Borg was the first human to make the list and from this point on killing him was the thought I woke up to every day.

27

Noki's lust for bingo was stoked by her twenty dollar win a couple weeks back, so it frustrated her that Sugar Ray was fighting on two Saturdays in a row, when she had to serve beer and hot dogs instead of gambling at church. She pulled Winthrop and me aside to ask if we'd go play her lucky twenty for her. Gloria said we could go if we did the cleanup after the fight. It's not that Winthrop wanted to play bingo so much as he wanted to drive the Ford on a Saturday night. And I was hoping to catch another glimpse of Louise. Noki kissed the twenty, gave it to Winthrop, and off we went, down the curves on Prospect Road so fast a couple wheels tipped off the ground.

The woman with the hat was selling bingo cards beside the sign saying "Children admitted with parents only." "Your folks'll be right in, won't they, kids," she said with a wink.

Winthrop held out the twenty but yanked it back and pulled me aside: "Let's skip out and tell Noki we won this twenty for her so we can drive around instead."

I said wait a minute cuz coming through the door with her mom was Louise with her hair in a long pony tail. She saw me and rolled her eyes toward the punch bowl so I met her there. "The wolf howls at midnight," she whispered, pouring punch.

It took me a second to remember: "The rabbit runs for cover."

"So you're in, then?" She acted like we were spies.

"In what?"

"Big Baasha. Full moon. Night before Christmas."

"What about Big Baasha?"

"Don't be an idiot. Moondog said you were an ally."

"Kohana?"

"Shhh! We don't say their names!" She was so wrapped up in the secrecy she didn't notice she was overfilling her cup.

Or that Winthrop was right behind us: "Whose name don't you say?"

Louise spilled her punch: "Oh shit, look what you did."

She didn't say "oh shit" real loud but Father Matthias, who was sitting in the back row with his bingo card, had an ear for that kinda language. He stood up, red faced, and pointed to the door, meaning we had to leave. Which was fine, cuz we needed to talk in private.

"Can he be trusted?" Louise asked.

"Of course I can be trusted," said Winthrop. I nodded.

"The Baasha Bust is on for Christmas Eve," she said.

"Bustin' it?" I said.

"Bust," Louise said, "like a sculpture of a head. Get up to speed, Cowboy."

"Cowboy?" wondered Winthrop.

"That's what we call him from now on. I'm Cricket."

"Why Cricket?" Winthrop asked.

"Because you can hear 'em but they're so sneaky you can never find 'em."

"What do you call me?"

"Dead Meat if you screw this up." Honest, this is how Louise was talking. She wasn't shy like I thought the first time I saw her in the hardware store window. "We have to go see the Dogs."

"The dogs?" asked Winthrop.

"Must be Mato and Kohana," I said, but regretted it cuz Louise slugged me. "Oh yeah, we don't say their names."

"I'll tell Mom I'm going to make sure I locked the store, then we can run over to the Flats to see if Mad Dog's home."

"Why run when we could drive?" said Winthrop proud-like, patting the Ford we were leaning against.

"Oh my god, you've got a car!" said Louise, and Winthrop was suddenly part of the team. He got pissed when the car got muddy on the road up to Mato's trailer.

Butterfly came to the door. "Here's trouble," she said. "What do you want?"

"Is Mad Dog home?" asked Winthrop.

"He means Mato," said Louise.

"Mato! White folks to see you." Mato appeared. "Don't sign any treaties."

Louise hit Winthrop three times before he could duck away. "You called him 'Mad Dog'!"

"You said that's what we were supposed to do."

"Not in front of his mother!"

We convinced Mato it was okay to include Winthrop, which was easy with the car sitting right there. We picked up Kohana, then Louise let us into the hardware store.

Painting Big Baasha was complicated cuz things needed to come together into a plan. Louise had to sneak out at least five gallons of paint with brushes and turpentine, which she'd do by fiddling with some paperwork and hoping her dad didn't see a lack of money coming in for the paint going out. If Jerry found out, he might try to beat her again but Louise was at the point where she could hit back. Maybe stealing the paint was her version of "fuck you."

To confuse things, it wasn't clear which paint was needed cuz the Dogs were still arguing about the color of God's eyes (Kohana wanted red, Mato blue), and if God had white or black eyebrows to go with his white hair. Kohana was upset there'd be no unconnected fist but started a new argument by demanding an eagle feather in God's hair. "They have to know this God's an Indian!" he yelled.

"If it looks too much like an Indian, they won't think it's really God!" Mato yelled back.

By Mato's calculation we needed four hundred feet of rope—a hundred each to suspend the artists and two hundred more to move buckets up and down. Louise took us to the back room, where spools of rope were waiting for shelf space. Mato unwound some, checking for strength and mouse nibbles, and chose a spool he figured contained at least four hundred feet. We decided to move it up to Big Baasha right away to save time on Christmas Eve. The spool was so large we had to drive up Prospect Road with the trunk open, hoping nobody would notice.

We took the dirt fork along the edge of the bluff and stopped on top of Baasha. The moon was new so we were looking into pitch black except for Hertzville's dim lights. The Indians lit two old lanterns Louise had pulled from a junk pile in the basement. We unwound the rope, cut it in half, then in half again, looped it around trees for leverage, and covered it with leaves. Louise and I hid the spool behind some rocks.

There were other questions, like how to get out late at night on Christmas Eve. That wasn't a problem for Mato and Kohana, who could say they were at Indian Town. The rest of us didn't have time to plan right then cuz Louise needed to get back to church before bingo ended. All we knew is we'd meet on top of Big Baasha at midnight on Christmas Eve. We raced back to the store to hose off the Ford, let Louise off at the church, and drove the Indians to Ho Chunk Flats but let 'em off on the highway so the car'd stay clean.

As Winthrop pulled into the garage we realized our story had a flaw. If we gave Noki the twenty she gave us, she'd suspect something cuz it was unlikely we spent exactly twenty bucks on bingo cards and won exactly twenty in return. So I contributed twenty cents and Winthrop had to put in a buck since he didn't have coins. We'd say that was the money left from the original twenty. The math was correct since bingo cards cost twenty cents each.

When we walked in, the fight hadn't even started so we had to serve food and do the cleanup too. It took Sugar Ray only four rounds to knock out the guy from Holland, who crumpled like a Model T meeting a freight train. The announcer said "They never come up when they go down like that." The crowd was pissed it didn't go ten rounds.

Winthrop and me cleaned up by ourselves. He stashed the leftover beer behind the workbench in the garage. "I take a few each time," he said, "sometime we'll have our own party." While we were out there we planned how to get out on Christmas Eve.

Noki was thrilled she came out a dollar and twenty cents ahead and asked us to play her money again the next Saturday, which gave us cover for a dry run. At the top of the rock the Dogs fashioned a harness at the end of each rope and we let 'em down, feeding the ropes around the trees. The artists did some measuring to space out the eyes and other features and made marks with charcoal. We still hadn't figured out how to get the paint up there; we couldn't do it before Sunday cuz it would freeze.

Sugar Ray beat a Polish guy that night but at least it went ten rounds. Ray's got a quick uppercut. After cleanup was done, Noki looked at us wide eyed and we gave her twenty two bucks.

28

The next day I glanced up at Big Baasha from the church parking lot. If you looked hard you could make out the charcoal marks and imagine how the face would take shape. Folks weren't looking up, though, cuz it was the week before Christmas, when they decorated the Christmas tree. They rushed inside with their ornaments. Lots of families brought angels, hoping theirs would go on top. The Larkins passed out chocolates. Father Matthias talked about Baby Jesus and how simple beginnings can lead to big things.

Louise was there with her folks. We tried not to let on we knew each other, let alone were planning the prank of the century. On the way out she did that thing with her eyes, meaning I should meet her on the steps. "Cricket doesn't know how to get up there," she said. Winthrop and I knew how to get outta the house but we didn't dare use the car cuz the noise would wake his folks. We planned to walk the half mile to the rock. Louise, on the other hand, would have to walk a couple miles, the worst part being the hike up Prospect Road, and even have to carry five gallons of paint. If she could do that, she wasn't only the one I dreamed about seeing naked, but Wonder Woman to boot. We needed an idea. That night I got one.

The next day after school I went running. I got to Old Man's store at five o'clock, which was when he and Lettie closed on Mondays to clean and restock. I pretended I was there to buy bananas but told 'em I could play checkers after they locked up. Old Man beat me in a flash, raising his fists like he was Jesse Owens crossing the finish line.

I said "let's play another" but this time I talked more'n I played. "When's the last time you did somethin' exciting?"

The question took him by surprise. Lettie came closer. "We rode horses and camped in Wyoming," she said, "that was a long time ago."

"How'd you like to scare the bejesus outta Hertzville?"

"Hell yeah," Old Man said. Turned out the McDonalds were old and frail on the outside but fulla the devil inside.

I took a big risk and told 'em about the Baasha Bust. When I was done, Old Man and Lettie burst out laughing. "Seeing God's face on that rock'll be the most fun I've had since Lettie and I were alone on a beach in California."

"Oliver!" yelled Lettie, and he shut up but he was grinning. "He was young once. So was I."

I thought they might be hooked so I took the next step: "How'd you like to help? We need to get three people and five gallons of paint up to the top of Big Baasha on Sunday night and we need a car to do it."

"Sunday night, hmmm," Old Man said, "seems like there was something happening Sunday night."

"Christmas Eve," said Lettie.

Old Man got excited: "So when people look up on Christmas morning, they'll see God looking down at 'em?"

"That's right," I said.

"Holy Christ, they'll shit their pants," howled Old Man.

"Oliver!" yelled Lettie, but she grinned.

"Can our Ford make it up the hill?" asked Oliver.

"If not I'll get out and push," said Lettie.

They were in. I told 'em to meet me in the church parking lot at eleven thirty Sunday night and we'd pick up Mad Dog, Moondog and Cricket. I didn't tell 'em the real names.

"Do we get names?" shouted Old Man as I left.

"Sure, think of some." You might say I played 'em like Old Man played checkers but I'd say I helped 'em recapture their youth.

The next day after school I ran to Ho Chunk Flats and found the Dogs at Mato's kitchen table with religious picture books from the library, working out colors for God's face with a box of Crayolas and still arguing about the feather and the fist. They'd decided to add a white beard.

Kohana still wanted red eyes cuz his god was pissed and about to shoot fire. Mato wanted blue eyes cuz red eyes were too unrealistic. And by "unrealistic" he meant it didn't look like the pictures in the books. They colored one eye red and one blue to compare, then settled on blue but narrowed like he saw the evil inside you.

I told 'em Old Man and Letty were in on the plan, which caused some concern but I assured 'em those two were good accomplices. Kohana was upset the white people would now outnumber the Indians five to two but I told him it might be four to three but that wasn't for sure.

Butterfly got home early from her job cleaning houses. When we heard her on the steps we quick hid the books and the drawing. She walked in to find me and the Crayolas and I'm not sure which worried her more. "You make dinner," she told Mato, "make enough for Moondog and Cowboy."

Damn, I thought, she knows our bandit names—what else does she know? Mato cooked a stew with gravy to soak the bread.

I plum forgot about the time so I was late getting back to Larkin's. Gloria scolded me and said I'd get no supper. I made a pouty face but laughed inside and went to my room to read the end of the play. It was too bad the two of 'em had to die. I added poison to the list of ways I could kill Borg even though it didn't kill the girl. The next day in Severson's class we talked about how revenge multiplies itself. Turns out I didn't apply that to my own life.

29

When Sunday night came we were jittery waiting for the Larkins to get to sleep. At eleven Winthrop heard snoring at their door so we dressed warm and climbed out my window and down the trellis. Winthrop set out for Baasha and I ran down Prospect Road to where Old Man and Lettie were parked at the church.

We drove to the Flats, picked up the Dogs by the highway, then turned back to the hardware store, where Louise was waiting. We loaded two gallons of white paint, two of black, a quart of blue, a gallon of turpentine, and buckets for thinning the paint so it wouldn't seize up in the cold. Kohana grabbed some red, restarting the argument about the eyes but he got away with it. When we were ready to go we realized a Model A Ford is too small to hold six bodies and five gallons of paint. Louise ended up on my lap in the back seat. She mighta felt the lump in my pants.

On the way up Prospect Drive Old Man turned out the lights cuz the full moon was bright enough to light the devil's dark heart. Lucky it was a Sunday night so the tavern was closed and there wouldn't be drunks weaving through the parking lot, wondering why a Ford with no headlights was sputtering up to the rich folks development at midnight. I'd be lying if I said we thought of that in the planning process. Winthrop was waiting for us, shivering.

"I'm Cricket," said Louise. The McDonalds knew who she was, of course, but never said her name.

"I'm Shadow," said Lettie, "and this is Spider." Old Man tipped his hat. Or rather stretched it out from his forehead, cuz he and Lettie wore black stocking caps to go with the charcoal on their faces.

"This is Dead Meat," said Louise.

"Can I get a new name?" said Winthrop.

We had to work fast to get done before daylight. We mixed black paint and turpentine in a bucket. The Dogs stuck brushes in their pockets, strapped into the harnesses and inched down the rock with me and Louise feeding rope around one tree, Winthrop, Old Man and Lettie around the other. We lowered down the buckets so they could outline the eyes, eyebrows, nose, and chin. They called for blue for the eyes, then both gallons of white so each of 'em could work one side of the face, painting hair, eyebrows, and beard. They went from top to bottom so they wouldn't get footprints on the paint, planning to swing wide to get back up. Every few minutes they'd yell "down" and we lowered 'em a couple feet.

In between thinning the paint and working the ropes, Old Man and Lettie kept warm by dancing and singing "I'm wild again, beguiled again, a simpering, whimpering child again. Bewitched, bothered and bewildered am I," which they musta heard on the radio. Old Man said "I love you, Shadow." Lettie said "Come here, Spider," and kissed him. If you read that in a book you'd swear it was too corny to be real, but I'm telling you they did it. They had a thermos of coffee and poured us a cup, making us feel sorry for the Dogs hanging below in the cold. When the white was done, more black was needed to "mottle" the hair and beard, which was Mato's fancy word for streaks to make it stand out, and there was black around the white areas to set 'em off. When that was done it was four o'clock by Old Man's watch and we'd set five thirty as the latest we needed to be done to get home without suspicion. We pulled up the painters.

"Give me the red," said Kohana. "Don't worry, I'm just gonna put a little red on the lips." Mato argued with him. "I'm an artist, damn it, give me the red!" Kohana shouted, and Mato gave in.

We lowered Kohana but he kept saying "more," so we knew he was below the lips, but didn't know exactly what he was doing. When we got him back up it was almost five o'clock and we felt pretty good about our chances of getting away with it, but we hadn't figured what to do with the paint cans, ropes, and lanterns, which would be easy to trace back to the hardware store.

"We'll take 'em," said Old Man, so we loaded the stuff into the Ford, which is when I noticed the lanterns looked like the ones the railroad uses. Dead Meat and I ran for the house while Spider and Shadow took off with Cricket and the Dogs.

Winthrop left his boots under my bed so's not to leave wet prints down the hall. I did the same and didn't wake up till I smelled bacon. We made quick work of Noki's breakfast, then sat around the Christmas tree to open presents.

Urs and me never gave presents on Christmas or any other day. We just gave whatever we needed whenever we needed it that was in our ability to give. I'd give him the first tomato from the garden or I'd patch the holes in his extra britches. Sometimes I'd chop logs into wedges to chink up the cabin walls. The biggest thing he ever gave me was the used rifle and then he bought a scope for it. Or maybe the best thing was the pair of running shoes he ordered from the Mercantile. He paid actual money for 'em, along with a pair of thick wool socks. And the jackknife I keep in my pocket. These were the useful things I prized most cuz they made life fun and comfortable.

So it felt weird when Dominic handed out boxes wrapped in fancy paper, which was a waste since it got ripped up. Each time something was pulled out there was a thank you sounding like it was the greatest, most useful gift ever. Dominic and Winthrop got reindeer sweaters. Noki got a pair of thin black gloves that weren't waterproof or warm. Larkin got a watch with diamonds to replace the one without diamonds.

Dominic handed his mom the smallest box of all, which, you'd think, woulda been the least impressive gift, but everyone gasped when she pulled out a glittery necklace. I don't know what good that was since you didn't eat it or play with it and it didn't make your life any easier, so I still thought it was the least impressive.

Until I opened my box and found a tie. "It's silk," said Gloria. Now I had two ties and I could live ten lifetimes without needing even one, but I said "thank you" cuz I was supposed to.

Larkin led us out to the crates by the garage and gave Winthrop a pry bar and hammer. He hammered and pried till the lid came off and shrieked when he uncovered a red and black Harley Davidson motorcycle.

"The sidecar's so you can give your brother a ride," said Larkin.

"Can I ride it now?" Winthrop asked over and over.

It had to wait till spring, when the roads were clear, Larkin said. Besides, we had to get to church.

We dressed up fancy for the special Christmas service, which was at noon so families had time to open presents. When we crested the hill we saw the church parking lot was full and cars overflowed into the tavern lot.

"Look how many people showed up for the Christmas service," said Gloria. When we got closer, we saw it wasn't the usual church crowd.

"Those aren't people," said Larkin, "those are In ..." He caught himself before saying "Indians."

Winthrop and I looked at each other wide eyed. It took about a second to understand what happened: Kohana and Mato couldn't keep their mouths shut. They bragged about their artwork and almost every Indian in Ho Chunk Flats and most of 'em from Indian Town now stood in the parking lot with big smiles, pointing up toward Big Baasha.

God's hair flowed in the wind and his eyes glared at us like he was royally pissed. The black background made the whole thing pop out. The brown face had depth owing to the shading that brought out the wrinkles under the eyes and nose. There were even hairs in his nostrils.

But the thing that sent a shiver up your spine was the word scrawled in red on God's white beard: "Sinners!" So that's what Kohana painted on his last trip down the rock.

People's brains had to know it was just paint on a rock, or an act of vandalism, as Sheriff Pope would say, but you could tell some of 'em were panicked deep down in places the brain don't prevail. A few even drove off with an uneasy look, probably to hide from God's vengeance.

Father Matthias was rattled. He had to ring the bell twice to get people inside. There were lots of Ojibwas, which threw the flock outta balance. A few white faces got red when Indians sat in pews normally occupied by the regulars, causing some to stand.

The sermon was about Jesus being born but if the Father was thinking, he woulda switched horses midstream and talked about the part of the Bible before Jesus—the part where God did horrible things to sinners. I bet he woulda got double the normal collection.

Laurence Larkin was quiet. He had to be thinking how property sales on the bluff would be affected and what he'd like do to the perpetrators. When we got home he called Sheriff Pope.

There was no school the week after Christmas so Winthrop and I were having a late breakfast when Pope showed up the next day. "There's no question who did it," he said, "those punks from the Flats. They got their hands slapped before, but this time they're going away for a while. If I know Fitzgerald, he'll send 'em to Virmeer for a couple years. We'll pick 'em up right away."

Suddenly the prank turned serious. Virmeer School for Boys was forty miles east of Onawah and was more a prison than a school, judging from the barb wire fence. I heard the kids there got beat for the slightest misdeeds and there were no Okemoses to give 'em gum.

I ran down Prospect into town and used the back door to Old Man's store. Lettie was happy to see me: "Cowboy!" she yelled.

Old Man joined us in the back room, looking younger than two nights ago but of course he'd washed the charcoal off his face.

I told 'em how the law was gonna send the Dogs to the Virmeer School, where they'd practically be tortured.

"Oh dear," said Lettie, "I didn't think it would come to that."

"The police were here," said Old Man, "asking if we knew anything. I told them no and they left. They assumed we couldn't know anything cuz old folks go to bed early and don't hear well."

That last part was actually true.

30

Church next Sunday was packed, including more Indians than usual. I'm guessing they wanted to hear what the Father would say about God's brown face after thinking about it for a week. Sheriff Pope and Linus Hooper were there, which was not strange, since they went to churches around the county to pick up votes.

The Father said nothing about Big Baasha—just waved things around and said words only he and Felix would understand. Then came a surprise. Matthias invited a special guest to the front, that being the sheriff, who wasn't there to give the blessing.

"Folks," said the sheriff, "my name is Pope, but I'm not *the* Pope." People laughed to be polite cuz they'd heard that joke before. "But I'm sure if the Pope was here, looking up at that monstrosity, he'd want us to catch the hoodlums who did it. It's my job to do just that. It's pretty obvious who the perpetrators are—those two that did the other paintings around town. Raise your hands if you know who I mean."

Most of the white folks raised their hands. The funny thing—five of us knew exactly who did it and none of us had our hands raised.

"We have a critical piece of evidence," continued Pope. "We found a large spool that must've held the rope they needed for this crime. There was a label on it saying 'Ship to Christianson Hardware.' So the little devils broke into your store, Jerry, to steal rope and who knows what else."

Once This River Ran Clear

Oh shit, I thought, we forgot about the spool. If Jerry's hair wasn't already standing up straight, that woulda done it.

"We looked for these two in the Flats and up in Onawah to no avail so I'm asking for your help," said Pope. "Tell us if you know where these lowlifes are hiding. I'll have a deputy parked outside the church at noon every day from now till ..."

Pope's voice trailed off cuz something strange happened. Old Man McDonald got up from his pew and walked down the aisle. "They didn't do it," he lied.

"Lettie," said Pope, "can you help Old Man back to his seat; he's a little confused."

Lettie stood beside her husband. "He's not confused, sheriff. They didn't do it."

The sheriff chuckled: "How do you know this?"

"Because we did it," said Old Man. Now most everybody was laughing. "You want the proof? The paint cans and rope are in the dumpster back of our store." The laughing stopped.

Pope's face got red: "You're telling me you lowered yourself down that rock in the middle of a cold night and ..."

"Yes sir," said Old Man. "I stole the paint from Jerry's store." He turned to Jerry Christianson: "Sorry Jerry, I'll pay you for it. You need a better lock on the back door." Jerry was probably wondering if he could get by with whupping Old Man.

Seeing those two old folks standing there stirred something inside me that was somehow connected to the loss of Viv and Gaetan and Felix. I walked up and said "I helped 'em do it." I heard a squeal from the front row that had to be Gloria.

Suddenly Louise Christianson was by my side: "They didn't steal the paint—I gave it to them. And I helped paint the rock." The audience gasped. Folks probably wondered what Jerry Christianson was gonna do to his daughter cuz it was rumored that the reason she always wore pants, even to church, was to hide the scars from years gone by. She stood there so fearless I wondered if folks should worry about Jerry insteada Louise. I felt a surge through my body, not cuz I was afraid but cuz Louise was holding my hand.

I heard Winthrop breathing hard in the front row behind me. He had to be thinking about his punishment if he joined us, probably losing the Harley. But maybe he knew if he joined in the confession it would all but ensure nobody was gonna get punished. His mom caught her breath when he got up. "I was there too," he said.

The crowd was stunned. Five white people were confessing to a crime that was supposed to be done by Indians. Never mind we were all liars; it was one of Noki's little white lies meant to keep the Dogs from torture.

Pope gathered his wits and tried to save the situation with humor. "Anybody else wanna confess?" He shouldn'ta said that.

Big Jim was suddenly at my side: "Yep, I did it." The crowd didn't dare laugh. Linus swallowed so loud you could hear it. He was probably thinking that putting cuffs on Big Jim was a death wish.

Then Doya was by Jim's side, followed by a rush of Indians like a dam'd broke. There were at least fifty of us claiming responsibility. Sheriff Pope no doubt wished he was at a different church. Was he gonna arrest us all and were there enough jail cells to go around? Or would he laugh it off cuz white people were involved, two of 'em being the oldest people in the county, and one of 'em the son of a rich man who paid to get him elected. Besides, it wasn't clear what crime we committed—vandalism maybe, but Big Baasha wasn't owned by anyone so who was gonna press charges? The main reason he was in church that day was to bring justice to Indians for being Indians. He was a loser no matter what he did next.

"Well," said Hugo Pope, trying to sound decisive, "we're gonna put this matter on the table for further consideration. I'm turning this meeting back to the good Father." He walked to the door, followed by most of the crowd.

"Wait," shouted Father Matthias, "you haven't received the blessing." He yelled it at our backs. "The Lord bless you and keep you. The Lord make his face shine on you, and be gracious to you. The Lord turn his face towards you and give you peace and the blessing of God almighty, the Father, the Son, and the Holy Spirit, be among you and remain with you always. Amen." He sank into a chair and whispered "oh shit."

I wonder if he understood the irony of saying "the Lord turn his face toward you."

By the time Winthrop and I got to the parking lot, the Larkins had left, which was fine by us, since Gloria would be screaming all the way home. We wandered to McDonald's store, where Old Man and Lettie were amid a crowd of people expressing opinions regarding Big Baasha. Hotel Harriet thought it was heresy since it didn't look like the real God. Skeeter Turlough thought it should be sand blasted cuz it might cause drunks to mend their ways (but I think he was kidding). Library ladies Gertrude and Frances thought we should leave it for the same reason. None of the opinions were expressed in anger out of respect for Old Man and Lettie's age. Quite a few folks bought groceries, which was a hint at the prosperity that would come to Hertzville due to curious outsiders.

Winthrop and I hung around Old Man's till dark, drinking free Cokes, debating where Mato and Kohana might be and whether they'd actually seen their creation from out front where they could get the full view of their artistry. Finally we took a deep breath and made a long slow walk up Prospect Drive.

Dominic was out front making snow angels. "You're gonna get it," he said.

Larkin and Borg were waiting inside. Gloria was drunk. "Beat the shit out of them," she yelled and slammed her door.

"Go ahead," said Larkin.

Borg pulled the club from his coat and took a couple steps toward me. I stepped forward, causing him to pause between steps. I took another step so I was close enough to stick my finger in his eye but I kept my arms loose at my side. "You raise that club to me," I said, "and I will take it and beat you like you beat my dog."

It's true I'd grown muscle and stature since Borg and I met on the cabin porch six months before, so maybe he was worried I could actually do what I said. More likely he was thrown off cuz I knew he killed Woof with his club. I held my stare cuz the first one to blink was the loser. Finally Borg glanced at Larkin.

"Let it go, Borg," Larkin stuttered. Did he know Borg killed my dog, I wondered. Borg gave me a look that said we would meet again, then stormed out with Larkin.

Winthrop collapsed into a pile: "Holy shit!"

I spent the rest of the evening in my room. When Gloria stopped yelling, I packed what little stuff I wanted into my shoulder bag, picked up the guitar, crept down the stairs, and jimmied the gun cabinet lock with my knife. I slipped the twenty two out of its case, laid the case back in the cabinet so it looked like the rifle was still in it, and left the box of shells, hoping nobody would suspect the rifle was gone. I left out the front door, not caring if the bell rang.

I walked the mile and a half to the cabin, hitting the ditch when a car went by, cuz a young man toting a rifle at midnight might cause some concern.

The trail down the hill now had a gravel base and the cabin was in a pile. I could see pretty well by the half moon and wandered the place, remembering everything that happened there. Shadowy thoughts had spun through my mind for months, but you might say this is when they started coming together into a plan.

I climbed to my ledge and sighted the rifle to the island. I'd have to get closer cuz a twenty two bullet at that distance wouldn't have enough velocity to pop a balloon. I slid the rifle under a ledge and blocked it up with rocks. It started to snow.

I got back on the highway and ran north, which musta been a curious sight—a kid running into a snowstorm in the wee hours with a bag over his shoulder and a guitar case in his hand. At Farmer Fred's I decided I needed shelter so I ran to Dash's barn and spent the night huddled next to my donkey.

In the morning I snuck out, leaving tracks in the snow that would make Fred wonder what was missing from his barn. I hitched to Indian Town and knocked on Big Jim and Doya's door, which was opened by the giant in his underwear.

"Um Um!" he said, "we've been expecting you!" He pulled me in for a bear hug and breakfast. It was January first.

31

Next day the trailer was busy with neighbors since Jim was off work and since Doya made such good fry bread fixings. People buzzed about Big Baasha and what to do if the law showed up. The general feeling was the cops'd leave us alone, but Mato and Kohana should stay hidden just in case. The police could find me any time they wanted, but I guessed Larkin was glad to be rid of me since he already had Urs's property. "You're old enough to be on your own," said Jim.

Truth is nobody knew for sure how old I was, including me. Urs didn't keep track of actual birthdays, just figured a person was a year older when January first rolled around, so, by his logic, I was seventeen. The law mighta said I had to be eighteen to be on my own and I coulda represented myself as eighteen except I didn't want anybody thinking I was old enough to be drafted. There was no paperwork anywhere saying I was even born so maybe the army didn't know I existed and maybe nobody would tell 'em. I had lies ready depending on the situation. In any case I was adjusting my thinking towards a possible life on the run and I was watching my back like Farmer Fred told me to do. I didn't know what I should watch for except I was sure Borg didn't like the way our last meeting ended. I asked folks to let me know if they saw a gray Nash in the area or noticed a tall man with yellow eyes.

When Doya and Jim left for work on Tuesday, I ran on icy roads to Lundeen's Market in downtown Onawah and spent almost all the Prince Albert money on onions, carrots, cabbage, beans, celery and spices. When Doya and Jim got home I had soup waiting. Over dinner we talked about my future, which was unplanned, except for killing Borg. I didn't tell 'em about that.

Doya asked if I wanted to go to Onawah High School. That was a tough one cuz Louise went there, but I said I'd get a job instead cuz if I was gonna stay with her and Jim I should pay my way.

"You can cook," said Doya. I perked up. "There's a couple places might need a dishwasher and maybe they'd let you cook your soup once in a while."

"We go to Chief's fish fry some Fridays," said Jim. "Owner's Ojibwa. I can vouch for you."

Two days later I was standing in front of Chief. His black braid stuck out a hole in his Yankees hat but I'm sure he was never at Larkin's to watch baseball.

"Call him Um Um," said Jim. Chief studied my features for a good ten seconds and said "Unnh," which is about the only thing he ever says.

"That means you're hired," whispered Donna the waitress. I think I got the job cuz Big Jim vouching for you is like getting baptized by the Pope but I'm also guessing Chief sensed I had some Indian blood.

Chief's is two miles west of Indian Town in downtown Onawah. It opened at five to take advantage of early morning shift workers who liked greasy sausage with their eggs and Chief's badass coffee, and closed at two o'clock cuz Chief had better things to do at night, meaning he went to bed at sundown in his room above the restaurant. The exception was the Friday night fish fry, which fetched a few Indians who could afford it along with some Catholics.

Hitching there was miserable cuz it was bitter cold some days and ankle deep in slush others. Most days I got a ride in one of the Indian Town Chevies and Hudsons serving as buses. Crazy Eyes Sam usually drove me and three or four others to work on her way to Timeless used store, where she patched up dresses and britches. My job started at six so she'd drop me first, then get one or two to the power plant. She'd be back in town before Timeless opened at eight so she'd stop at Chief's for coffee, compliments of Chief, then hike across the street to work. Sam's eyes pointed different directions; it was a miracle she could drive and sew. She found me some used boots, which I sorely needed cuz my running shoes weren't good in the slush.

Scraping caked eggs and sausage grease off plates wasn't fun but I did it. The first couple weeks I kept quiet and took directions from Chief. Donna taught me how to interpret his "Unnhs," and pointed fingers along with the look in his eyes.

When the breakfast crowd thinned out I got to sit with Chief and Stumpy the cook. Donna would bring us leftover scrambled eggs and coffee on a tray. She needed the practice cuz her sense of balance was off, resulting in spills. Sometimes people would get their own hot coffee to be safe. I got to chop stuff up for lunch and I tried to impress Stumpy by dicing the potatoes into exactly bite size and forming the hamburger into perfect quarter pound patties. Chief even weighed 'em a couple times and said "Unnh" when they were right on.

Stumpy approved of me chopping things since he was missing his left arm up to the elbow. He wasn't an Indian so folks mighta thought it was curious Chief employed him, but he was a Gypsy so he was familiar with suffering. It was a pity the combine caught his left arm cuz it cut the tattoo of Carmen Amaya in half.

After a couple weeks I got brave and told Chief I could cook soup. He looked at Stumpy, who shrugged, which was my invitation to go ahead. After breakfast Chief washed the dishes himself while I cooked up my usual blend of vegetables. "We'll call it 'Um Um soup'," said Donna.

Chief tasted it, said "Unnh," and pointed to a stack of bowls, meaning we could serve it for lunch. He held up ten fingers, meaning it'd cost ten cents.

"Guess it's on special," said Donna.

Folks liked the soup so I got to make it a couple times a week. They also liked the fish Chief let me cook on some of the Fridays using the spice mix Viv invented for the carp. I mixed it into a beer batter like I saw Penny do and fried the fish hot and quick so the outside was crispy but the inside wasn't tough.

The truth is it was catfish; only a few people could tell it wasn't walleye. On Thursdays Chief drove to a fish farm up river, brought it back frozen and let it thaw overnight in the icebox. Penny coulda bought the same fish but folks in Hertzville thought catfish was just as evil as carp cuz it was popular in the south, proving there's prejudice against fish the same as against people. So when walleye wasn't available Penny kept serving fishhead soup and people kept running to her bathroom after they ate it.

32

Winter at Jim and Doya's was easier than at the cabin, where snow could pile up against the door making Urs and me go out through the window to fetch water or use the biff. Some days Urs'd fish on the ice for hours. If he came back empty we'd eat veg from the space under the floorboards or I'd shoot a squirrel that forgot to hibernate. We'd pass the time playing cribbage, which I could usually win cuz Urs got distracted with worries like would the roof blow off. Doya and Jim knew cribbage too and we played on cold, dark evenings. Sometimes the neighbors came over to tell the stories they'd prefer to tell round the fire.

I told the skunk story which gave Jim an idea: "Tell that story to Chief. If he likes it maybe he'll let you tell it when there's a crowd—could be good for business."

I didn't have to ask Chief myself cuz Jim got off work early the next day and showed up at closing. "Hey Chief," he said, "this man's got a story for you."

Chief loaded a tray of coffee for Donna to bring us.

The story was firm in my mind and getting better cuz I was adding playful details like Felix taught me. I asked Donna if it'd be okay if I said "motherfucker" once. She said twice would be better.

I have a way with stories (I hope you agree). I didn't just tell it, I performed it for the four of 'em, drawing laughs and applause. Stumpy slapped his right hand on a table.

"He should tell that at your fish fry." Jim was promoting me again. "Could be fun, get people in the mood for more beer." Chief nodded. "Expect a big crowd this Friday," said Jim.

That was a safe prediction considering Jim brought most of the crowd with him. Chief's could seat thirty people at tables and six more at the bar. When Jim and fourteen of his friends arrived, the place was overfilled by a bunch. Good thing Chief bought twice as many catfish as usual. Stumpy and I fried fish as fast as we could and flipped fry bread on and off the griddle to warm it up before slathering on a mixture of beans, onions and hot peppers. Chief cooked up a huge batch of mashed potatoes and stirred the gravy so it didn't burn. He couldn't keep up drawing beers so he set out mugs and yelled out "pour your own," which was a day's worth of actual words. Donna broke out in a sweat running plates to the tables and to those standing for lack of chairs. She wasn't actually running, though, cuz she was trying not to spill. When she was about to cry, Doya and Jim rescued her and ferried plates back and forth while she went out back for a smoke.

"Who ordered the fish!" Jim yelled to a big laugh, since fish was the only thing being served.

A few folks ate and left but more came in, which is when we realized we were outta clean dishes and too busy to wash the dirty ones.

"Who wants to eat for free tonight!?" yelled Jim. At least ten hands went up. "You and you!" shouted Jim, "get in there and wash dishes." Chief showed 'em to the sink.

About eight o'clock we ran outta fish, disappointing a few late arrivers. To make up for it, Chief gave 'em the potatoes, fry bread, and a beer for a quarter.

Jim musta told everyone something special was gonna happen at nine o'clock cuz the place was still full, even though it was closing time. He dragged me from the kitchen and said "Um Um here's got a story for you."

I had a sudden dizzy feeling from nerves but also cuz I hadn't eaten in spite of all the food passing in front of me. The first thing I said was "I need somethin' to eat," which got an unexpected laugh.

Chief brought me fry bread to chew on and I used it to gesture. The skunk story took a good half hour cuz I made up new details, like how we had to dodge bullets and how our Ojibwa dog could sniff out evil and bit the farmer on the ass.

When I was done I sank into a chair, sweaty and exhausted, but swelling with pride cuz I had an effect on the crowd. Chief laid his Yankee hat on a table and threw in a quarter. Others followed with coins adding up to three dollars and seven cents. It was then I started thinking storytelling might be my calling. So far that's working out; I hope you agree.

When the noise died down people got up to leave but sat down again when Clyde Youngbird took my spot. "I got a story," he said, and talked about hitching rides out to Montana to see the back country where his people came from. He got lost in the mountains but his horse knew the way home.

After him, Wildcat Adams told a story about making whoopee with a white woman that left her upset. "That's cuz you were doing it wrong," yelled Donna to the biggest laugh of the night. "My husband could give you lessons." She would know since she was a white woman married to an Ojibwa man.

Then Lonetree Johnson told how his ten year old son drowned in a barge's undertow. You might think that story ruined the night for everyone but it was the opposite. The tears seemed to drain the suffering from your soul.

It was almost midnight before the stories ended and Chief's was empty. Donna and Stumpy had to get home, leaving me and Chief to clean up and get ready for breakfast. I slept on Chief's floor upstairs and woke to the smell of sausage and the quiet voices of folks who had to work on a Saturday.

That was the start of Chief's Fish Fry and Story Time. Donna wanted another story the next Friday cuz it made people more forgiving if she spilled.

Chief pointed to his head and said "blueberry pie," meaning he wanted dessert on the menu.

"We don't know how to bake pie," said Stumpy.

"I know someone," I said, and told 'em about the Lutherans. Chief nodded, so Wednesday I went to the evening service of First Lutheran Church looking for the soup ladies, and sat two rows behind 'em. I pretended to sing and be moved by the sermon, but really I was eyeing the two ladies, looking for their weakness. After the service I made sure we crossed paths.

"Why, Eltha, look who's here. I didn't figure you for a Lutheran," said flower smelling lady.

"It was your pie turned me to God," I said. They laughed. "I tell people it's the best ever."

"That's so kind of you," said Eltha. "Say, how's your friend doing—the one who needed the nickels?"

That caught me off guard and I had to think for a second. "Oh, he's in a good place now," I said, and changed the subject: "Speakin' of pie, I just had a crazy idea. I know a restaurant's lookin' for someone to bake ten blueberry pies tomorrow. They'll pay good money. I don't suppose you'd be interested."

"Son, we can bake ten blueberry pies in the blink of a cat's whisker." I wasn't sure what that meant but I convinced 'em to be at Chief's at three o'clock, even talked 'em into bringing the ingredients. I was concerned they'd object to a place that served beer and catered to people with various beliefs, including some who thought eagles carried their prayers up to Gitchie Manitou. But they were Lutheran so I guessed it was okay.

As I left the church and headed down 33, a gray Nash slowed as it passed, and sure enough it was Borg staring straight at me. How did he know I was at the church? Did he follow me from Indian Town? I guessed he was out to run me down and I figured he'd try it on Indian Town Road, where there wasn't much traffic. When I turned toward home I slowed to watch for any clue he was waiting. The moon was only half full that night but that was enough to light up the exhaust from his car behind some weeds. The February air was below freezing and he had the car running to keep warm.

I crouched in the ditch, thinking he'd get tired of waiting. A dog's year passed and the Nash didn't move and I was getting cold. I could work my way around him through the woods, I thought, and leave him sitting there all night. Maybe I should crawl up to the car and slit a tire.

Instead of that, though, I did the dumbest thing ever. I blame it on Old Man and Lettie, Louise, Gaetan, Viv, Urs, Kohana, Mato, and even Winthrop cuz they all did things that were stupid and gutsy at the same time. I pictured the McDonalds standing fearless in church, inviting the wrath of the law; Gaetan insulting a large white man with a song and Viv punching that same man till his face was red mush; Kohana and Mato dangling down the face of Big Baasha to shame Hertzville; even Winthrop, who was destined to trample people for profit just like his dad, owning up to the prank that was likely to get him beaten. And Louise, holding my hand as she confessed, which was a big "fuck you" to her dad and to the people of Hertzville for letting him beat the crap out of her and her mother. Common sense gave way to defiance and I did a foolhardy thing.

I felt around for a rock and found one that was the right size and weight to smash a windshield. I stood and closed the fifty yards between me and Borg at a quick pace to limber up my joints for a run. I knew I could beat the train for a quarter mile but could I beat a Nash. I knew it wasn't the fastest car on the road.

When I got to the car I stood for a second to be sure Borg saw me, then kept walking. I musta took him by surprise cuz I was maybe forty yards away before he got back on the road. He turned on the lights and I ran. For a few seconds I kept the forty yards between us. Was the Nash that slow or was he toying with me?

When I saw the lights gaining on me I turned and stood like that kid in the Bible musta stood before the giant. Borg closed fast, leaving no doubt he wanted to run me down. At thirty yards I raised the rock and waited maybe three seconds before I threw a fast ball through his windshield. It wasn't Big Baasha smashing down on Hertzville but it was still a rock full of righteousness. The Nash swerved and fishtailed a few times before turning over in the ditch.

I walked to the car and watched Borg struggle out. I let him get a few yards away from me before I took off. He chased but gave up in a few seconds. I guess you could say I was toying with him. I ran all the way to Big Jim's, fulla confidence I would know what to do when Borg and I met again.

The next day the Lutheran ladies arrived at Chief's with six bags of stuff. "Who's in charge?" asked Eltha. Chief raised his hand. "We're supposed to bake some pies." Chief showed 'em to the kitchen.

"We paid eleven dollars and seventy two cents for groceries," said flower smelling lady. Chief got money from the cigar box and put it in an envelope.

"How much are we getting paid?" asked Eltha.

"How 'bout sixty cents a pie?" I said. I looked at Chief for approval; he looked away.

"Well then, let's get cookin'," said Eltha.

We helped 'em unpack their stuff—sugar, flour, cans of blueberries, lemons, Crisco, cinnamon, ten pie plates, a rolling pin, and rum.

"Rum?" Stumpy asked.

"Oh, we brought that by mistake," said flower smelling lady, "but as long as it's here we could drink some."

They showed us how to roll out the dough, cook the filling, and drink the rum with Coca Cola while the pies baked. By six o'clock we had ten spectacular blueberry pies. By six fifteen one of the pies was missing six pieces and we were all smiling. Chief stuffed six bucks in the envelope, and handed it to Eltha: "Good pie," he said. The ladies left with the rum.

As expected there was a big crowd on Friday and I was ready. I'd been rehearsing the bear in the dumpster story and I told it with "panache," to use a Felix word. I had the bear saying things like "come here you big galoot" with a weird twang cuz of her sideways jaw. I know I'm bragging again but it's the truth.

Someone asked if Urs was a real person. "Yup," I said—he could snarl an alpha wolf into submission and filet fish better'n anyone. But that's all I said cuz I wasn't ready to tell a sad story. I was working up to it, though, cuz I was starting to think that sadness ties people together. That feeling grew stronger when Roy Onehorse told about drinking so much whiskey his wife and kids left him. His story wasn't great for beer sales but it mighta influenced some people toward sobriety.

On Thursday Donna and I baked pies cuz now we knew how and Friday the crowd heard about Dash being the meanest, stubbornist donkey that ever lived, which was pretty funny, but then I told about him getting burned in a fire just to see how folks would react. Suddenly they loved him and the guy who said we shoulda shot him took it back.

On Fridays Chief's was crowded by seven o'clock. If you didn't get a chair, too bad—you had to hold your plate while you sat on the floor or leaned against the wall cuz nobody left. Chief stopped open the doors with wood wedges to help Donna get back and forth to those who had to eat outside and listen through the window screens. He turned off the lights and lit candles for drama.

I was proud to see people leaning in to catch every word and then gasp or laugh when I surprised 'em or tickled their funny bone. They loved the goats and pigs and cows getting nooky in Farmer Fred's barnyard and I even sang part of Gaetan's song. I said plug your ears if you don't like dirty words. The reason they plugged their ears is cuz I can't sing.

Every Friday more and more people spun tall tales or reinterpreted history or confessed minor sins. There were stories about a sturgeon longer than the boat, a snakeoil salesman who sold actual snake oil, a house that took five years to build then got hit by a tornado, a tour boat sinking in a storm killing ninety eight people, some awful stuff people ate during the depression, friends who died in the war, a ninety seven year old great grandma who still had all her teeth, a fight over which was better for farming—tractors or horses, a child dying of diphtheria, and plenty more. It was a sympathetic crowd and people owned up to things they or their ancestors done wrong—thieving, swindling, moonshining—to a point. I confessed some of the lies I told but wasn't about to let on I was planning a murder. We discovered we lived out the same pleasures and sadnesses. It wasn't unusual to hear folks say "I know how you feel." I wondered if they really did know how I felt about one particular thing though. I aimed to find out on the Friday before Easter.

"There was this hobo woman," I started. "She was stronger of body than half the men she traveled with and stronger of willpower than all of 'em put together." Folks giggled cuz they thought it was a story about a superhero like in the comics.

"She came from misfortunate stock—people who dug and scraped on other people's land for crops. She was the youngest of four children and the one who was supposed to save the family from total misery in their old age, so she went to school in addition to sweatin' in the fields, in hopes she would learn enough to be a waitress or secretary. But her education came too late. When the land dried up and the country went to shit, her family fell victim to disease, starvation, and lack of wantin' to live. One by one her father, mother, two brothers and sister faded away, leavin' her, age sixteen, in a tumble-down shack with five wooden crosses out back. She had made it through the tenth grade but could not continue cuz stayin' alive is even more basic than bein' educated. She fit her few useful possessions into a gunny sack and stood on dusty roads, thumbin' rides, not carin' which way they took her as long as it was to a city where she might find one or two people who cared. She lived with stray dogs and stray people in parks and dark alleys in southern cities, once in a while in someone's spare room if she cleaned their house. It was hard times and even well to do folks tended to be stubborn with their money, so findin' houses to clean was a struggle. Findin' people who needed to ease their misery with booze was easier, which led this woman to an arrangement with a moonshiner, whereby she ran cheap hooch to down and outs who used it to numb themselves, and to private clubs where you needed a password to get in. By age eighteen she was numbin' herself as well, not only with the hooch, but also with the intimate companionship of the moonshiner and a few others. When sober, she displayed an unusual will to learn and spent her spare hours in whatever library would tolerate her ragged appearance, hidin' in corners and favorin' books that carried her away."

"Real life carried her to half a dozen cities around the south, the moves made necessary by predicaments her friend manufactured outta pure stupidity. Truth be told he was not a moonshiner, just an unskilled hanger on who sometimes drank the spirits he was supposed to sell and reported 'em stolen. He was horsewhipped and run outta town more'n once, each time takin' her with him, or rather beggin' her to go cuz she propped him up. They traveled by boxcar, learnin' the art of train hoppin' and panhandlin' from seasoned veterans of the rails. By the time she was twenty two, the same story had played out so much that she was sick of it. In the spring she broke out on her own, and jumped on trains headed north, where, she had read, the summers were cool and the rivers ran pure. There was a month of ridin' trains, beggin' food in cities along the way, and takin' comfort next to men with similar needs to hers. In June, as she felt a freighter slow down for perhaps the twentieth time, she looked out the boxcar to see a wild river cuttin' through a forest, felt cool air on her face, and decided this was where to stop. She was in Onawah."

When they heard "Onawah" the folks clapped their hands or let out a "yeah," suggesting they thought their city was gonna lift her up. "What did she do next?" someone shouted.

"Onawah was friendlier than the south," I said, "but not by much. She took up with a native man named Noodin, who had a house deep in the woods—shack, really—and lived with him through the summer till it came to light the shack didn't actually belong to him but to two men who used it to hide from the law. They showed up in September with a bag of what mighta been cash, and ran the squatters off with a shotgun. Noodin headed north without her, sayin' he needed to travel fast. Once again she loaded a gunny sack and headed south, hopin' to hitch a ride. Nobody stopped and she was seven miles and two hours down the road when she saw a breach in the trees with a long trail leadin' down to a cabin. There was smoke and even at a few hundred yards she could smell cookin'. She made her way down the trail, hopin' for a free meal, not expectin' to stay till the snow flew. The man who was cookin' fish was large and strong, with a gentle, quiet nature. She shared his home, his food and his bed till the snow flew and winter turned the cabin into a prison. With deep regret, she rode the trains south, where she found the moonshiner as she had left him, drunk and hapless. She made friends with a petty thief, who worked his craft with a blend of skill and carelessness. The three of 'em together made up the equivalent of one human being able to provide the materals needed to keep a creature alive. The group was missin' a conscience, though, which was provided by a smart but thick and awkward hobo man who loved knowledge but not women, except in a brotherly sense. At a delicate time in her life he became her protector, lacking as that was, since a nimble wit goes only so far in a fist fight. He was the one who traveled north with her in July of 1934, this time not by train but by the generosity of car drivers willin' to help a woman in need. After weeks of thumbin' rides and beggin' food they took the trail down toward the large, hairy man diggin' a trench for spring potatoes. He turned to find her lookin' at him, with a sling around her neck and a baby in the sling."

"'I think he's yours,' she said, 'I'm not sure, but I hope so.'"

There were whispers cuz a few'd figured out this was a true story.

I told 'em how she stayed through the winter, even after the smart but awkward hobo left; how they struggled to eat, since there were three mouths to feed; how the chickens quit laying eggs in the coldest stretch; how the man had to freeze for hours on the ice to catch dinner; how there weren't enough blankets and warm clothes since he hadn't expected company; and how the long cold nights drove her next to crazy. She survived one winter and then another, but knew deep down that would be her last winter in the north. And she knew she had a terrible decision to make.

"She made it in November when an early snow turned her blood cold. 'I have to leave,' she said, 'or I will die.' He knew she was right. The only question was about the boy."

"'He needs to stay with you', she said. 'It's a better life here than with me. I love this boy, but he can't be raised in boxcars and back alleys.' Just before Christmas she hopped a southbound freighter and cried goodbye to her two year old son and the man holdin' him up."

"She was back the next summer and every summer after that, bringin' books and bein' the boy's teacher and defender. She helped with the things survival demanded but mostly she loved and educated the boy the best she knew how, schoolin' him in practical things like cookin' and buildin'; readin' stories of adventure and wisdom to him; and lyin' on the beach with the dog between 'em, wonderin' about the stars—all this time never lettin' on she was his mother cuz of her shame at leavin' him behind. The third summer she brought the moonshiner with her, to save him from bein' killed by real moonshiners. The summer after that it was also the pickpocket and the brainy hobo. When the boy was twelve, the group was joined by a young black man who had a guitar and a voice to make angels cry. It was a curious group, knit together by the need for family but not so tight that flaws could be overlooked. She was the one who held it together with common sense, quiet affection, and sharp scoldings. They settled into a rhythm, the hobos doin' just enough work and creatin' just enough good times to make up for their inconvenience and failures. There were ups and downs, friendly disagreements turned to arguments, good ideas and bad, dancin' and poutin', laughin' and …"

I had to take a breath before this next part: "And there was cryin'. There was a fire, the same fire that burned the donkey I mentioned a couple weeks back. But he wasn't the only one in the barn that night. There were two goats, three chickens … and two humans. She was there comforting a man who got beat up only cuz he was black."

The crowd was stunned. "Her name was Vivian," I said. "She was my mother."

I put Viv's story together from what Felix told me at the Wild Card Motel and scraps I overheard from Urs, Moonshine, Eddie, and Viv herself, although others talked more about her past than she did. Far as I knew at that moment none of it was a lie.

The crowd did not clap or cheer. Nobody else told a story. A few came up to embrace me; others dropped coins in Chief's hat and left silently with a nod to me. Chief, Donna and Stumpy worked quietly in the kitchen.

I sank into a chair and didn't notice the white haired man till he slid up a chair and sat like he was horseback. It was Joshua, barefoot and wearing the Indian Joe hat, living on the streets now since the weather was warmer.

"I heard through the window," he said in his slow, raspy voice. "His name was Eugene Redfeather. They called him Noodin because he could run. It means 'like the wind.'"

"You knew him?"

"I know plenty. He would put a stone in his shoe to cause a limp and bet men for money he could beat them in a race. Without the stone he was the fastest man around. He ran like the wind and disappeared the same way."

"Why?"

"Those two men with the bag of money—they weren't the ones with the shotgun. Noodin had it. He was waiting for them."

"How do you know?"

"Wesley told me."

"Who's Wesley?"

"Wesley Proudfoot. He was there."

Joshua said that last name like it should mean something to me but there were so many things spinning in my head I couldn't put my finger on it. He waited till I got it. "Your name is Proudfoot," I said.

"Yes."

Holy shit, I thought, Joshua's son was one of the men with the money bag. "Where's Wesley now? Can I talk to him?"

"Disappeared." Joshua winked.

"How about the other man?"

"Noodin shot him. He woulda shot Wesley too but the woman wrestled the shotgun from him and Wesley got away."

"The woman? Vivian?"

"I don't know that part of the story. But I know plenty other shit."

I was stunned. Viv switched around the story she told Urs and Urs later told me. We shoulda known it was too simple. She was hiding the real story and that's why she never said much around the fire. Any tale she spun would be trivial cuz she was withholding the biggest one of all. I wondered if I would ever be able to track down Wesley to get the whole story.

Joshua cleared his throat and looked at the coins in Chief's hat, then up at me, making it clear there should be a reward for the information, so I turned the hat over into his cupped hands. "What happened to Wesley and where's that bag of money?" I yelled at his back. He waved without turning around as he went through the door.

I thought about the possibilities: Viv wrestled the shotgun away from Noodin, told Wesley to run, and held the gun on Noodin as he buried the body. Or Noodin grabbed the money and ran, leaving Viv to bury the body. Or after Wesley ran, Viv shot Noodin and buried him with the other body—pretty sure that's not what happened. Or Wesley grabbed the money as he ran. Maybe he gave some to his father and Joshua was really rich as hell and had just suckered me out of a couple bucks. Whatever happened, there was a chance Viv saved Wesley's life.

Something else caused pressure in my chest. It might be Noodin's blood running in my veins. Did it carry killing with it? Eddie said once it wasn't his fault he was a thief cuz his father was one before him and his father before that. "It's in the family," he said, "there's nothing you can do about your blood." If destiny was at work, was killing Borg decided for me cuz Eugene Redfeather's blood flowed through my veins?

33

On April first I left Chief's after the morning rush and ran to the jail to see Urs and Moonshine get released. Monroe ran through the door, sank to his knees, and yelled "praise Jesus!" Urs walked out slow and hugged me but it wasn't a back slapping bear hug thanks to six months alone in a cell. At least his hair was back and his feet healed. Harvey Moss was there, beaming cuz two of his clients were free. Never mind that one of 'em hung himself and another was still in jail.

To celebrate I took 'em all to Chief's for a late breakfast and told 'em it was on me, which was funny since Chief gave us leftover eggs, fry bread, and coffee for free. I hadn't seen Urs since the fall so there was a lot to talk about but Moss had legal stuff to do first. He had the thousand dollars from Larkin in cash since Urs didn't use a bank, but Urs had to sign a paper saying it was paid and another paper saying he'd never set foot on his former property again.

Moss left and Monroe borrowed five bucks from Urs to buy used clothes at Timeless, leaving me and Urs alone. I was dying to tell him what I found out about Viv and Noodin but I held it back. "What are you gonna do?" Urs looked blank. "You got money so maybe you could rent a place."

"It's Larkin's money," he said in the same voice he used to describe the filthy carp.

"You could get a job. Captain Jack said he'd hire you."

"And put me in a uniform with a little hat."

"There's the power plant. Jim works there."

"Who's Jim?"

That's when I realized Urs knew nothing about my life since I saw him at the jail in the fall. I told him about everything—the Larkins, the bulldozer (which made him smile), painting Big Baasha (which made him smile even bigger), living with Jim and Doya, and the stories at Chief's. He already knew about Felix.

"They call me 'Um Um,' by the way."

"Is that Ojibwa?"

"Kinda."

His eyes got wet. I'd done a lot of growing up since he saw me last and he wasn't there for it. He probably wondered how bad he screwed me up by going to jail. Or by being a dirt poor loner.

"You're seventeen now." His meaning was really about me being ready to live my own life. "This Jim and Doya—you okay there?"

"I'm fine there. Jim's big and he hugs like you. He could squeeze the sap out of a two by four."

We left Chief's to take care of practical things, meaning where was Urs gonna live. Monroe followed us around town, looking through a kaleidoscope from Timeless. It was obvious from Urs's slumped shoulders he wasn't keen on city living.

"Maybe we could live here," said Moonshine at a small two story house with a sign saying: "Upstairs For Rent, $15 per week, see Shirley inside."

"Ain't you heading south?" I asked.

"How about I stay awhile and take care of you and Urs." That's all we needed—Moonshine shouting "praise Jesus" every five minutes. He'd stay as long as Urs's money held out.

We made a wide loop back to Chief's. Stumpy and Donna and Chief were behind on lunch since I took a couple hours off. I sat Urs and Monroe down with bowls of soup and helped in the kitchen. When the lunch crowd thinned out we talked across leftover blueberry pie.

"Good pie," said Monroe.

"Lutherans showed us how to make it," I said.

"Praise Jesus." See what I mean.

Moonshine eyed the beer tap. "I bet it'd go good with beer. But I don't drink any more."

First off, blueberry pie and beer are terrible together. Second off, if Moonshine stayed sober for another month I was the one gonna shout "praise Jesus." Only reason he was sober this long was they don't serve booze in jail.

"Maybe I'll live in town till I figure out what to do," Urs said.

We went back to the house and talked to Shirley, who came to the door in a headscarf, carrying a mop. She squinted. "Yeah?"

"You got an apartment for rent?"

"Yeah. Are you clean? Can you pay?" You could tell we weren't the type of renters she was hoping for.

"We have money," said Moonshine, "and we love Jesus, we learned that in jail."

"Jail?!"

"Only for six months and they did nothing wrong," I said.

"I'm done with the moonshine business," said the idiot Monroe.

"Only way I rent to jailbirds is a week at a time" she said. "First time I have to call the cops, you're out. And no women!" She shook the business end of the mop at us. "Rent's twenty bucks a week."

"The sign says fifteen," said Urs.

"That's for law abiding people," she said. "Go take a look." She sent us up the back stairs with a key. The place had a bathroom with a flush toilet, a bedroom with a single bed, and a gas stove.

Moonshine flopped onto the couch: "I could sleep here."

It wasn't bad if you don't mind living indoors. Urs paid the twenty bucks, then we went to Timeless and got a cast iron fry pan, soup pot, forks, spoons, bowls, and a mattress that Urs carried on his back. At Axel's Hardware Urs bought a couple fishing poles and some Rapalas.

That Friday Urs and Moonshine sat in the back corner at Chiefs while I talked about how carp crowded honest fish outta the river. Urs cracked a grin when I used his words—"shit brown, mud sucking fuckers." I told how the lake had become a cesspool of garbage eating rough fish ruining it for walleyes and northerns. I knew carp were evil, I said, since I saw the devil himself sticking 'em with a three pronged spear and throwing 'em on the bank to rot and smell like a fat man's poop. Our secret blend of spices and smoke could make 'em good enough for poor people to choke down, I said, but not good enough for the well-to-do, who'd take a sniff and wretch. I told how the same spices turned Chief's fish into a king's dinner.

Someone yelled "Can we get the recipe?"

"Didn't you hear me say it was secret?" I yelled back and folks laughed. Like I said once or twice, Urs can talk with his eyes and right then they told me I was grown up, even at seventeen. I was feeling the same thing: I could tell stories that made folks laugh and cry, cook a pot of soup, run like the wind, shoot a varmint in the eye at fifty paces, and lie my way out of most situations. And my hair was long again.

34

With warmer weather, the Friday night crowds thinned out in favor of people telling stories around their fires. I told Urs he should tell his stories at Indian Town, but he stayed away, choosing instead to associate with ladies at a bar called "Elmo's." Some nights he never came back to the apartment, making us worry about him and his money. He kept it in a wad in his pocket so it'd be easy for someone with Eddie's skills to fleece him. By summer he was a sorry sight. He had no job and wasn't looking for one. He took no pleasure in anything. I said once we should hunt morels and he looked at me like I was crazy.

Other than drinking at Elmo's, Urs's only ambition was to see God's angry face on Big Baasha. He kept saying I painted it even though I told him I just manned the ropes. One evening we coaxed a ride to Hertzville outta Sam, which pleased Moonshine since he was sweet on her. I dreaded the drive since we'd pass the cabin, or rather where the cabin used to be, and I feared what Urs would do when he saw nothing left of his life. He was apparently afraid to look cuz he stared straight ahead as we passed.

I looked, though, and was startled by the changes since I was there five months before. Big trees were stacked in a burn pile. Trucks passed over a makeshift bridge to the island. Cement pillars to support the permanent bridge stood tall enough to let Captain Jack's sidewheeler underneath. I didn't see all this in the instant we drove by. I'm recalling some of it from when I sat on my ledge a few weeks later watching the construction through my rifle scope, wondering how close I'd have to get to kill Borg.

Traffic on Main Street in Hertzville was heavy. There were cars in the church lot, which was strange for a Wednesday, and cars lined the street. People stared east, where God looked down like he wanted to wipe the town off the face of the earth.

Urs was impressed: "You did that?" I reminded him I only worked the ropes. "Still ...," he said.

Moonshine was impressed too: "That scares the bejesus outta me."

I bet it scared most Hertzville folks too, cuz God was looking at them in particular. The out of towners were probably more curious than scared as they pointed their cameras at Big Baasha and sermonized the locals under their breath for being sinners or maybe just dumb enough to be panicked by paint on a rock. The business owners on Main Street had a different attitude, though, owing to the surge in sales.

Sam dropped Urs and me at the back door of Old Man's store and drove Monroe to the church.

Old Man and Lettie waited on customers, but when Lettie saw us we got hugs and Coca Colas and a chair in the back room while she and Old Man finished out front. They posed for photographers, hoisting up a gallon sized plastic likeness of Big Baasha, pretending it was heavy. When the crowd thinned out Lettie came back and gave us one: "It's yours," she said, "see where Old Man and I signed it on the bottom. We get a buck for 'em and they only cost us ten cents each." She held it up at the back window so we could see how it resembled the real Big Baasha. "Larry had them made over in Pressworth."

"Larry?"

"Larkin. He had a sculptor shape the mold and the face is a decal we paste on. Then we sign 'em."

Old Man rushed in: "Come outside quick." We followed him across the street. God was glowing red from the setting sun and angrier by the minute. There was a hush, then the sound of folks exhaling as the bluffs swallowed the sun.

Down the block cars left the church lot. "That's the church crowd," said Old Man. "On Wednesdays Father moves the pulpit to the east windows so the congregation can see God looking over his shoulder when he says they're going to hell if they don't watch out. He gets quite a haul in the collection plate. On Sundays he still talks about Jesus; makes money there too."

"It's better than bingo," said Lettie. "Here I thought we were going to jail and now we're sitting on a gold mine. We sold twenty seven Baasha rocks today, dear."

"Pretty soon we can buy a new car," said Old Man. He led us inside, put the "Closed" sign in the window, and pulled large pickles from a barrel: "Larry's going to buy the store, in fact he'll buy the whole downtown and renovate it soon as he can get Jerry to agree to a price. Hertzville's going to give Bluffton a run for best town on the lake. And we're going to change that name—sounds like a town in pain. Larry put suggestion boxes on main street and we're going to vote for the name on Labor Day."

When Urs heard that he said thanks for the pickle and headed out the door, leaving the plastic rock. We walked down Main Street and found Sam and Monroe at the church.

As we drove back toward Onawah I had an impulse and told Sam to turn in at Farmer Fred's. Fred and Mrs. Fred were cleaning up the barnyard. In the twilight it was hard to tell 'em apart since they wore the same overalls. Up close you could tell Fred was shoveling manure and Mrs. Fred was hosing off animals.

"Sorry folks, we're closed for the day," yelled Mrs. Fred.

"It's okay, hon," said Fred, "it's the boy with the donkey."

"Well then, come on over and say hi to the donkey," said Mrs. Fred. "Give him this carrot, he's a good boy, pulled kids in the cart today." I gave the carrot to Urs and made him hold it out for Dash. They eyed each other but finally Dash took the carrot and looked almost happy as he munched.

"He's got a gash on his leg there," said Fred. "We tried a potato poultice but it ain't workin'; gonna need the vet and that's gonna cost."

"How much?" Urs wanted to know.

"Usually about twenty bucks including the medicine."

Urs pulled Larkin's cash out of his pocket, peeled off two twenties, and gave 'em to Fred. "Take care of him," Urs said, and got in the car.

That's the last I saw of Dash and the Freds. And Hertzville too, except for a couple months later when I saw it from the river, glowing red.

35

One afternoon Urs and Moonshine were at Chief's when there was a racket on Main Street. "A parade!" Moonshine yelled.

Down the street came a guy clanking cymbals loud and often, followed by a dozen or so old men in army dress, waving flags. "Fourth of July," Donna said. Independence Day caught us by surprise again. Urs cursed and left.

Five men rode circles on motorcycles, almost crashing into the army guys, who walked slow and stopped to shake hands. There was a clown on a one wheel bicycle, and after him was the Onawah High School band, which was smaller than the Bluffton band. They didn't sweat as much, though, cuz they wore shorts and t-shirts instead of stupid uniforms. They couldn't keep the beat or play in tune but it was the best band I ever saw cuz of the clarinet player in the second row—Louise. I ran out and walked along side, looking down the row till she saw me and giggled so much she couldn't play.

By Bluffton standards it was a sorry parade, but at the tail end was the grandest sight in any parade. A white horse with red circles around the eyes and flames on his nose, and a black horse with white eye circles and lightning flashes on his neck, arched their necks and pranced, looking proud, but not as proud as the riders—Mad Dog and Moondog. They looked straight ahead like they had their minds set on a distant ambition but Mato peeked at me and grinned. As they passed the bulge in the crowd there was applause and whistles. Those two were heroes in Onawah even though it was Hertzville experiencing fame and fortune from their artwork. The parade turned the corner, but the Dogs rode back and tied the horses in front of Chief's.

"Cowboy!" they yelled, and that began an hour of stretchers about how they outfoxed the law for six months. I knew better, of course. The law quit caring about them and me too when it became clear the artwork on Big Baasha was a godsend (so to speak) for Hertzville. I knew all they did was hide out at the rez, leeching off Indians up there insteada their moms. You could tell being idle was gnawing at 'em. Six full moons had passed without an adventure.

"We need to take coup," said Kohana.

"Shut up about takin' coup," said Mato, "we were in a parade; that's like takin' coup."

The two argued about the definition of "taking coup," Kohana saying you had to touch the enemy, Mato saying any kind of heroic deed would count.

"There's a full moon in two weeks," said Kohana, "what're we gonna do?" They tossed around the possibilities: painting God's face on a church (not the Lutherans, I said); wrecking the bulldozer (already been done, said Kohana); cutting a hole in the fence at the Virmeer School for Boys (we'd end up in the school, said Mato).

"The moon's full in exactly two weeks?" I asked.

"Yep," said Kohana. I swear he kept a calendar.

"That would make it a Wednesday," I said.

"You're one smart white man," said Mato, but he meant it as an insult.

"That's when the Girl Scouts have their big fire down river," I said.

That was all they needed. Within minutes it was agreed we would meet at the river at six o'clock, get down river in

Donna's husband's canoe, and terrorize a buncha twelve year old girls, not figuring they were the ones gonna terrorize us.

"Louise has to come too," I yelled as they rode away.

Chief handed me a bucket and shovel and pointed to the street.

* * *

It was anybody's guess which would give out first, Urs's money or his patience with city living. You could tell he was roiling on the inside like a slough fulla carp. He formed no friendships outsida Elmo's. He looked in store windows at useless stuff. He flinched and cursed when cars honked, 'specially when they honked at him for being in the street. He read signs advertising "Salesperson Wanted" or "Cashier Needed" and kept walking. He slept in and spent late nights at Elmo's, where painted women snuggled up to him for free drinks and repaid him with affection.

Once in a while me and him went fishing in Donna's husband's canoe, but it was mostly to get away from Monroe (we lied and told him it was a two person canoe even though it would hold three). The fishing wasn't exciting cuz our lives didn't depend on it. The weekend after the parade he asked if I felt like a man yet.

"I can take care of myself," I said, and I told him how I stood up to Borg when he went to beat me and how I caused him to wreck the Nash. "Not bein' scared is half the fight," I said, "I learned that from you."

"You learned it from Viv; I just kept you alive."

"Isn't that the most important thing—stayin' alive?"

"You didn't get any of the finer things."

"I was at Larkin's for three months. That's all the finer things I can take."

It wasn't like Urs to talk about the finer things. You could tell he was leading up to something.

"I need to leave," he said.

"To where?"

"North."

"Colder there in the winter."

"Keeps people away."

He was really asking for permission to leave me, so I gave it: "You don't have to worry about me. I'm grown up and you got me there. You're my father no matter who was with Viv the night I was conceived." He cried. We both did.

The fastest way to get north was on the freighter, which went forty miles up to a little town called Hanko, just fifty miles or so from Canada, to pick up lumber. Urs had never rode a train so he called on Moonshine for pointers, which made Monroe puff up with pride. He sat us down like school kids and lectured.

"Hoppin's not for the faint of heart," he began, "you gotta be strong of body and mind to pull it off. Best to travel with a partner for protection and that makes it easier to get on cuz you boost the first guy, then he pulls you up. Best to have a shoulder bag for your gear so you have both hands free to grab the hardware on the boxcar. Best to get on and off at a stop or a side out, but if you have to catch it on the fly, you wait on the inside part of a curve, when the train slows down and banks a little. If you're goin' north the best place to get on is the power plant in the afternoon, but it doesn't stop there on the way back so if you're going south you either have to catch it in Onawah or on the fly or get down river to Parker's Crossing, where it stops to switch crews at night. Careful to get on the right train, though. The tracks split and one takes you to Chicago, which you don't want; the other one goes straight south. If you get confused there's a night guard there named Eustis who doesn't mind helping folks out."

Urs had no use for pointers on southbound trains. I did, though.

The next day Urs went to Indian Town to make sure it was okay if I stayed with Jim and Doya, even offered 'em money but they refused since I was already paying rent out of my salary from Chief's. It was the first time Urs and Jim were side by side and you'd swear the floor boards would crack.

The day after that Urs found a shoulder bag at Timeless and jammed in everything he owned except the cast iron fry pan. He paid Shirley for the next week so Moonshine had a place to stay while he decided on his future, and we walked the tracks to the power plant. There was a good hour before the freighter arrived, which was spent with Urs recalling moments from his life. Urs wasn't a sentimental person but he was fulla tears as those memories poured out. Moonshine and I said nothing, just cried or laughed along with Urs. When the freighter squealed to a stop, Moonshine led us down the line to a suitable boxcar. He showed Urs how to grab the hardware and swing himself up.

There was an awkward twenty minutes as the train uncoupled hopper cars. Urs gave me three twenties off his roll. "If you happen to see that lawyer, ask him if he can get a deal for Eddie. This can help with his fee." It's true, we didn't talk about Eddie, maybe cuz we figured he belonged in jail and maybe cuz we blamed him for getting everybody else in trouble.

The train creaked and lurched northward. Urs looked back at us like a lost dog. I haven't seen him since.

36

Moonshine milked every last minute outta the extra week at the apartment. On Saturday he stuffed his bag and said goodbye to Sam, explaining his skills were more suited to the south.

I walked him to the Onawah station and boosted him onto a boxcar, where he dangled his feet. There was an uneasy moment that happens when people split, due to the possibility they'll never see each other again. On impulse I pulled out the three twenties Urs meant for Eddie's lawyer and gave 'em to Moonshine. "Here," I said, "I think you'll use this better'n Eddie would."

Moonshine cried. As the train pulled away I realized he'd been sober since he left jail. "Praise Jesus!" I shouted after him.

That night Mato and Kohana told the Big Baasha story to the largest Indian Town crowd yet, which included Noki cuz there was no bingo in July. Some details I didn't recognize, such as it being so cold their piss froze on the way to the ground (which was ridiculous cuz the paint woulda froze too) and how an eagle flew past the moon over and over, (they shoulda said it was an owl since eagles don't see well at night). When they were done, Butterfly, who was hiding in the crowd, grabbed 'em both by the ear. "Why haven't you been home to see your mama!" she yelled, but it was more funny than mad.

"Oh mama, you're the best," said Kohana, causing her to give 'em both a hug. She was Kohana's mom only in the way every Indian woman's the mother of every Indian kid.

Noki headed in. As she walked by me she said "Winthrop wants to show you his motorcycle; makes more noise'n the train."

"Tell him I work at Chief's," I yelled at her back.

She musta heard me cuz Winthrop roared up to Chief's Tuesday afternoon. He was on the Harley, wearing cowboy boots and a Yankee hat turned backwards, revving the machine to the annoyance of everybody on the street. Chief went to see what was making the racket and said "nice hat."

"Get in," he shouted. Chief said "unnh," meaning I could leave early, so I got in the sidecar. It was my first time on a motorcycle and it was scary fun. Winthrop sailed over the road like it belonged to him alone, like his mom in her Jaguar. He went airborne over the humps on County 33, giving my stomach the willies, passed slow cars, and took the bumpy bridge way too fast. We zoomed down River Road and did a noisy trip through Bluffton, ending up at Tony's Pizza.

"The usual?" said Tony.

"Yep," said Winthrop. He filled me in on a few things. He'd finally seen a naked girl thanks to a hole that Waldo Larson—the kid in the wheelchair—bored through the locker room wall. He also kissed a girl, that being Tammy, who probably kissed half the boys in school. His dad was getting him into a college so he wouldn't have to go in the army. "Good thing I got the Harley," he said, "cuz I don't get to drive the Ford. Borg's got that full time, now cuz something happened to the Nash."

"What?"

"He hit a deer," said Winthrop. "He's always at the island. They want to get the resort done by Armistice day so they can have a bunch of vets at the grand opening."

I was sure Borg would not admit the crash was caused cuz he was trying to kill a kid, but I was relieved to hear it just the same. I also listened for any clue the Larkins knew my rifle was missing from the case but heard nothing.

Tony brought over this thing with a crust and tomato sauce with meat under a thick layer of cheese. So that's a pizza, I thought, and I ate half of it. On the ride back I concentrated on two things—not throwing up and thinking how to get Winthrop to put me together with Louise. "Hey," I said as he dropped me at Chief's, "there's a full moon tomorrow. The Dogs wanna do somethin'."

"The dogs?"

"Mad Dog, Moondog. They wanna take coup on Girl Scouts."

"They want to scalp some Girl Scouts?!"

"It's just an expression. Maybe you wanna come along."

"Hell yeah."

"Oh, hey, how about we get Louise to go. It'll be a Baasha reunion, except for the McDonalds."

"I'll let her know, and I'll bring the beer!" he yelled over the rumble of his machine.

"Six o'clock at the dock," I yelled back.

I wangled that one pretty good, I thought, and ran to the bathroom to throw up. "Pizza," I told Chief when I came out.

The next day I stayed at Chief's after closing, cooked some fry bread, jawed with Sam at Timeless, then met the Dogs at the river.

"That's a small canoe," said Mato, "three people max. So Louise ain't comin'?"

I told 'em both Louise and Winthrop were coming.

"What the fuck, you think that canoe'll hold five people?"

Mato was right, I didn't think ahead.

Winthrop howled up in the Harley with Louise in the sidecar, looking deadly in shorts and a loose fitting top that sagged like Penny's blouses. And she was holding a bucket of beer, which musta come from Winthrop's stash.

"This here is Scooter Man," laughed Louise. Winthrop's new name was only one step better'n "Dead Meat." She looked me in the eyes and said "you got your hair back."

The beer caused the Dogs to quit being mad. We agreed the canoe wouldn't hold all of us so we spent an hour drinking and rehashing the Baasha adventure.

After two beers each, our opinion regarding the canoe shifted toward optimistic. Kohana said "Oh shit, it'll hold five people, just nobody stand up" and we piled our five bodies and the beer into the three person canoe, bringing the gunnel down to a foot above water level. Mato let the current push us a couple miles down river to the beach. A fire flickered inland and songs drifted through the trees.

"Here's the plan," said Kohana, "we sneak up and surround 'em. Hide in the bushes, then on my signal run in and take coup."

"Cut the shit, Kohana, we ain't takin' coup," said Mato, "we just sneak up and watch 'em. This ain't the Little Big Horn and you ain't Crazy Horse."

"And you ain't a real Indian," said Kohana.

We started into the woods but Louise grabbed my hand: "We're staying here. To guard the canoe. And the beer."

"Up to you," said Kohana, and the three of 'em disappeared into the trees.

Louise turned to me: "Well..."

"Well what?"

"You're an imbecile," she said, and pulled me in for a kiss. "Open your mouth." She taught my tongue to play, then pulled me to the sand, unbuttoned her shorts and guided my hand into her panties. "Press. Harder." She moved against my hand, looking me square in the eyes till her eyes rolled up and she made a sound like pine trees make when the wind sneaks up on 'em. She stopped moving, sank against me and finally giggled: "You can take your hand out now."

Father Matthias was wrong—God did make us animals. I looked up and thanked Him.

"What can I do for you?" she whispered. Before I could answer there was screaming from the trees. Mato and Kohana broke onto the beach like the devil was chasing 'em. Winthrop tried to keep up.

"Get the canoe!" Mato yelled.

"What's goin' on?!"

"Girl Scouts!" yelled Winthrop, "they're trying to kill us! There's a million of 'em."

I laughed.

"He's not kidding!" yelled Mato, "get the canoe in the water!"

Seconds behind Winthrop was a swarm of girls, their yellow neckerchiefs glowing in the moonlight. A couple stopped to throw rocks. Louise and I pushed the canoe into the lake and the Dogs slid in. Winthrop lurched toward us and fell face first in the water so we had to drag him over the side. We were thirty feet out when the girls got to the shore, hurling rocks and cuss words young girls shouldn't know. Behind 'em a couple older women panted like overheated dogs, shouting stuff like "stop, girls!" and "this isn't how Girl Scouts behave!"

Apparently it was how Girl Scouts behave cuz they were Girl Scouts and that's how they were behaving.

We paddled like crazy, me in back, till we got to the middle of the river and stopped for a breather.

"Oh man," said Winthrop, "you missed it! We snuck up on 'em."

"Like Injuns," said Kohana.

"Yeah, like wild ass Injuns," said Mato, "we were in the bushes twenty feet away. They were singin' and they never woulda caught us except this asshole" (meaning Winthrop) "started singin' along."

"It's a catchy tune," said Winthrop.

Kohana laughed and sang: "It was sad, so sad, it was sad when the great ship went down ..."

Mato joined in: "to the bottom of the ..."

Winthrop and Louise jumped in: "Husbands and wives, little children lost their lives, it was sad when the great ship went down." The song was way too happy considering all those people drowned.

"They always sing that one at camp," said Louise, and she started in again with the others filling in the "so sads" and "to the bottom of the's." The noise bounced over the Naawakamig River, crashed into the rocks on both shores, and probably woke Alliconda. It was all I could do to keep the canoe balanced so we didn't tip over into his soup.

"So you were a Girl Scout?" I asked Louise.

"Yep, I learned some dandy things in the scouts," she said with a grin meant for me alone, "but you don't mess with our ceremonies."

When we beached the canoe Louise whispered in my ear: "Get to the store Saturday at seven o'clock. I'll be there alone."

37

I didn't sleep. In the middle of the night Doya got up scowling cuz I was trying to play a sweet melody on guitar and slamming my hand against the strings when I couldn't get it. She stood with folded arms while I put on shoes and left, running to nowhere in particular on moonlit roads. Over and over I called up the feel of Louise's tongue in my mouth but it was her eyes looking straight into me that stirred me in ways I never felt. My mind went wild imagining what might happen Saturday night in the hardware store. Louise would be tallying the week's sales by herself cuz her father would be at a bar down river getting drunk enough to set off his mean streak. Her hair would be in a pony tail but when she saw me at the door she'd undo it and let it fall to her shoulders. There's more to this fantasy but it belongs to me alone.

My thoughts turned to Borg. It's a mystery that he and Louise were in my head at the same time, maybe cuz deep down I knew I had to make a choice. If I killed Borg I couldn't pretend to Louise I was anything but evil. She seemed to have Urs's ability to stare the truth right out of a person. It was Louise or Borg and I chose Louise. Someone else would have to kill Borg.

On Saturday I allowed myself two hours to run to Hertzville on the train tracks. My stride had lengthened over the past year and I hit every other tie on a dead run. I'd be early, I knew, and I'd watch Louise through the store window till seven. Never mind that I didn't have a watch—when she looked out the window for me, it would be time.

Have any of you had a shock that changed the course of your life in an instant? That's what happened to me the night of the barn fire and that's what happened when I got to Urs's nine acres on my way to meet Louise. I knew the cabin was gone, of course, but the mutilation of the island grabbed at me. The tall pines were down in a tangled mess. In their place was a structure that sat so heavy on the land you had to wonder if the island would crumble beneath it.

The bridge pillars I noticed a few weeks before now held an arc of steel that stabbed into the island but rose enough in the middle so Jack's sidewheeler could get under. A tarred parking lot held twenty cars, give or take, and a lumber truck. Hammer sounds bounced across still water; the crew was working late on a Saturday so Larkin could have his grand opening on Armistice Day, probably with flags and army guys and Father Matthias saying how Jesus had sent Laurence Larkin the Third to rescue the town.

I crept up to the edge of the woods and waited. It musta been six thirty when the hammers stopped and the voices hushed as men with lunch pails straggled out to their cars and drove over the bridge and up the steep hill to County 33. As the cars drove off I recognized a screwup in the engineering of the road. Where Urs and Dash had to climb up the rock bank to get over the tracks, there was now a tunnel underneath with huge timbers holding up the tracks. The cars passed through easy but the lumber truck was a tight fit. It was a flat bed and the wood was stacked up to the height of the cab but not over it like you see sometimes on a farmer's tall hay wagon. Fire trucks were taller than the lumber trucks and would get jammed in that small opening. If someone set fire to that building, I thought, the fire could have its way.

And then I discovered something that had been hiding behind the lumber truck—a green Ford Crestliner. And sure enough, Borg was driving it. He emerged a good five minutes after the last worker left, locked the door, and drove up the hill. Jesus just showed me how to catch two rabbits with one dog, I thought, and was immediately ashamed cuz I knew it was the devil on my shoulder, not Jesus.

I crossed the bridge and circled the building till I found an opening where the window wasn't placed yet and crawled in. I climbed the wide, curving stairs to the next floor, then another stairs to the top. Larkin was right, the view in the distance was grand. Rich folks would see it from behind glass. In the foreground was the wreckage of a once magnificent piece of creation.

I left, hoping the workers wouldn't notice the tracks my running shoes made in the sawdust, which were different from their work boot tracks. I located an oak tree with a perfect view of the front door, sighted an imaginary rifle to the door, whispered "pow" like you see in the comics, and saw Borg fall. But he fell too fast, died too soon. I sank against the tree and planned a more painful way for him to die.

I climbed the new road up the hill to County 33. It was only as I stuck out my thumb to hitch a ride that I remembered Louise. I know you find this hard to believe considering what was waiting for me at the hardware store, but my lust for Louise gave way to my obsession with killing Borg. Louise would be pissed beyond imagining. Or maybe I just told myself that so I could put her out of mind and concentrate on the upcoming murder.

Over the next few days I invented the story I wanted to recite to myself in old age, when my life consisted of remembering but not doing. I took inspiration from Kohana and decided killing Borg had to take place under a full moon.

Call it taking coup if you want. A full moon was coming up on a Thursday in the middle of August.

The next three Thursdays I ran the tracks back to the island to make sure Borg was there. I climbed to my ledge, pulled my rifle from behind the rocks, and sighted to the island through the scope. Each time was the same—quitting time about six thirty and Borg the last one out. On the last trip I looked in the windows and saw what I wanted—the interior doors were hung.

I needed twenty two shells since I left mine in Larkin's gun case. I didn't want people to know I needed 'em, so I stole 'em at Axel's. He's a good guy but I had to do it. He was tipped back in a chair by the door, sound asleep, so I woke him and said I was thinking about buying one of those Schwinn bicycles, which was in the back room. When he went there to bring it out, I slipped behind the counter, got a box of shells outta the drawer and put two quarters on the floor like someone dropped 'em. He came back with the bike and we jawed. I told him I'd consider it and left. I really was thinking about a bike for my getaway but figured a canoe was more inconscrip ... damn, that word. Besides, bikes are pretty expensive. I went to Timeless for a five gallon bucket, a rubber tube, and a floppy broad brimmed hat, and hid that stuff in the alley back of Chief's.

It was hard leaving good people behind but of course I couldn't tell 'em what I was up to. I confess I wavered right up to the day itself. When I left for work that morning, Jim saw me carrying Gaetan's guitar and my shoulder bag. "I won't be home tonight," I said.

"I knew it!" he yelled. "Doya, look at this, he's gonna sing to his woman tonight and take her to bed."

"I hope she's deaf," said Doya.

I blushed like it was true and ran out to Sam's car.

When the lunch cleanup was done I said I was gonna stick around and practice singing. Donna and Stumpy hurried out and Chief got up the stairs. I sang a bit to back up my lie, then stuffed fry bread and fixings into my bag. I wrote down Viv's spice recipe on one of Chief's envelopes. Under it I wrote "Good Chief." On another envelope I wrote "Donna's husband for the canoe," put forty bucks in it, and slipped both envelopes into the cigar box, leaving about fifty bucks in my pocket. I stole a box of matches and two of Chief's door stops, got my stuff from the alley, and wore the floppy hat to the river.

The next part was tricky cuz people saw me with the guitar and bag in the canoe. "You gonna sing 'em to death?" someone shouted. I laughed with him but kept my back turned.

I paddled slow and hid my face under the hat when I passed river traffic. I calculated it would take two hours to go the seven miles and let the current take me as much as possible to conserve energy. I thought of Big Jim when I saw the power plant's smoke stack. One of my biggest regrets is not saying a proper goodbye to him and Doya and Noki. Or the Dogs. Or Chief and Donna and Stumpy. Or Winthrop. Or Old Man and Letty. Or Louise.

When I got to the mouth of the lake I steered east into the stumps and tangled roots of the backwater, climbed up to my ledge for the rifle, loaded it, paddled to the island, trying to look casual in case anyone was watching from the top floor of the building. I beached the canoe, carried the rifle and bucket and hose to the oak tree, and waited.

Finally the hammering stopped and weary men drove away, leaving the Ford. After an eternity Borg stepped into the twilight. As he locked the door I snuck behind him on cat's feet like Viv taught me. When he turned I was ten feet away and he was looking down the barrel of the twenty two.

"Unlock the door," I said in the commanding voice I'd been practicing.

"You're over your head," he snarled.

I lowered the rifle and sent a round at his feet, then reloaded the chamber quick but slow enough it didn't jam. "Unlock the door," I repeated.

He pulled out the key and turned to the door. "Wait," I said, "take out the club."

He hesitated so I sent another round even closer to his feet. He took out the club.

"Did you kill my dog with that club?"

He didn't answer till I lined up the rifle with his heart. "Yes!"

"Throw it down." He did. "Did you know there were people in the barn when you burned it down?"

"No, I swear!"

"Then why did you wedge the door shut?!"

"I..."

"Get inside!"

I followed him into the building, keeping ten feet between us cuz I knew he could wheel and kick.

"Into that closet."

"What are you going to do?"

"Just get in the closet!" I slammed the door, standing to the side in case he flung it open on me. I took one of Chief's door stops and jammed it between the door and the frame, then hammered the other stop under the door with the rifle butt.

I ran to the Ford, took off the gas cap, stuck one end of the hose in the tank, sucked on the other end till gas hit my mouth, filled the bucket, and walked it back inside, holding the rifle up in case Borg had got out.

He was screaming. "Shut up!" I yelled, "or I'll shoot you through the door," which was a hollow threat since it was a twenty two against a solid oak door.

I splashed gas around the main floor and up the staircase, leaving a space by the front door to get out.

"What are you doing?" he yelled. I'm sure he smelled the gas.

"I'm doing what you taught me!" I yelled back.

He pounded on the door: "You won't get away with this!"

"I know!" The chances of getting away with it were slim. That gave me pause but I lit the match cuz there was no going back.

The flames played around the gas trail and skipped up the stairs. Smoke gathered fast. "Damn," I thought, he might die from the smoke, not from burning up like I wanted. I smashed windows to give the fire air and watched the flames eat away at the building and Borg's life and Larkin's greed.

But I couldn't walk out. Was hell a hot place like Moonshine thought? Was hell right here on earth like Felix said? Right here in these flames? Borg deserved to die but did I deserve to kill him?

I went to the closet and hammered out the stop between the door and frame with the rifle stock. The wedge underneath was jammed in tight. "Stand back!" I yelled. I shot the wedge three times before it splintered and Borg flung open the door.

"You son of a bitch!" He came at me but stopped when I pointed the rifle at his chest.

"You killed two people!" I yelled.

"A hobo and a black man!"

"My mother and my friend!"

I aimed the rifle at his knee. "I lasted five strokes when you beat me. Can you last five bullets before you beg me to kill you?! On your knees!"

"You're not man enough to pull the trigger!"

He didn't move so I sent a bullet past his ear. He sank to the floor. I walked up and pressed the barrell against his forehead. "You deserve to die."

"Then we all deserve to die!" he yelled.

That gave me pause. "Did Larkin put you up to it?"

"He's the boss, what do you think?"

"Did Jerry Christianson let you into his store to get the lantern?"

"Yes."

"Did Virgil Dickerson give you kerosene?"

"No!"

"No?!" I pressed the barrell against his forehead.

"Gas! He gave me gasoline!"

Shit, I thought, that's why the fire took hold so easy. It was gasoline, not kerosene. The lantern was just to make it look like an accident. Viv and Gaetan didn't have a chance.

I suddenly realized I'd have to kill at least a dozen people to make things right. More than that if you count the folks like Hotel Harriet and Father Matthias whose inhumanity flowed under a skin of respectability. In a way they were all guilty of killing Viv and Gaetan and Felix.

An animal sound swelled up from my gut, causing Borg to shrink back, wide eyed. I grabbed the rifle by the barrel, swung it over Borg's head, and heaved it through a window. "Stand up!" I yelled. He snarled and raised his fists but I stood with my hands at my sides, thinking I'd know what to do when he attacked. I took a step forward, then another, till I was within his reach. I stared into him like Mato and Kohana's wolf stared into you from the back of Harriet's hotel, like their horse on Jerry's store stared with fiery eyes, like Urs stared the truth right outta you. Borg turned suddenly and lurched out the door, into the Ford, and squealed away on whatever gas was left.

I paddled hard. Down river I stopped and let the current take me past the buildings on Larkin's Main Street. Looming over 'em was Big Baasha, glowing red from the flames a mile and a half back. God's blue eyes turned black in the red glow.

By then Laurence Larkin the Third was certainly screaming into his phone call to the sheriff and Gloria was certainly screaming into her wine and Winthrop was no longer my friend. Maybe Noki understood.

Soon the sheriff and fire marshall and all who made the gears turn toward progress would shit their pants cuz fire trucks wouldn't fit through the tunnel under the tracks.

Past the town, I took stock of my possessions—fifty bucks, a jackknife, a shoulder bag with clothes, and a battle weary guitar, the things that would sustain me until my stories earned hatfuls of change while southern folks like you eat catfish and grits.

The river carried me like in my dreams. I let it take me south toward the train stop at Parker's Crossing, where I hoped to find a helpful man named Eustis, who would show me the train headed for a city with two shelters, three parks, a library, and, hopefully, a man with a long white beard and hickory walking stick.

Acknowledgements

Thanks to David Solheim and Buffalo Commons Press for accepting me into their family and guiding me through the publishing process; to Sherry Quan Lee for invaluable critique and advice; to Dr. Lawrence for an insightful read; to Barbara Laman for publishing guidance; to my friends Donna and Bill Curry, Joyce Johnson, Barb Minar, Holly Jorgensen, Jayne Zell, Roland Trenary, Kris Schaefer, and Marissa Eastling for their insightful readings of early, ragged manuscripts; to my daughter Adrienne for being a constant inspiration. Thank you to Victor R. Volkman and Modern History Press for book shepherding services. And thank you, Mom and Dad, for a perfect childhood in the small Minnesota town that would become Bluffton which looked across the lake that would become Delacroix to the town that would become Hertzville (but in my childhood it was not a town in pain; I made that part up).

About the Author

Peter Martin lives in Minnesota. In addition to *Once This River Ran Clear* he has written twelve plays for families, most of them a twisted take on a classic story, and produced them ninety times give or take. He is writing those scripts into long stories for parents to read to their children or for children to read with a flashlight under the covers. Pete can be reached at petermartinliterary@gmail.com or in person in one of the canyons in southern Utah, which he considers his second home.